THE HARBOUR

CUMBRIA CRIME
BOOK 1

RACHEL MCLEAN

JOEL HAMES

ACKROYD
PUBLISHING

Ackroyd Publishing

ackroyd-publishing.com

❀ Created with Vellum

THE HARBOUR

CHAPTER ONE

AISHA PULLED her jacket tight around her and shivered.

It wasn't all that cold, thank God, because the jacket's job was to look good more than to keep her warm. But she'd been inside and on the dancefloor most of the night.

Now she was outside, standing still. It was dark, and the wind coming in off the sea didn't care that it was October and only an hour or two till sunrise.

"Come on," she muttered. Claire, standing beside her, giggled.

Claire was drunk. Simon was a few feet away, looking at the gate, and didn't hear.

It was quiet. They were less than a minute's walk from half a dozen bars and clubs and more chicken and kebab shops than you could get through in a year, but Aisha could barely make out the shouts and music and the occasional sound of someone emptying their guts in the street. Just the wind and the splash of water on hull.

"Nah." Simon was back, buzzing with energy. She

wondered what he'd taken. Not just weed, whatever he claimed. "Reckon they've changed it."

Had they changed it? Aisha wasn't sure Simon had ever known it. He'd lured them here, out of the club, to the marina – OK, maybe not *lured*. She'd asked if he had weed, he'd said yes, she'd suggested going outside to smoke it, he'd proposed the marina. She'd dragged Claire along with her, of course. She and Claire dragged each other everywhere.

Simon had claimed he knew the code for the gate onto Bulwark Quay. That was one of the things she loved about Whitehaven: wherever you were, you were never more than a few minutes from the middle of nowhere. They could find somewhere quiet. The shore would be dead this time of night. Or morning. Aisha opened her mouth to suggest it, and realised Simon had gone again.

"Kneel before me!"

She followed his voice. He'd climbed the gate.

Idiot.

Anyone living on the right side of Pears House who happened to glance out of their window would see him standing on it, hands raised, grinning like he'd conquered Everest. Aisha found herself grinning back.

He hopped down the other side with surprising grace and beckoned them over. "Come on. It's easy."

Aisha looked at Claire. "Shall we…?"

Claire already had a foot on the base of the gate. It wasn't high, but there were spikes on top. While Aisha argued it back and forth with herself, Claire was already over.

Fuck it.

Simon was right: it was easy. Within moments they were walking along the quay, the three of them in a line. The marina building stood low and dark to their left, but most of the boats were lit. Yellow and white lights rolled back and forth with the waves.

"How about here?" asked Claire, but Simon pressed on.

He had hold of their hands, both of them, one in each of his. Aisha wasn't sure how she felt about that. This was just a smoke, then home. And the three of them had known each other for years.

Another gate rose to their right, the blue-painted metal picked out against the darkness. More blue railings on the other side. Aisha had lived in this town nearly half her life, walked around the marina a hundred times, but it was different at night. Even the gulls seemed quieter, with mating season finally over for the year. She shut her eyes and let herself be pulled forward, to move as part of a group, to—

"Wake up, mate!"

Aisha opened her eyes, confused.

Simon had stopped. Was he talking to her?

She blinked and turned to her right, but he was looking down. She followed his gaze.

There was something there, a few feet in front of them, at the far end of the quay.

"Come on, mate, you'll catch your death," Simon said.

It was a person. Lying there by the capstan, pale skin on the cold dark ground.

Too much skin.

"Simon," Aisha said.

He was still talking, ignoring her. Beyond him, Claire stared down, eyes wide, mouth open in horror.

"Simon!" Aisha repeated, louder.

He turned to her, frowning. She held out a hand. *Stay where you are. Shut up.*

She dropped into a crouch and edged closer. There was

precious little light anywhere else at this end of the quay. She reached into her bag and grabbed her phone, creeping forward as she coaxed its torch into life.

Yes. There was someone there, definitely someone. But whoever they were – whoever *she* was – she wasn't going to be waking up anytime soon. She wasn't going to be catching her death, either.

It was a bit late for that.

CHAPTER TWO

Only day three, and DI Zoe Finch had a routine. The first challenge today, as always, was to find the cat.

Yoda hadn't taken the move well, and Zoe could sympathise. Yoda was a Birmingham cat, just like she was a Birmingham copper. Being exiled from the city at the dead centre of the country and dragged a hundred and fifty miles to its edge would be a challenge for anyone, human or feline.

For Zoe, this had come out in complaints: the terrible weather, the god-awful takeaways, the lack of decent coffee. But *she'd* had a choice. The cat had had no say in the matter, and communicated this by hiding wherever she could inflict the most damage. The tally so far was one shirt, one tablecloth, and Carl's favourite tie, which he was still annoyed about.

There would be no checking for damage this morning. No time.

Zoe tracked Yoda down inside a box of shoes at the back of the room that would be her son Nicholas's, when he was home from Stirling.

Home. She wondered if Nicholas would ever see it that

way. If *she* would ever see it that way. It was nice enough, bigger than her old terrace. Nice rooms in a nice modern semi in the middle of a nice development of similar nice modern semis on the outskirts of Whitehaven. Which didn't seem too bad either.

But *outskirts* meant something different here.

Back in Brum, it could take an hour to get from the edge of the city to the centre. Bad weather, a motorway accident fifteen miles away, or a football match could add another hour.

From Holly Bank, she could be anywhere in Whitehaven in ten minutes. At the police station in fifteen.

She'd be putting that to the test shortly.

"Here you go, love." Carl stood in the kitchen, holding out a plate and a cup of coffee. Zoe took them, forcing a smile. She sat down at the small round table they'd brought up from Carl's place.

The coffee, at least, would be tolerable. She'd spent long enough teaching him how to make a proper brew. The toast she ignored.

"Feeling OK?" He put his hands on her shoulders.

Zoe leaned back into his warmth. She closed her eyes and sighed. "I am now. Thanks. What about you?"

It was Carl's first day, too. Both of them starting on the same day, and on a Saturday to boot. She turned to look him in the eye. She wasn't sure if his smile was real.

"Oh, you know." He shrugged. "Good luck to both of us."

"You'll be fine," she told him. "They wanted you up here, remember? You're doing them a favour."

"I hope so. And you, love. Someone with your record, you could have had your pick of DI jobs."

"Well, this is the one I've got, so let's hope they appreciate me as much as you do."

He smiled, more sincerely this time. "They will."

Zoe sipped her coffee, checked her watch, and took a gulp, almost burning her mouth. She stood up. "I have to run. See you later?"

He nodded, serious. "Just promise me one thing."

"What?" She was in the hallway, throwing on her warmest coat, looking for her bag and the keys to her Mini.

"Promise me we won't be running into each other at work, OK?"

So this was what he was worrying about.

Carl worked for PSD. Professional Standards. His job was to root out corrupt police officers, and he was good at it, as more than one of Zoe's former colleagues knew to their cost.

She swore under her breath and returned to the kitchen to put her arms around him.

"You know I wouldn't do anything to risk your position."

"Not deliberately, no. It's just—"

"It's just you think I have a habit of, what, being in the wrong place? Finding out the wrong things?" Zoe took a step away. She didn't have time for this.

She took a breath. "I had a dodgy boss, Carl. You knew that. You were involved from the start, you knew what I knew. If your old colleagues got it into their heads that anyone who worked for Randle must have been tainted by him, that's their problem, not mine. It's bad enough the man's shadow followed me all over Birmingham. I'm not having it follow me up here."

"I'm sorry. You're right."

She leaned forward, kissed him, and turned. Not the best start to the first day of her new life, but she could only play the hand she was dealt.

CHAPTER THREE

DETECTIVE SERGEANT AARON KEYES checked his watch again, and cursed.

"OK," he said, looking back up at the end of the quay and the area marked off with police tape. Half past eight. People would be wanting to get at their boats, get cracking with the day's work, or what was left of it. They'd been waiting a while. Even longer if he stood there like an idiot, watching the gulls and doing nothing.

It wasn't raining, at least. Not much wind either, and the cordon was up. Any evidence should have been preserved.

"We'd best get started."

"Don't you want to wait for the boss?" asked Nina.

Aaron turned to face her. Detective Constable Nina Kapoor was usually keen, sometimes too keen. He frowned, not that she'd see much of his face through the forensic suit.

"This isn't like you, Nina."

"I know, Sarge. But it's her first day. I'm sure she'll be here soon. She might have her own ideas."

"I've no doubt she does. But if she wants them put into practice, she'll have to show up, won't she?"

Nina grunted an agreement. He detected surprise, which was fair enough. Most days, Aaron didn't go in for insubordination, or anything approaching it. But most days, they didn't have a dead body in the marina and a new DI who hadn't shown up.

"So what have we got, then?" he asked.

Nina had arrived nearly half an hour before him, so should have some of the answers already. Uniform had been on site since soon after the call had come in, not long after four. The call to Nina and Aaron had been delayed because the new DI wasn't in place yet. Uniform had had no choice but to stand there watching the gulls and doing nothing for four hours already.

Not quite nothing. They'd got the tape up.

"CSI are on their way, Sarge," Nina told him. "Pathologist too. Roddy's taping around the body."

Aaron squinted towards the end of the quay. He could see the outline of a man. Low and squat, solid and immovable. No one would be getting past PC Roddy Chen.

"That's good, but I don't want anyone on this quay at all."

"We've made sure the gate's locked."

That was true. Nina had let Aaron in. He didn't know who'd let Nina in.

"Good, but there's a code, isn't there? And people know that code. So get Roddy to put up another cordon. He can stand at the gate and keep an eye on things from there. Tell people the bare minimum, get them to go away, look out for anyone showing undue curiosity or who seems to know more than they should."

"Got it, Sarge."

Nina turned to walk away. Aaron held out a hand to stop her. "Who's with Roddy?"

"Harriett Barnes, Sarge. She's checking the boats and the buildings on the marina, making sure there's no one here who shouldn't be. There's sixty-three boats in at the moment, and we haven't found anyone yet. After that, I've told her to knock doors on Pears House and anywhere else with a view. We've already got some CCTV, but someone might have seen something."

"Good work. OK, show me the body, then you can have a chat with Roddy."

They hadn't managed two steps up the quay before a shout from behind brought them to a stop. Aaron tried to keep the exasperation from his face.

"Please, officers, can I have a word?"

A man approached from the gate, which he'd left open.

Aaron sighed. Nina took a step towards the intruder.

"I'm sorry, Sir, but this is a crime scene. You'll have to wait outside the gate."

"Yes, yes, I understand that." He stopped in front of them. He was tall, wearing the distinctive green marina uniform. He rubbed his hands together. "But I'm responsible for security. I thought I might be able to help."

Nina's expression shifted from bored to interested. Nina had been on the team for nearly a year, and Aaron was impressed by her. She was smart and hard-working, enthusiastic, too, if a little full-on sometimes. Her mouth was masked, but her eyes gave her feelings away. She'd have to learn to hide those.

"What's your name?" Aaron asked.

"Raoul Fournier. I'm head of security."

French name, Aaron thought. *No accent, though.* "Just the man. How long have you been here?"

"Just got here, spotted something going on." Fournier pointed behind him. "I live just on the edge of town, got a good view." He gave them a nervous smile.

"Did you see anyone here last night?"

"Sorry. My shift finished at midnight. I locked up, checked the boats. No one around, not even anyone in their boats, for once."

Aaron shivered. *Who does that in October?*

"Have you got CCTV?" Nina asked.

Raoul nodded. "Yeah. There's only a couple of cameras on the entrances, but I can show you."

Aaron gave Nina a look. "You talk to Chen. I'll go with Mr Fournier."

"Before the DI gets here?"

"Before the DI gets here." He looked towards the town again. Still no sign of her. Did she even know this had happened?

Aaron followed the security guard to a low hut near the entrance to the marina. Fournier unlocked the door and ushered him inside. Two monitors sat on a flimsy table.

"I can give you the tapes."

"VHS?"

"Yeah."

Old-school. Aaron approved. It was so much easier to take tapes away than to get digital footage downloaded and transferred. He took the two tapes the guard offered him. "How thoroughly did you check the marina when you finished at midnight?"

The man squared his shoulders. "I know how seriously the boat owners take security, and I know how useless those cameras are. I checked it top to bottom. Always do."

"The quay?"

"Of course. It was empty." Fournier glanced out of the window. "I swear it."

"And what about overnight? Is there anyone else around to keep an eye on the place after midnight?"

The security guard shook his head. "Cutbacks," he said. The universal explanation.

"OK. Thanks."

Aaron left the hut and approached the quay. He could see some sort of structure behind Nina and Chen.

As he approached the end of the quay, Aaron realised it was a tarpaulin supported by three metal poles and an umbrella.

"Whose idea was this?" he asked.

"Mine," replied Nina.

Aaron nodded. It would protect the body from the attention of the gulls before CSI turned up with their tents and protective gear.

"Good work. Now, what do we have?"

Roddy Chen stood silent, staring back down the quay towards the gate as if expecting a horde to attack at any moment. Aaron lifted one edge of the tarp and looked down.

Lying on her back, staring sightlessly up at the sky, was a woman. She was young – twenties, at a guess. She was naked. And she had a deep wound across her throat.

The two of them looked at her for a minute. Aaron resisted a prayer.

"When's the bloody pathologist getting here?" he snapped, regretting it immediately. This wasn't Nina's fault.

"Sarge."

There was something off about Nina's voice. He turned to see her frowning, staring down at the body. But not at the throat. Nina was looking at her side.

"I think you might want to take a look at this," she said.

CHAPTER FOUR

SIXTEEN MINUTES, with the last part of the drive along the ominously named Steel Brow. Not bad, but Zoe reckoned it could be improved. The car park was quiet too. Bonus.

She sat on a surprisingly comfortable metal chair in the reception area of the new Cumberland Police Hub, in the fields outside the village of Frizington, a short drive east of White-haven. From the outside it was an impressive-looking building, all concrete, steel, and glass surrounded by low rolling hills. She'd admired pictures of it when she'd been considering the job. But inside, it felt uninhabited, as if there weren't enough police to fill it. The team she'd be heading up had been here nearly a year. She wondered if there was anyone else here at all.

"Zoe, it's great to meet you at last."

Detective Superintendent Fiona Kendrick hurried towards her. Her heels clattered on the tiles and loose grey hair fell to her shoulders.

Zoe had met Fiona, but only on Zoom. Her new boss had seemed pleasant enough: happy to talk about the unit, the station, the team, her own background, a Geordie copper moved west. Another Lesley, Zoe hoped.

She followed Fiona into the lift – more steel and glass – up four floors, and along a short corridor.

"Call me Fiona, when it's just us," the super said as she opened the door to her office. "Super, when there's anyone else about. Got to keep up appearances."

Fiona's office was a large corner room with deep carpets, a dark wooden desk, a few chairs, and big windows. Fiona laughed as she spotted Zoe looking. "Uninterrupted views of the car park and the A5086, Zoe. Forget the fells. This is why people move to Cumbria."

"It's a bit different from my last boss's office."

"I can imagine. Thanks for coming in on a Saturday. Coffee?"

Zoe felt her cheek twitch. It would be bad coffee. "Yes, please," she replied. *Get it over with.*

Five minutes later, a pale woman in a green trouser suit brought a tray with a cafetière and two cups. Zoe watched as Fiona poured, then sipped, wary.

Wow. This was good. Maybe she *had* found another Lesley.

"I thought this would be a good chance for you to meet another of our DIs," Fiona said. "Alan Markin."

Zoe nodded. She'd checked the website and knew the names of her new colleagues.

There was a knock at the door, making Zoe wonder if someone had been outside listening. A short, bald man wearing a too-large suit entered, along with a woman who was a good head taller than him.

"DI Finch," he said. "Pleased to meet you."

Zoe took the offered hand; his handshake was limp. "Call me Zoe please, Alan."

"I know you're used to the big city, but we aren't as slow up here as you might expect. So don't go getting any ideas." DI Markin smiled, his eyes narrowed.

"I'm sure you aren't." Zoe looked at the woman. "You're DS Giller-Jones?"

"Yes, Ma'am." She stood behind her boss, saying nothing more.

"Good, that's done." Fiona stood up.

That was brief, thought Zoe.

"Let's show you your office, then," said the super.

Zoe followed Fiona to the floor below. Her office was smaller than Fiona's, with bare walls and a similar view. She took in the glass desk, the computer already set up with her own ID flashing on the screen, the distant view of the fells.

There was no sign of a team room. She was used to working in an office that was separated from her team by a glass partition. In Birmingham, she'd initially resisted using it, preferring to be with her team until realising that there were times when a DI needed privacy.

"Where's my team based?" she asked.

Fiona smiled. "Just a couple of doors up. Not too far."

Zoe frowned. She wouldn't be able to communicate with her team using waves and hand signals. She'd have to actually stand up and walk to them.

"I'll show you," Fiona said, still all smiles. "I asked the team to come in for the morning, so you could meet."

Fiona opened a door and stood back to let Zoe through to a larger room with equally bare walls. One man in his twenties was slumped in a chair behind one of four wooden desks, intent on the screen in front of him. She had a sudden memory of Rhodri Hughes, back in Birmingham.

Zoe cleared her throat. The man jerked up, looking guilty.

"I'll leave you to it." Fiona closed the door and Zoe heard her footsteps – those heels – recede.

"I'm Zoe Finch." She walked towards the man, her hand out. "Your new DI."

A nervous smile broke over his face. "DC Willis, Ma'am. Tom Willis."

He stood and shook her hand, grinning. He had a couple of days' stubble, and under his mop of curly hair he looked exhausted, which wasn't promising. Zoe hadn't liked being called *Ma'am* back in Birmingham – too serious, too distant, too *old* – but this was a new start. A little distance might help.

"So, where's everyone else, Tom? Saturday morning lie-in?"

He shook his head, anxious. "No, Ma'am, it's not that."

"Then what is it?"

He looked blankly at her, then composed himself. "There was a body, Ma'am." He smiled, as if this explained everything.

"A body?"

"A body. Out at the marina. You know it?"

"Not yet. A body?"

"Yes. You... you really don't know the marina, Ma'am?"

"I've been in Whitehaven for three days. The body?"

"Oh, yes. Sorry. Aaron – that's DS Keyes – went out there first thing. With Nina. DC Kapoor. Young woman. Found about four in the morning by some clubbers."

"So they're on the scene. Good. What have you been doing?"

"Going through CCTV from nearby, Ma'am."

"And who told you to do that?"

"The sarge, Ma'am."

This Sergeant Keyes, she thought, *should have tried to get hold of me before going to the scene.* And all this time, she'd been sitting in Fiona's office and drinking coffee.

Had Fiona known?

"Any leads?" she asked.

"Well, you know. Friday night, the town was buzzing."

Zoe stifled a laugh. She hadn't experienced a weekend in Whitehaven, but suspected that it wouldn't match even a slow Monday afternoon in Birmingham.

"And?"

"Up by the marina it's dead quiet at night," Tom said. "Even though it's close to all the bars and everything. The quay is full of blind spots, but just outside, there might be something."

"Where from?"

"There's a building opposite the marina." He looked up. "Pears House. Flats upstairs, shops and the like downstairs. There's this salon – hairdressers – and they had a few break-ins last year, so I know the owner. It's called *Merveilleuse.*"

Zoe winced at his French accent. He carried on, oblivious. "Soon as she saw there were police about, she called me to ask what was going on, and I asked her if she could send me her footage. That's what I've been watching, Ma'am."

"And you think you've found something?"

He pointed to his screen. "Here. This is near the entrance to Bulwark Quay."

"Which is?"

"Sorry. It's the bit of the marina where the body was found. Like, a bit of land sticking out into it. Boats either side, but nothing up where the body was. I'll rewind from four o'clock, OK?"

Zoe grabbed the nearest chair. There was some sort of cover on it, a piece of white material with a design sewn into it. Was that supposed to be a bird?

She pulled the chair over to Tom's desk and sat down, following his finger to an image of a dark, empty patch of ground. In the background, she could make out railings. In the foreground, nothing. He tapped at his keyboard and the fuzz of high-speed rewinding appeared, followed by three figures. He paused and tapped the screen.

"That's the kids who found the body. Aisha, Claire, and Simon. Shitting themselves, they were. Oh, sorry, Ma'am."

"You don't have to apologise. So, have they been questioned?"

"Uniform took statements. I reckon they're OK. They called us, they were terrified."

He was probably right. But Zoe didn't like to let a lead go before she'd tested it herself, especially with a new team.

Tom's fingers were back on the keyboard. The three figures skipped across the screen and were gone. A longer gap, then four other people appeared.

"Stop it there," Zoe said.

Tom paused the video.

"You know this lot?" she asked.

"Nina might. She knows everyone. This is half past two. They just walk past, see?" He started the footage again, going forward this time.

The figures lurched across the screen. Drunk, or similar. The quality of the footage was good; Zoe could make out individual features. If DC Nina Kapoor didn't know these men – all men, all four of them – someone would.

"And then, about twenty minutes earlier," Tom said, "there's this lot."

The screen emptied again, the fuzz returning for a second or two before another group appeared.

There were five of them moving across the screen. This time, Zoe couldn't see features.

Their faces were obscured. Hoods, or hats of some sort. And they were looking away from the camera.

Did they know it was there?

They all wore the same clothes, Zoe realised. Some sort of... Was that a robe?

"What's that?" She pointed at something on the ground between them.

"That's what I wanted to show you, Ma'am. It looks like a bag, doesn't it? A holdall or something."

Zoe nodded. It did.

It looked like a holdall, and if she was any judge, it was big enough to put a body in.

CHAPTER FIVE

AARON SQUINTED.

"What *is* that?" he asked, more to himself than anyone else.

Nina answered anyway. "Looks like blood, Sarge."

"I can see that. But it doesn't look like it got there by accident."

He started to crouch for a closer view, but was interrupted by a familiar voice.

"Step back, Sergeant. The grown-ups are here now."

Aaron turned and stood up. Stella Berry, Crime Scene Manager for the Cumberland area of Cumbria Police, advanced along the quay towards them, her assistant in tow, both clad in the same white protective suits.

Stella was a short woman in her fifties with a loud voice and peroxide blonde hair, something that had initially prejudiced Aaron against her. That, and her habit of treating the police like interfering toddlers. But he'd worked with her long enough to know she knew her business back to front. He stepped away and gestured to the body.

"Morning, Stella. Caroline."

Stella nodded. Caroline Deane gave him a shy smile.

"What have we got here, then?" Stella stepped towards the body. "Young woman, looks like she's had her throat slit. Was this how she was found? How long's she been here?"

"Nina can tell you everything we know," Aaron replied, "but I warn you, it's not much."

It took Nina less than a minute to explain things, in which time Aaron had sent Roddy Chen to the main gate and spotted the latest arrival. Bulwark Quay was getting busy.

"Aaron. Stella. You other two, whoever you are. I'd say good to see you, but it's never good for someone, is it?"

"Dr Robertson." Aaron stopped the pathologist. Stella and Caroline would want a few minutes to examine the scene before Chris Robertson got to grips with the body. Caroline would need to take photos, too. "Are you alone?"

"My lad'll be here soon enough. You keeping me away, Aaron?"

"Stella's only just got here."

"Fair enough. I can wait. It's not like there's a queue of living patients waiting for me at the hospital, right? Oh, no. There *is* a queue of living patients waiting for me at the hospital, and I'd quite like to get back to them before they're not living anymore. I'll give you five minutes."

"Seen this?" shouted Stella, as if on cue. Aaron, Nina, and Dr Robertson all approached.

"These markings on the body," she continued. "I don't want to move her, that's your job, Chris. Could you...?"

Dr Robertson obliged. Stella and Caroline had replaced the tarpaulin with a small white tent, and Caroline was already dismantling her camera. The pathologist turned the body onto its side. Aaron heard Nina exhale beside him. This was what she'd pointed out to him.

"They're right across her back," said Chris. "Some sort of symbol. Looks like blood, but might not be. There's very little blood around the wound. Was she killed here, or brought here?"

Aaron shrugged.

"Depends how she died," said Stella. "If that wound's what killed her, it didn't happen here. Not enough blood around."

"Okay. I think my lad's here," said Chris. His *lad* was whichever intern had been unfortunate enough to be assigned to him that week, and would be *the lad* regardless of age or gender. "You ready for me to move the body?"

Stella opened her mouth to reply but was interrupted by a loud clatter.

Aaron looked back towards the gate. A car had pulled up outside the quay, just behind the vehicle gate. The gate swung slowly, grinding against the ground.

Aaron sighed. Some rich boat-owner, thinking their right to play on the water was more important than a murder investigation.

He sprinted along the quay and stopped in front of the car, hand out, breathing heavily.

The driver's door opened and a tall red-headed woman in black jeans and a leather jacket got out. She didn't look like Aaron's idea of a rich boat owner.

"I'm sorry, Madam," he began.

"Ma'am." She smiled at him.

"I beg your pardon?"

"You can call me Ma'am. DS Aaron Keyes, is it?"

Aaron found himself frowning and nodding at the same time.

"Great. I'm your new DI. Zoe Finch. Mind showing me what we've got?"

"I'll..."

He wasn't sure what to say.

Her ID. He had to check she was legit. "I'm sorry, Ma'am, but I'll have to see some proof of that."

"Of course, here's my ID. Now why don't you let me see my first Cumbrian body?"

Aaron watched as she returned to her car. He checked his watch. There was... Was that a sandwich in her hand?

She'd turned up half an hour late in a ridiculous green Mini, and now she was going to examine the body eating a sandwich.

•"Shut the gate, Roddy," he said, and started walking back up the quay, glancing back at the new DI just in time to see a gull swoop away with half the sandwich in its beak.

CHAPTER SIX

"Oh, for Christ's sake," muttered Zoe as her sandwich was snatched from her hand.

She'd asked Tom to grab her something from the canteen in lieu of her missed breakfast, and he'd returned with an inoffensive-looking cheese sandwich just as she was leaving for the scene.

She'd been nervous as she drove to work. Nervous meeting Fiona, nervous heading to her first crime scene. It had taken a while to persuade the constable at the gate to let her in – she didn't even have a phone number to call ahead. She'd been talking to him long enough to take in her surroundings, the wide road behind her, its gutters still full of last night's kebab wrappers. The marina itself was bigger than she'd expected, this central spit a hive of activity amid near-silence.

She'd been looking forward to that sandwich, was planning to eat it before she put her forensic suit on. And now it had been ripped away right in front of her new DS.

The DS was leading her towards the body, his expression hostile.

She didn't know much about the team; she'd asked Tom, but he'd been cagey. From her website trawl, she knew Aaron Keyes had been a DS for about two years. And now she knew he was Black with a short, neat hairstyle, around six foot tall. And that he didn't seem impressed with his new boss.

She'd eat later.

She grabbed her paper suit, thinking of her old boss Lesley and her chocolate bars. Maybe Zoe would keep food in her car, now she was away from the city and its familiar cafés.

"Aaron," she said. "Let's start again."

"Ma'am."

She smiled. "Can you talk me through what you've found, and make some introductions?"

"Of course."

They approached the body, and Aaron worked around the group. Stella Berry, Crime Scene Manager. Caroline Deane, her assistant. Dr Chris Robertson, the pathologist. There was something familiar about him, but Zoe couldn't place it. And DC Nina Kapoor, a short woman whose long black hair was piled up on her head in some sort of quiff.

"Right. First impressions, Stella?" Zoe asked.

The coffee was starting to wear off, the hunger fighting through, and it was colder here than she'd expected.

"Of what?" asked the blonde woman.

"Of the evidence. Is there anything obvious? Is there anything you might be able to get from the body?"

The woman nodded. If this was a test, Zoe had passed. "I was saying earlier, and Chris'll be able to give more detail, but if the cut to her throat is what killed her, it didn't happen here. No spatter. But the body's in good nick, by the look of it. See the nails?"

Zoe crouched down. Chris Robertson, who'd been staring at her with an odd sort of frown, lifted the victim's right hand.

Stella continued. "Long nails, genuine, a few jagged edges. Might be defensive, and if so, we'll get whatever was left behind. And obviously, she's naked."

Zoe could hardly have missed that.

"Which means she was probably stripped after death. If so, they'll have left something we can work with on her skin. And then there's these marks." Stella pointed to the symbols. "Difficult to do something like that without leaving a trace."

"Right." Zoe turned to Dr Robertson. "Where are you taking her?"

"West Cumberland. We can do the PM there. It's a fifteen-minute drive."

Zoe knew where the West Cumberland Hospital was. And where Stella's lab was. She'd done her research.

"OK," she said. "Aaron, Nina. Any suspects?"

Aaron took a step back. "We've only just found the body, Ma'am—"

"I know it's early days, Aaron, so I'm not expecting you to say *yes*. I'm just asking."

"Oh. OK. Sorry."

Zoe turned a slow circle, checking the surroundings. There was overhead lighting further down the quay, but not here. Near the body was a squat blue metal cylinder with an ancient metal chain looped around it. A capstan? The marina wall and two other deserted quays reached out into the harbour.

She pointed to the nearest quay. "Anyone likely to have been there?"

"Not at night-time, Ma'am," replied Aaron.

"CCTV?"

Nina stepped forward. "Yes, Ma'am. We've got footage

from the marina, but we've been warned it won't be much use. Uniform's checking the boats and flats, just in case. Tom – that's DC Willis – he got some off a woman who runs a salon over there." She pointed past Zoe to a large building over-looking the quay.

"He showed me that. Have you looked at it?"

"It's in the team inbox, but I haven't seen it yet, Ma'am." The DC looked nervous. "Want me to take a look?"

What had Tom Willis said? *She knows everyone.* "Yes, please," Zoe told her. "Work back from four am. There's three groups. First the ones who found her, then at half two there's another lot. Tom thought you might know them. Then another group twenty minutes earlier. You take a look while I talk to the DS."

Nina walked away. Zoe turned to Aaron. "Tom told me she was found by three clubbers. They'd come out here to take drugs?"

"They were so freaked out by what they found, they forgot to get rid of it. But there was barely enough to give a seagull the munchies."

Zoe raised an eyebrow. Had he seen what had happened to her sandwich?

"I really don't think we need to worry about them," he continued.

Zoe nodded. "Good. Leads are useless if they don't take you anywhere."

Dr Robertson passed her, the body rolling on a stretcher between him and a young woman Zoe assumed was his intern. There was definitely something familiar about the man.

She turned back to Aaron. "Right. Let's see if Nina can help us."

Nina approached them, her phone held out. "I think I can, Ma'am. This group, here."

The image on the phone was frozen on the group of four. The ones Zoe had thought might be drunk, captured mid-lurch across the screen.

"What about them?"

"I know them. Well, these three, anyway."

"And?"

"Came across them when I was in Uniform. Had to pick them up a few times, but never anything serious. I can't tell you they're squeaky clean, Ma'am, but *this*?" She gestured towards the quay, where the body had been. "They're just kids. A bit of fighting, some break-ins, low-level drugs. They're trouble, but I don't think they're killers."

"Bad luck, eh?" replied Zoe. "Can the two of you go and pick them up, bring them in?"

Aaron frowned. "You want us to arrest them?"

"Definitely not. I want you to bring them in voluntarily."

"I think... I'm sure Nina can manage that by herself, can't you, Nina?"

Nina gave a small nod.

"And I can stay with you, Ma'am," he continued. "Get things started, you know?"

"I'd rather you go with Nina. Get Uniform assistance, in case of trouble. I'll see you back at the station. Office. Whatever you call it."

"Just the station, Ma'am," said Nina. Aaron was staring at her, silent.

"Good," said Zoe. "Everything OK, Aaron?"

He nodded.

She'd wanted to stamp her authority, to make sure everyone knew who was running the show. She'd been SIO on plenty of investigations in Birmingham, but that had been with a team she'd known for years. This was new.

Had she been brusque?

"Can I have a quick word, Aaron?"

Zoe walked a little way down the quay, listening for his steps behind her. She stopped and turned towards him.

"Is everything OK?" she asked, making sure she sounded like she meant it this time.

"I think so, Ma'am. I'm just... Are you sure you don't want me with you? I mean, you don't know this place, I can help you figure out—"

"And you will. I'll be relying on my team. You, most of all. Right now, I just want to get back, have a bloody sandwich, and start putting things together. And Nina might be confident about these kids, but I'd rather she had you there as well. OK?"

"OK." He nodded.

Thank God for that.

Zoe turned and walked back towards the gate. Chris Robertson was still there, with his colleague, and the body. She'd remembered, at last, where she knew him from.

CHAPTER SEVEN

THE BODY WAS ALREADY inside the van as Zoe approached. Dr Robertson raised a hand in greeting.

"Wait," she said. "Can we chat?"

"Sure."

"You don't remember me?"

His brow creased. "Well, I know who you are. Everyone's heard about the new DI."

She raised an eyebrow. "That's not what I mean. Back in 2003, West Midlands CID. I was new. We fished a couple of bodies out of the canal."

His expression cleared. "How could I forget? Zoe Finch. I knew that name rang a bell." He held out his hand, and she shook it again. "So what brings you to the back of beyond, Detective Inspector?"

"Please, just call me Zoe."

"OK, Zoe. Why Cumbria?"

"Long story." She shook her head. "What about you?"

"I'm a local. Or at least, I was born here. Went to school here. Got out, went to university, worked in London, worked

East Midlands, got seconded to your patch. Last year I heard they were moving post-mortems back here from Carlisle. So, I applied for a job, got it, here I am." He shrugged.

"Excellent. You can be my man on the inside."

"Eh?"

"You can tell me what this place is really like. You're like... Well, you're local, but you're not, at the same time."

"I suppose so." He tipped his head towards the van, parked between two cannons pointed townwards. "And meanwhile you've got a little excitement on your very first day."

"Mind if we have a quick look together?"

"Be my guest."

He pulled open the rear doors, and she climbed in after him. He began to offer her a hand then decided against it.

The victim was lying on her back, in almost the same position she'd been in on the quay. But here, under the internal light, Zoe could see more. Early twenties. Long, dark hair. She'd have been pretty.

"What's this?" She pointed to the left shoulder.

"Tattoo. A red rose. And there's another one." Chris pointed at the woman's right ankle. There was a blue figure there.

"Is that a mermaid?"

"I think so. Now, this wound." He pointed back up at the victim's throat. "It isn't what killed her. Not nearly enough blood around it, not enough blood lost."

"So what *did* kill her?"

He shrugged. "Let me get her back, run a PM, then we might have a better idea. Reckon she'd been dead a while before she was found, though."

"How long?"

Another shrug. "Again, not clear yet. Maybe around midnight, maybe even earlier."

Zoe's legs were feeling the strain of crouching. She straightened up as much as she could without hitting her head on the roof, and rubbed at her calves. "So someone cut her throat *after* she was dead?"

"Looks like it."

"But why? Could they have thought she was alive? Cut her throat just to be sure?"

"You're the detective, Zoe. I can tell you what I think happened to her. Maybe when, if we're lucky. I can't tell you who or why."

He was right. "Anything else, before you take her away?"

"These." He turned the body onto its left side. "These marks."

"I saw them. Blood?"

"That's the thing, it's not blood. I don't know what it is. I'll get samples and Stella can figure it out, but it's not blood."

"Right." Zoe crouched again. There was something familiar about those markings. "It's writing."

"It's what?"

"Writing, Chris. Dr Robertson."

"Chris is fine."

"It's Arabic. I don't know what it says, but I'm ninety-nine per cent sure it's Arabic writing."

"OK." He backed away and stood, removing his gloves and wiping the back of a hand across his face. Zoe watched him. "OK," he repeated.

"Is this going to be an issue?" she asked.

"What do you mean?"

There was a bench seat along the side of the van. Chris dropped into it with a sigh.

She looked at him. This kind of thing would be more straightforward in Birmingham.

"Are people going to jump to conclusions when they hear about this?" she asked. "Am I going to have to lecture my team about racial profiling and that sort of thing? You know them better than me."

He shrugged. "I've met Nina once before, and the other chap, Tim, is it?"

"Tom."

"Him. So them, I've no idea. I've worked with Aaron a bunch of times. He's smart, but he won't put a foot out if there's any chance of it being the wrong foot. Apart from that, it's your team. I don't think any of them are secret racists, but you're going to have to get to know them."

Zoe nodded, thinking back to her interactions with Aaron Keyes that morning, and hoping she hadn't already messed things up.

CHAPTER EIGHT

"Hello, Jay," said Nina.

She was pleased to find him at home. Not that Jay Whitwell was an inspiring sight anywhere. His hair was a greasy mess, his face pitted with acne scars, his eyes slits against the morning light. But the boss had asked her to pick these lads up, and she was relieved that they'd all been where they should be.

"Well, if it isn't Elvis herself," replied Jay. He laughed, then stopped when he noticed the sarge beside her and the imposing figure of Roddy Chen behind them both. "What... what's up?" He turned and called, "the police are here, fellas," then turned back again.

Nina gestured behind her colleagues. Next to her Fiesta, PC Harriett Barnes sat in the front of a response car. A small figure waved from the back seat.

"Is that Mal?" Jay asked.

"Mal's kindly agreed to come to the station for a little chat about last night."

Jay took a step back, towards an open door with a sign taped to it that read "Keep this door shut at all times."

The sarge shook his head.

"What about last night?" Jay asked.

"Wondering if you saw anything in town," Nina replied. "You, Mal and Davey, and the other lad you were out with."

"Dunno what you're talking about."

"Look, Jay, I just want a chat. I don't care what you've got in there, but if you won't help us, then maybe me and my friends *will* take an interest. It's simple, really. Mal understood."

Jay blinked at them. "Mal's mum must've been well pissed off."

Nina nodded. They hadn't had the friendliest of welcomes on Glenridding Walk, where Mal McDonald lived with his mum and his brother. This bit of Cumbria wasn't all lakes and stunning views, and the McDonalds' house had marks on the front door where it had been kicked in and the locks broken over the years.

"No one wants the police at the door, do they?" she said. "Come on, Jay."

He looked between the sarge and Nina. "OK. Give me a minute."

"We're not going anywhere," the sarge told him. After Jay had disappeared upstairs, he turned to Nina. "Elvis?"

She smiled. "You know I do a little karaoke."

"Oh, *I* know. I just didn't realise half the villains in White-haven knew too."

"Villains? If this lot's all we've got to worry about, we can quit right now."

Jay was back, two others at his heels.

"Hello, Davey," said Nina.

Davey Grant was the good-looking one of the three, not that that said much. Tall, broad-shouldered, blond hair looking like it had seen shampoo sometime in the last year.

"Alright, Detective Constable Kapoor?" His voice was surprisingly high-pitched. "What's up, then?"

The DS jumped in. "I'm DS Keyes. You're Davey Grant, right?"

Davey nodded. "You're the one who's..."

Nina glanced at the sarge, who was shaking his head. There weren't many gay officers in Whitehaven – she wasn't sure there were *any* others who were out – so the sarge had given up being surprised when his reputation preceded him.

"And you?" the sarge said to the third man, the fourth if you counted tiny Mal McDonald. This one was older, shaven-headed, with a red-brown beard covering half his thin face. Nina hadn't recognised him.

"Richard." The man stepped forward, hand outstretched.

The sarge looked at it but didn't take it. "Richard? Is that it?"

"Richard Madsen."

"You live here? With these two?"

Davey shook his head. "Ricky-lad crashed with us last night, after we was out, weren't we? Late night." He scratched his head. "Not sure why I'm awake now, to be honest."

"Are we under arrest?" asked Richard Madsen. Nina pegged him as in his mid-twenties. What was he doing with these kids?

"D'you think you should be?" asked the sarge.

Madsen shook his head.

"Good. No need to arrest anyone, provided you help us out."

CHAPTER NINE

It was quiet in the team room, but Tom didn't mind that. He'd had a call from Nina, warning him they were heading back in with four men. He'd got the names and was trawling through HOLMES, but so far there was nothing of interest. Affray, shoplifting, vandalism, minor drugs offences for McDonald, Grant, and Whitwell. He'd come up blank on Richard Madsen.

His phone rang. He answered without looking up from his screen. "Tom Willis."

"Tom, it's Melanie at the front desk. I've got a walk-in for you."

"For me?"

"Says he wants to talk to whoever's investigating the Marina incident."

"The *Marina incident*?"

"That's what he called it. Sounds like a disaster movie, doesn't it?"

Tom laughed. "Well, the others are out, so I suppose that's me. Who is he, anyway?"

"Mick Halfpenny. Ring any bells?"

"None."

"I'll put him in four and tell him you'll be right along. That OK?"

"Thanks."

Tom grabbed his jacket and left a note on his desk before heading to the bathroom to check his appearance. There were dark patches under his eyes and he needed a shave. No worse than usual.

A man in his late fifties or early sixties was waiting in interview room four, the comfortable one with the nice chairs and slightly subtler cameras. He was slim: a man who either worked or walked, but didn't sit on his arse all day like Tom. He had curly, greying hair, and his clothes were nothing to write home about apart from a set of thick-framed red specs.

"Mr Halfpenny? I'm Detective Constable Tom Willis. I understand you want to speak to someone about the marina?"

"You're part of the team looking into it, are you?"

"Can I ask, Mr Halfpenny—"

"Call me Mick. Mind if I call you Tom?"

Tom blinked. "Can I ask what you know about what happened at the marina last night?"

"Well." Mick leaned forward and cleared his throat, a gentle *ahem*. "I don't know what happened, but I can tell you what I saw, Tom."

Tom felt his foot twitch. "And what was that, exactly?"

"Well, it was busy in town, Friday night, but the marina's usually quiet, isn't it?"

"I suppose so. Were you in town last night, then?"

"Oh, well, you know me. Or, no, you probably don't, do you? Well, young man, I suppose you'd say I'm a historian. Local history. More of a hobby than anything else, but some nights you'll find me just walking about, soaking it all in. Better that than staying home listening to the warehouse clanking and scraping all night, right?"

"I suppose so. So, you were around the marina area?"

"That's right. Fascinating history, the marina. The whole town, really." He cleared his throat again. "You do know it was invaded by the Yanks during the War of Independence?"

Tom nodded. You couldn't grow up in Whitehaven without learning about John Paul Jones and his raid.

"Well, anyway, there I was. And I wasn't the only one, I can tell you." Mick raised both eyebrows in expectation.

"And who did you see, then, Mick?" asked Tom, trying to remember everything he'd learned about interviewing people while trying to keep the questions coming at the same time. *Sit up straight and look confident. Look them in the eye. Use their name.* He'd been using the name. Had he been using it too much?

"Well, there were two lots, as it happens. Both sets around the marina, in front of Pears House. There was a bunch of drunks, four of them, staggering about the place, and as I say, Tom, I don't know what actually took place last night." He paused, waiting. Tom said nothing.

"But whatever it was," he continued, "I doubt they could have managed it. Struggling to walk in a straight line, they were."

Tom nodded. "Thanks, Mick. Two lots, you say?"

"There were the others, a little earlier. About two o'clock. Very strange, all in white. Five of them, wearing the same white clothes, almost like robes, and they had a great big bag they were dragging along with them."

Tom nodded again, more keenly. "Can you tell me anything else about them? About either group?"

"Alas, no. I wish I could be more helpful. But when I heard about all the excitement down at the marina this morning, I thought it was my civic duty to come in and let you know what I'd seen."

"You did the right thing, Mick." Tom thanked him and made sure they had one another's contact details before accompanying him back to the front desk, where he thanked him one last time before watching him leave the building.

He hadn't learned anything they didn't already know. But if this Mick had been on the scene, it was possible he might have something more locked up in his memory.

And with people like Mick Halfpenny, it never hurt to show a little gratitude.

CHAPTER TEN

"Want us to stick around, Sarge?" asked Harriett Barnes.

Standing in the entrance to the Custody Suite, Aaron eyed their cargo: four young men with a penchant for minor acts of violence. It wouldn't hurt to have Harriett around. It definitely wouldn't hurt to have Roddy Chen there.

But they were here voluntarily. To provide information, if they had any. Roddy's presence might not help with that.

"It's OK, Harriett. Thanks for your help this morning. Can you head back to the marina and carry on with the door-to-door?"

"Sir." She summoned Roddy with a tilt of her head and walked away.

There was the sound of a scuffle behind Aaron. He turned to see one of the youths – Jay? – holding another's head under his arm and preparing to punch the lad in the face.

"Stop that!" he shouted.

Jay released his victim, Davey, who was laughing and, it seemed, uninjured.

"Just messin' about, Your Honour," said Jay, followed by "Ow!" as he received a punch in the arm from Davey. Aaron shook his head as he approached the desk, where Sergeant Clive Moor stood and surveyed his empire.

Clive 'Ilkley' Moor was a refugee from Yorkshire who'd been in charge of the Custody Suite since before Aaron had joined CID. He had one rule, which was *Don't fuck about*, and he applied it equally to the freshest of constables, the arrestees, and the most senior officers in the building. Aaron explained what he was after, and Ilkley told him what he could have. Rooms one and two, not too shabby but hardly comfortable, plus a couple of plastic chairs in the corridor outside them.

That would do.

The lads were still talking behind him. He called Nina over.

"What the hell are they on about?"

"Come on, old man. It's not that complicated."

"I'm thirty-two, Nina. What's a Goldie? What the hell is a Plumber?"

Nina laughed. "Names, Sarge. They're just winding each other up about their shoes."

Aaron looked blank.

"Trainers. For some people, it's important."

Aaron looked down at his and Nina's feet – both sensible work wear – and at the four lads'. Trainers. Big. White. You wouldn't run far in those. And you wouldn't enjoy wiping the mud off them. He watched them for a moment. Banter. Minor acts of violence.

It wouldn't hurt for them to know how serious things were.

He leaned over and muttered to Ilkley then turned back to the lads, raising his voice. "Thanks for coming along with us, lads. DC Kapoor and I will be speaking to each of you individually in a moment. In the meantime, wait here with Sergeant Moor. He'll look after you."

In the corridor outside, he and Nina discussed tactics. He kept an ear on the reception area: more banter, more minor acts of violence, and then a quiet word from Ilkley. The word was *murder*.

The reception area went quiet. The messing about stopped.

These lads hadn't done anything serious. But they might know who had. Aaron wanted them to take things seriously.

Half an hour later, he and Nina reconvened in the team room.

"What did Jay and Mal have to say?"

She surveyed her notes. "The bunch of them were out all night. Drinking. Smoking weed, according to Jay. He took that back quickly enough."

Aaron nodded. He'd spoken to Davey, and to Richard, the older man. "Same here." He listed the pubs. Gallacher's, the Corner Bar, the Candlestick. Another one they couldn't remember.

"I've got the same, Sarge. It fits."

"No mention of five figures in robes dragging a big bag around?"

"Plenty of people mentioned. But not them."

"Me neither." He sighed. "I guess we'd better let them get home."

He went back down to Ilkley's empire. Two response cars had been summoned; there were no buses out here.

Aaron watched as they piled into the cars. Banter, again. A touch of violence. But not from Richard Madsen. The older man held himself back.

"You sure you've never come across him before?" he asked Nina.

"Sorry, Sarge. He's new to me."

Aaron sniffed. Madsen looked like the lads' leader. So how come they'd never seen him before?

CHAPTER ELEVEN

Zoe sat in her Mini outside the station, looking up and trying to identify her new office. She had a murder to deal with already, but it wasn't that which was playing on her mind.

She still wasn't sure about the team.

Tom was pleasant enough, but seemed reluctant to get out from behind his desk. Nina looked capable and wasn't prepared to sit back and let things happen.

She'd been impressed by Aaron, but disappointed by the tension between them. She wasn't expecting another Mo – that was too much to hope for – but she needed a DS she could count on. Someone who understood her, who'd do what she asked and, if they had doubts, would save them for a private conversation.

At least Fiona had seemed welcoming.

She climbed out of the car, her stomach rumbling. *Let's hope there's a bloody vending machine somewhere.* Maybe Tom could find her something again.

Inside, she made for the stairs. A man was descending.

"DI Finch?" he said.

Zoe nodded.

"Inspector Keane. Morris Keane. You can call me Minor, everyone does, I don't hold it against them. Been looking forward to meeting you. Hope you're settling in alright."

He spoke quickly and his tone was friendly. He was in his mid to late fifties, his shirt stretched across a generous stomach.

"Thanks," she replied.

"Let me give you my number. You want extra help from Uniform, you can go all the way up the chain like you're supposed to, or you can give me a call and I'll sort you out."

He smiled and walked past her to the reception area. Zoe watched, trying to make sense of him. Hopefully his offer was genuine. She didn't think she'd be calling him *Minor*.

She carried on up the stairs, passing a bald, long-faced PC in his forties. He gave her a passing glance just short of being a leer, then continued walking.

Aaron was outside the team room, at the top of the stairs. "You've met Tel Cummings, then."

She looked back. "The man I just passed? I wouldn't say *met*."

He raised his eyebrows. "PC Cummings, not the most forthcoming of men. Be wary of him. That's all I'm saying."

"OK. I'm glad you're here. We can get the team together, kick things off."

He nodded. "Just give me a moment. I'll fetch Nina."

The team room was empty, just a note on Tom's desk Zoe struggled to decipher. She slipped out and back to her own office.

The room was bare. Gleaming, but utilitarian. Should she personalise it? She'd never been good at keeping plants alive. A photograph? Not of Carl, who might end up investigating people who entered this room. Nicholas? Maybe Yoda?

No. She wasn't that kind of woman.

Zoe went back out to the corridor. She needed coffee.

After opening and closing four doors, including a fire door, she found it. Another featureless room, with modern but cheap kitchen units and a fridge that contained nothing but a carton of milk.

She chose the blandest mug in the hope it didn't have an owner, and the least offensive-looking instant coffee. She'd bring in her own mug tomorrow. Some better coffee.

As she poured, her phone rang. She glanced at the screen and snatched it up, wincing as boiling water splashed on her hand.

"Mo!" she said. "God! How are you?"

"Great, Zo. All good. But I wanted to hear about you. I wanted to say good luck on your first day."

Wind noise almost drowned him out. Mo would be in his car, racing between loch and mountain to some majestic windswept crime scene. Zoe closed her eyes and pictured him as she turned on the tap, shaking out her hand. She smiled.

"It's been OK." She plunged her hand under the water while squeezing the phone beneath her chin. "Big change. You know what it's like."

"Oh, I know what it's like. You've moved county. I'm in a different country, and they really *are* different here."

She laughed, then winced. She needed to be more careful. "Where are you, anyway?"

"I'm pulling up outside a chippie in Glasgow where some wee bastard's got himself stabbed in the guts. You?"

"The office. Making a coffee. Glasgow, then?" Not a majestic windswept crime scene. "And *wee bastard*? You gone native?"

"You'll be the same. Striding across the fells, chewing on

Kendal Mint Cake before the month's out. But really, is everything OK?"

"I think so. New team, new boss." Zoe went to close the kitchen door. "I miss what we had, Mo. You and me, Rhodri and Connie. I'm sure they're fine here, but I'm not looking forward to building all that up again."

"Be patient. You just said it yourself: they'll be fine. Give it time. Don't forget, you're a brilliant DI."

"You're biased. And what if I'm wrong, and they're not fine at all? What if they're a bunch of Ian Osmans and David Randles?"

"What are the odds of that? I can see why you're worried, but what happened in Brum, it's not normal. I don't think you need to worry."

She sighed. Down the line, she could hear Mo's engine cutting out.

"And how's Carl?" he asked. "You two getting on OK? All better since the move?"

"All good. And what about you? How's the job? How are Catriona and the girls?"

"Cat's OK; the NHS is just a little bit nicer to its GPs north of the border. And the girls are turning into haggises before my eyes. Nicholas came for lunch last weekend."

Zoe felt her heart dip. Mo was living in Stirling, minutes away from her son.

"How was he? He didn't ask you to do his washing, I hope."

"We're always happy to do his washing. Anything else he needs. Nicholas is family, Zo. Don't forget I was there when he was born."

"You were." Zoe turned off the tap and sucked her hand.

"Look, I've got to go. I need to kick off a murder investigation, and you're making me want to cry."

"I didn't mean to."

"In a good way, Mo. Give Nicholas a hug from me, next time you see him. I don't care if he tries to wriggle out of it. And tell him to come to Cumbria. It's closer than Brum."

"Will do. You look after yourself."

Zoe hung up and picked up her coffee. The team would be waiting.

Mo was building a life, up in Scotland. Her own son was part of it. She had no family here. Just her, Carl, Yoda, and, eventually, she hoped, Nicholas. But it was a start. It could be enough.

She hoped it would be enough.

CHAPTER TWELVE

CARRYING coffee in one hand and her phone in the other, Zoe made her way back, trying not to compare Mo's moving experience to her own.

"Shit," she said as a fire door sprang back on her and made her spill coffee down her shirt.

In the team room, Tom was slumped in his chair again, looking like he'd been working all night. Nina faced him, frowning into her screen, the back of her head resting on that strange cover Zoe had noticed earlier. Aaron stood between them. He turned as she walked in, clocking the coffee and phone but saying nothing.

Zoe smiled at him. If no one had spotted the stain yet, so much the better.

"Right," she began. "We've already started working together, but because of... events... I haven't had the chance to introduce myself properly."

"Murderers," muttered Tom. "Inconsiderate bastards."

She suppressed a smile. "My name's Zoe Finch. I was with Force CID in the West Midlands for longer than I care to remember, and now I'm here. I like to think I'm not difficult to work for, and I'll always be happy to listen to your ideas as long as you remember the buck stops with me."

She looked around the room. Tom was sitting up, at last, and nodding as she spoke. Nina was attentive. She paused on Aaron and he gave her a nod in acknowledgement.

"I appreciate it's not ideal being thrown into a murder investigation on my first day with you. You're right, Tom, murderers are inconsiderate, and that's not the worst of it."

A small laugh from Tom. Smiles from Nina and Aaron.

"But I've heard great things about this team, and I'm confident we can solve this and show Cumbria Constabulary that we're a team to look out for. OK?"

"OK," they replied in unison.

"Your turn now." She sat down at the empty desk and looked at Aaron.

He pursed his lips and walked to the centre of the room. "Detective Sergeant Aaron Keyes, Cumbria lad through and through—"

"*Lake District,*" Nina said, with a sneer.

Aaron gave her a look. "What Nina is alluding to, Ma'am, is that I come from a more salubrious area than Whitehaven. Proper fells and lakes round Elterwater, just not quite enough serious crime to keep me there."

"And three fingers on every hand," muttered Tom.

"I've been a copper for twelve years," Aaron continued. "CID for seven, a DS for two. I've had the dubious pleasure of working with these two since they joined CID, and I hope I can speak for us all when I say we're all really pleased to have you on board."

There was vocal agreement from Tom and Nina.

"And finally," Aaron said, "from a personal point of view,

Ma'am, I hope you don't mind me saying that I've heard great things about you too. I'm excited to work with you and learn from your experience."

Zoe eyed him, looking for sarcasm. But he was for real. "Thanks. Nina?"

Nina stood in the centre of the room. "Nina Kapoor, proper local, just under a year in CID, looking forward to working with you. Love being a copper, but nothing gets between me and The King."

Zoe frowned. "The King?"

"Uh huh huh," intoned Nina. Tom sniggered. Aaron shook his head.

"The King?" repeated Zoe.

"Elvis," explained Nina. "I don't want to blow my own trumpet, Ma'am, but it's fair to say I'm Whitehaven's number one Elvis impersonator."

Zoe looked from Nina to Tom, and then to Aaron. There was no sign that Nina was joking.

But the quiff made sense now.

"And is there much competition in that field?" she asked.

Nina shrugged. "You can only beat what's in front of you, Ma'am." She sat back down.

Tom stood up, remaining in front of his chair. "Tom Willis. Lived here since I was nine. Met this one" – he waved in Nina's direction – "at police training. Imagine how thrilled I was to find myself getting accepted into CID and finding out she'd done the same thing at the same time."

"Working for the same unfortunate DS," added Aaron.

"All you need to know about me, Ma'am, is that I'm the normal one." Tom sat down, then stood again. "I'm looking forward to working for you." He looked at the other two. "When you think it might have been Markin' Time."

"Markin' Time?" asked Zoe, wondering if this was another Elvis reference.

"DI Markin, Ma'am."

"Markin' Time?" repeated Zoe.

Aaron cleared his throat. "He has... It's just... Never mind."

Zoe nodded. *Laziness?* "Don't worry, Aaron. I get it."

There were disadvantages to stepping into a ready-made team. But perhaps there were some advantages, too.

"Right," Zoe said. "Now we've all got to know each other, let's catch ourselves a murderer."

CHAPTER THIRTEEN

There was a suitable photo in the team mailbox – Chris Robertson had sent through half a dozen – and Zoe had Tom print it off, along with CCTV stills showing the three groups who'd been in the area.

"Can you stick these on the board, Tom?" she asked, eyeing a board in the corner. "Pull it out, too."

"We've got an app, Ma'am," Tom said. "Takes half a second to add stuff, you can move it around, it's... A child could do it."

"What if I want to show you all something? If I want to draw connections with you watching while I do it?"

He smiled. "You can do all that on the app. And it's connected to this."

He was pointing at the wall behind Zoe. She turned to see a screen that was four times the size of the sad, lonely board.

It was an improvement, she had to admit. "OK." She'd have to learn the new system. Not now, though. "What have we got, then?"

Using his phone, Aaron displayed the images onscreen: the victim and each of the groups. "We've had a chance to look at the CCTV in a couple of the bars on Tangier Street. That's the centre of Whitehaven's nightlife." He brought up a photograph of a neon-lit club entrance. "And the three who found the body, they go straight from this place to the marina, and call us a few minutes later. Tallies with what they said in interview. I think we can rule them out."

Zoe nodded as the original screen returned.

"Now we have this lot," Tom said, "the ones you sent us to pick up." The other images disappeared, leaving just the four young men, faces turned towards the camera. "Nina?"

"Jay Whitwell." Nina drew a red ring around one of the figures using her own phone. "Age eighteen. Mal McDonald," another ring, "and Davey Grant," a third, "both nineteen. All at the same schools in Whitehaven, left without any decent qualifications, no proper jobs but some occasional bar work or unskilled labour. Previous for affray, shoplifting, vandalism, some minor drugs offences. They're the sort of lads that the expression *known to the authorities* was invented for. They're basically idiots, but I wouldn't have them down for murder."

"That's what Mick Halfpenny said," added Tom.

Zoe turned to him. "Who?"

"Sorry, should have mentioned. I had a walk-in."

"A walk-in?"

"Guy called Mick Halfpenny turned up at the station while you were all out. Told me he was at the marina last night. He saw two groups. The lads we pulled in earlier. Said they were drunk." Tom checked a scrap of paper. "*Struggling to walk in a straight line.*"

"Did he see the other group?" Aaron asked.

"Yes. About two o'clock. Described them as very strange, all in white. Five of them." Tom looked up. "Dragging a big bag around with them."

"Anything else?" Zoe asked. "I don't suppose he saw the actual murder?"

Tom blushed. "Sorry, Ma'am."

"Who is he anyway, this Mick Halfpenny?"

"Local historian, he told me," replied Tom. "Old guy. Well, sixty or something like that. Seemed nice enough, but he likes to talk."

"Anyone heard of him?"

Blank looks and shrugs all around.

"So, what was he doing in town in the middle of the night?"

Tom searched his desk to consult more scraps of paper. "He told me that some nights he walks around town to soak it all in, because it's noisy at home. Warehouse nearby."

"Does that sound likely?"

"It's possible," said Aaron. "Front desk gets plenty of complaints about noise at night. Businesses springing up all over the place."

"Right," said Zoe. "The four lads. Nina, you haven't mentioned the last one."

"Richard Madsen? Never seen him before today, Ma'am. Sarge interviewed him."

"Aaron?"

"He didn't have a lot to say," Aaron replied. "Older than the others, but he backs up their story."

"Let's see what we can find out about him. Tom, can you check for anything on the system?"

"Already did. He comes up clean."

"Well done. And the interviews?" Zoe looked from Aaron to Nina.

"Nothing really," said Nina. "They got into a bit of trouble, but that's normal for this lot. I've written up a report from us picking them up to sending them packing." She tapped on her phone. "I've sent it to the team mailbox, Ma'am, but I dropped a printout on your desk."

"Thanks, Nina. I'll look at it when I get a chance. But it's looking like this group isn't involved, like you and Aaron say. I spoke to Chris Robertson. He's convinced the victim's throat was cut after death. Then there's the symbols on her back."

"In blood," added Nina.

"Actually, not blood," Zoe pointed out. "Dr Robertson will be getting samples to the CSIs, but he was certain it wasn't blood. And it wasn't just random symbols. It was writing."

She looked around the room: three pairs of eyes, all focused. Even Tom looked like he was taking things in.

"Arabic writing," she said.

"Oh," said Nina, in a near-whisper. "The robes."

"The other group," Zoe said. "Get them up on that screen, will you?"

A moment later, they were onscreen. Five of them, all wearing robes, with a bag on the ground between them. Zoe couldn't make out their faces, but the robes were clear, and looked white.

"You know what this means?" said Nina. "This'll get out, and local Asians'll get blamed for it."

"Not if we find out who actually did it," Zoe told her. "And not if we find out who these people are. Any ideas?"

More blank looks and shaken heads from Aaron and Nina. Tom peered at the screen.

"It looks..." He tapped at his phone and the image zoomed in on the two figures nearest the camera. He circled something in red.

Zoe took a step towards the screen. "That's a design." Just below the neckline was what looked like a half circle and some more complex lines. "Good work, Tom. Any idea what it's supposed to be?"

"No. But I can check online."

Zoe turned, hearing Aaron mumbling. He was looking at her with an uncertain expression.

"What is it, Aaron?" she asked.

"It's like Nina says, I don't want to be jumping to conclusions. Getting people blamed just because of where they're from or what religion they are."

Zoe dug her nails into her palms. *First day*, she reminded herself. *First day, new team.*

"I can hardly work out if you're jumping to conclusions if you won't tell me what you're thinking, Aaron."

He pushed out a breath. "There's a brand-new Islamic community centre up by North Shore. Not far from the marina."

Nina nodded in agreement. "Near where the Conway development's supposed to be."

Zoe shrugged. Had they forgotten she didn't know the area?

"Exclusive development," Aaron said. "Executive houses, not very Whitehaven, but they'll sell, if they ever get built. Anyway, all I was saying is, there is a Muslim presence in town. I'm not saying it's anything to do with this lot." He gestured at the screen. "But they might know something."

Zoe nodded. "OK. What do you think, Nina? Any thoughts on the centre, or this group?"

Nina looked uncomfortable. "I'm not a Muslim, Ma'am. They might not be either, but the centre is. I'm a Sikh."

"Sorry, Nina. That's not... I meant that you seem to know everyone around here. Meanwhile, we need to identify the victim."

Aaron tapped again and an image of a woman's face appeared on the screen. The wound had been cropped out, and it almost looked like she was asleep. So pale, though.

"This one'll do if we need something for the public," said Zoe. "I take it your Mick Halfpenny didn't have any idea who she was?"

Tom shook his head. "He didn't even know there'd been a murder. Called it the *marina incident*."

"And your bunch of idiots, Nina?"

"When they heard the word *murder* they froze. It was news to them, I'd swear it."

"What about the CCTV from the marina?"

Aaron shook his head. "Blind spots, bad angles, poor light. You'd have to stand in front of it and wave."

"OK. Here's what we're going to do. Tom, I take it you're the person for online info, social media, image searches, right?"

"That's me."

"Good. See if you can find out anything about these people with the robes and the bag. And anything on the Arabic writing."

"You're sure it's Arabic, Ma'am?" asked Nina.

"Good point. It looks familiar, I think it's Arabic, but that's not enough. Start by assuming it's Arabic, and then spread out if you don't get anywhere. Meanwhile, Nina, I want you on the victim. Dr Robertson's sent through a whole bunch of images, and there are a couple of tattoos you can't see—"

"I've got them, Ma'am." Nina held her phone up.

Zoe was developing a healthy dislike for this app. "Get onto Mispers and anything else that might help. Aaron, I want you liaising with Stella Berry and Chris Robertson. Find out when the PM will be."

"No problem, Ma'am."

"Good. I think that's everything." Zoe hesitated. "No. I'm still not happy about your drunken idiots, Nina."

"I really think—"

"I'm worried your familiarity with them is clouding your judgement. Let's assume you're right about the ones you know. That still leaves Richard Madsen. He's older than the rest, doesn't say much, and comes up blank on our systems."

She looked from Nina to Aaron, waiting for a challenge. There was none.

"Good. In that case, Tom, do you think you can put your tech skills to work tracking down Richard Madsen, too?"

Tom nodded. "Easy."

"Really?" Nina said. "You willing to bet on it?"

A smile flickered on Tom's lips. He glanced at the white thing Zoe had noticed over the back of a chair. "Usual deal, right?"

Nina smiled. Zoe didn't know what was going on here, and she wasn't about to ask.

"OK, folks." She clapped her hands once, thinking of the times she'd seen her old boss DCI Lesley Clarke do the same. "Let's get to work."

CHAPTER FOURTEEN

AARON KNOCKED on the door to the DI's office. He'd left messages for Stella Berry and Dr Robertson and left the others getting on with their tasks.

He was still trying to figure out the new DI. Her record spoke for itself, and she seemed like she knew what she was doing, but *seemed* wasn't enough. Did she know he was gay? He knew it shouldn't matter, but he always dreaded having that conversation with a senior officer.

On top of that, he wasn't sure what impression he'd made. Yes, she was the DI, but he was the one who knew the station, the town, the way things worked around here. Perhaps he should make the running?

He heard a sigh, followed by, "Come in," and pushed open the door.

DI Finch was at her desk. There was nothing on it other than the PC and the phone.

"Ma'am," he said. Behind her, through the window, the sky was greying and rain had begun to fall.

"Aaron. What can I do for you?"

"I'm sorry, Ma'am."

"What for?"

"This morning. At the marina. I didn't know it was you, and when... Well, I might have been friendlier. More welcoming."

The DI frowned at him for a moment, then laughed. He breathed out in relief.

"It's OK, Aaron. You had a new DI missing, and then she shows up and gets her breakfast nicked by a bloody seagull."

"I didn't—"

"I know you saw. Must have been tough not to laugh out loud. And for the record, this isn't my first murder case; I'd have finished that sandwich before I got to the body." She leaned across the desk, her hands clasped. "Look, I know it's difficult. You've been running this team since Nina and Tom joined, reporting directly to Detective Superintendent Kendrick. You're used to your own way of working. I'm used to having my office right inside the team room. I'm sure we'll work it out."

"Thank you. Do you mind me asking," he said, nervous again, "what do you see my role as?"

"Your role?"

"Will you be getting me to delegate everything to the DCs, or will you be managing them yourself? Do you want me working on things by your side or running parallel tracks on investigations? It would—"

"Let's work it out as we go along, yes?"

"I just wonder..." He noticed the expression on her face.

"Look," she said, "I don't know you yet. And you don't know me. I have no idea where your strengths are until I've seen you all in action, and I won't get that after half a day on the job. I need to see it for myself."

"OK," he replied. "Thanks, Ma'am. I'll get back then, shall I?"

She nodded, her expression vague.

Aaron turned and left. *That could have gone better*, he thought as he headed back to the team room. *But it could have gone a whole lot worse, too.*

CHAPTER FIFTEEN

"Ma'am?"

Zoe sighed. The one advantage of an office away from the team room should have been privacy. She'd been about to call Carl and ask him how his day was going. But now Tom was easing the door open, looking excited.

"What have you got?" she said. "The mysterious Mr Madsen?"

He shook his head. "Sorry. But there is something I'd like to show you."

She followed him back to the team room, where the screen was divided in half. He pointed to the left-hand side.

"This is the website for the Whitehaven Islamic Community Centre." He circled a section in the corner. "This is their logo. Look familiar?"

A dome, with a tower; a minaret, Zoe assumed. Above that, a star and crescent, all white against a black background. Tom switched to the other half of the screen, a close-up of the robes.

It was the same symbol.

"And look at this," he said. He clicked on the website's *Facilities* link.

The page contained an image of the community centre, along with a description of bookable meeting rooms. In the image, three men were walking out of the centre. They were heavily bearded and serious-looking, all three of them wearing white robes.

She clenched a fist. "Tom, just because—"

"No." He circled a small area on one of the robes.

Shit.

There was no doubt about it.

Same design. Same placement.

Same robes.

"Great work," Zoe said, allowing herself to relax. "Aaron, let's pay them a visit."

Tom grinned.

"Carry on with your searches," she told him. "Keep looking for the writing, find out about this community centre, and call me if you think there's anything we need to know. You've got..." Zoe turned to Aaron.

"It's a twenty-minute drive. Maybe less."

She nodded. "You've got twenty minutes, Tom. Nina, any luck on Mispers?"

"Not yet."

"Keep going on that, but first can you grab an image of that writing the victim and clean it up as best you can? I want something to show people without them knowing they're looking at a dead woman's back."

Nina nodded.

"Great. Aaron, you're with me. Let's go."

CHAPTER SIXTEEN

AARON HADN'T DRIVEN a senior officer for a while, and found himself taking the roads more cautiously than usual. He glanced at the DI from time to time, trying to gauge her reactions, but her gaze was fixed on the window. It had stopped raining, and the clouds were breaking.

He took them in through Hensingham, but instead of swinging north around the centre of town, he decided to drive straight through it.

"So this is Whitehaven, Ma'am. This is Corkickle, where we picked up Davey and Jay and Richard Madsen."

He pointed at the block. She nodded but gave no comment.

Five minutes later, they were driving along Duke Street. Aaron took a right into Queen Street and round the block so he could show her St Nicholas' Church and its gardens.

"Lovely," the DI said. "That's my son's name, as it happens."

"Nicholas?"

She nodded as Aaron navigated the one-way streets towards North Shore.

"Is he moving to a school up here?" he asked.

"He's away at uni."

"Ah. Where's he studying?"

"Stirling. Miles away. Might as well be Sydney." She pointed towards the giant Tesco. "Can you pull in there?"

He stopped a few feet from the entrance.

"Sorry," she said. "I'm starving. Want anything?"

"I'm fine."

The DI emerged two minutes later with another cheese sandwich, eating the whole thing in the handful of steps between the exit and the car. Aaron smiled to himself. She wasn't giving the gulls a second chance.

"So we're near the marina, right?" she asked as they pulled back onto the road.

He tilted his head back the way they'd come. "Very close. There's a boatyard here." He pointed to one side. "Then the offices. Then we're onto the new stretch. The sea," he added, pointing the other way. There was nothing there, not even rubble, but three signs rose from the scrub. *Conway Homes.*

"Someone's building," the DI said.

Aaron nodded. "They've levelled the embankment here, ready for a few big houses. It'll be a decent site, if they ever get it started." They turned a corner. "And this is the community centre."

The Whitehaven Islamic Community Centre was a low, modern, domed structure with a tiny tower attached. There was a small car park, with just a four-year-old Škoda in it. The two of them left the car and approached the building in silence, broken only by the sound of the gulls and their footsteps on the gravel.

The DI was scanning the front of the building.

"What are you looking for?" Aaron asked.

"Separate entrances for men and women."

There was no sign of anything like that. Just a single door with a buzzer. The DI pressed it.

A middle-aged woman appeared, wearing a long, dark blue dress. Her hair was wrapped in a blue and white floral scarf. She smiled at the DI, then at Aaron.

"Can I help you?"

A bearded man wearing a white shirt and trousers appeared behind her. He put a hand on the woman's shoulder and echoed her smile.

"I hope so," replied the DI. "I'm Detective Inspector Zoe Finch, and this is Detective Sergeant Aaron Keyes, from Cumbria CID. We're investigating an incident near here last night."

"That poor girl." The woman frowned. "News spreads, unfortunately."

The DI nodded.

"Please, come in," said the man. Aaron took a step forward, but stopped, almost tripping over the boss, who'd bent down in front of him.

"No need to take your shoes off," said the man. The DI straightened up.

They followed the couple through a narrow corridor, past a kitchen and into a living room with two well-worn sofas and three mismatched armchairs. Zoe took one end of a sofa and Aaron took a high-backed chair. It was hard.

"I am Ali Bashir." The man sat on a sofa beside the woman. "I run this community centre with my wife, Inaya."

"Would you like some tea?" the woman asked.

"Please," said Aaron.

"Have you got coffee, by any chance?" the DI asked.

"Of course."

"Can I ask," she said, "what's the difference between a community centre and a mosque?"

"It's everything and nothing," Mr Bashir replied. "A Masjid will be bigger, and we hope to establish one eventually. In the meantime, we study here, we can pray. It's just a place that people know is there."

"So you're the Imam here?" asked the DI.

The man shook his head. "I have been an Imam, but here, I'm just the prayer leader. You can call me whatever makes you comfortable, but on the whole, I prefer Ali."

Aaron listened in silence. He'd never sat and drunk tea with an Imam before.

"Is there a significant Muslim community in White-haven?" the DI asked.

"Not really," replied Mrs Bashir. "But there are people dotted around the western edges of Cumbria. So we thought, why not give them a focal point here?"

"All we want," added her husband, "is to be a part of the community. The Whitehaven community. People think we're different. We want to show them that we're not, not really."

Aaron shifted in his seat. He sipped at his tea, putting it back down when he realised that his bladder was already full. Looking back up, he saw that the DI was showing the couple her phone.

"These words," she said, "I hoped you could help us with them. What does it say?"

"Is this—?" began Ali.

"I think we can all see what it is, Ali," his wife said.

She's right, thought Aaron.

Nina had sent through the photo, nicely cleaned up. But it didn't take a genius to realise this was a photo of the body.

"It was a woman?" asked Inaya.

The DI nodded.

"That makes this a mistake."

"It's... Well, it's not a nice word," her husband said, his brow furrowed. "You'll have heard it in the mouths of terrorists and demagogues. *Kafir.* It's an insult, meaning non-believer, or just someone who isn't a Muslim."

"How is it a mistake?"

"Arabic is a gendered language," the woman replied. "For a female subject, it should say *kafirah.* Whoever wrote this doesn't have perfect Arabic."

"People make mistakes," her husband pointed out.

The pressure on Aaron's bladder was becoming more than uncomfortable. He stood up. "I'm sorry. Do you mind if I use your bathroom?"

Ali led him out of the room, pointing to a door at the end of the corridor.

Aaron fought back an urge to justify himself; he'd often pretended to need the toilet so he could snoop around a suspect's property. This wasn't one of those times.

These people weren't suspects. And they'd been helpful.

He left the toilet and stepped back out into the corridor, his gaze downwards on the patterned tiles.

"Who are you?"

Aaron looked up.

A young man barred his way. He stood filling the corridor as much as he could, given his slim build. His face was set in a hard expression and he wore white robes.

White robes like the ones in the CCTV.

Aaron swallowed. "I..."

The man shook his head. He took a step towards Aaron.

"No. You need to tell me who the hell you are. And you need to tell me what you're doing in our place of worship."

CHAPTER SEVENTEEN

"Nothing local," Nina muttered.

"What?" Tom asked.

"Just talking to myself." She lowered her voice. "Only way I can be sure of an intelligent conversation."

"I heard that."

"You can add *good hearing* to your list of talents, then. Take it all the way up to two."

She ducked as he threw a scrunched-up sheet of paper, then bent to her screen to widen the search.

If the dead woman was local, she hadn't been reported missing. That didn't mean she *wasn't* local, just that she hadn't been missed.

She sighed. *Time to check the national databases.* Slow, dull, and equally depressing.

"Bloody hell."

Nina turned to Tom. "What?"

"Come and look at this. *Shit.*" He looked at his watch. "Too late to tell the boss. She'll be in there by now."

"What are you talking about?" Nina stood behind him to look at his screen. He had Twitter open.

He tapped the screen. "I've been searching Twitter. X, whatever it's called these days. Looking for stuff about the community centre." He pointed at a tweet from an account named *Dragonslayer*. Its avatar was a St George's Cross.

What kind of sick bastard slits a woman's throat? No Christian, that's for sure. #WestCumbriaIslamicCommunityCentre

"Shit," Nina muttered. "Is there anything else?"

He clicked to display other tweets from the same account. Predictably racist, predictably tedious, but nothing that would draw attention.

"How did they know about the throat?" he asked.

The first tweet had two retweets and a handful of likes from similar anonymous accounts with similar names. *Sons of Albion. White Knights. Men of the North.* The hashtag brought up four more tweets, from the same accounts, with similar phrasing. *Outsiders. Infidels. Invaders.*

Nina realised she was shaking. She forced herself to stand still.

Tom pointed at a tweet from *Men of the North*. "This isn't good."

This was done on a Friday night. After prayers. By men wearing white robes. Doesn't take a genius, does it?

"You need to call the boss," Nina said.

"I want to check the others."

Nina forced herself to return to her desk and pick up with Mispers. She couldn't concentrate.

"Fuck," said Tom.

Nina walked back round. He was on Facebook, yet another anonymous account with a stupid name, a similar message, and the same hashtag.

But this time, there was a photo.

It showed the five figures. Five figures in robes, dragging a bag through the streets of Whitehaven. Again, the faces were obscured; again, the backdrop was the area just outside the quay.

Nina inhaled.

The angle was different, not the one from the CCTV Tom had recovered. It was closer. No buildings in the shot, no structures.

She turned to Tom.

"Someone took that."

Tom nodded. "Someone who was there."

CHAPTER EIGHTEEN

ZOE WAS SIPPING at her too-sweet coffee and wondering where Aaron had got to when a young man dressed in a white robe stomped into the room. Aaron walked in behind him, looking shellshocked.

Ali stood up, facing the young man.

"Why are these people here?" the young man asked, looking at the older couple.

Inaya cleared her throat. "Sit down, Ibrahim."

"They're police, aren't they?"

"They are our *guests*, Ibby. How can you expect them to respect you when you treat them with such contempt?"

"They don't care about the likes of us, Mum. They're just trying to fit us up." He sank into an armchair, glowering.

"This is Ibby," Ali said. "Our son. I'm sorry—"

"You don't—" the young man began, then stopped as he caught the look on his mother's face.

Zoe took a sip from her coffee. "It's good to meet you, Ibby."

"Ibrahim."

At least he was talking to her.

"Ibrahim." She offered a smile, which he ignored. "I promise you, we're not trying to fit anyone up."

"Sure." He didn't sound convinced.

"Look, Ibrahim, I'm not supposed to be releasing this, but you'll find out eventually. There was a murder last night, in town. In or near the marina. I'm new to Whitehaven, so I've got no prejudices about you or anyone else. All I want is some help."

Ibrahim edged forwards a little. *Good.* "So, what's it got to do with us?"

She pointed at his robe. "Can you tell me what this is? The symbol on your robe?"

Ibrahim twisted his neck, his scowl dropping.

"That's just a traditional set of symbols," said Ali. "Basic shapes. The dome, the minaret, the crescent, and the star. It's been associated with Islam for centuries."

Zoe nodded. "But that precise layout." She gestured at the building around her. "Is that something specifically associated with your community centre?"

"Oh, no." Ali shook his head.

His wife was tapping at her phone. She passed it to Zoe.

The screen showed a page of Google shopping results. At least half included a symbol that looked identical to the one on Ibrahim's robe.

"It's common," explained Inaya. "You'll find that on a million robes."

"I'm sure you're right." But Zoe had to ask. "Ibrahim, can you tell me where you were last night?"

"See?" He looked at his mother. "What did I tell you?"

"He was at work." She turned to Zoe. "He works nights at a local warehouse."

"I wasn't, Mum."

Zoe felt a chill run down her arms. "You weren't?"

"Second Friday of the month. Place is shut for maintenance. I was at home. And before you ask, they didn't see me." He gestured towards his parents. "I was in my room. On the PS5."

"What were you playing?" asked Aaron.

"Modern Warfare. Call of Duty Modern Warfare Two. You can check my logs and everything if you don't believe—"

"Oh, I believe you," said Inaya. "You useless, lazy... You could have been doing something useful. But no. You waste your life, you sit there with your friends shooting pe—"

"With your friends?" asked Zoe.

"Online." Ibrahim stared at his mother. "And yes, I do work, and sometimes I like to play on the PS5."

"Please," said Zoe. "Ibrahim, you're not a suspect. None of you are suspects. That's not why we're here. We'd like your help. We need your help tracking down a killer."

Ibrahim stared, but seemed intrigued. Ali and Inaya looked uneasy. Aaron stood behind him, watching the young man.

"Please," Zoe repeated.

"Of course," said Inaya. "Of course we will help you, won't we?"

Her husband nodded. She turned to her son. After a moment, he nodded too.

Zoe turned to Aaron. "Can you get the team mailbox up on your phone please, Sergeant?"

She scrolled to the footage from earlier and found an appropriate frame.

"This," she said as she held it out for Inaya, "is a still from CCTV footage taken last night. We'd like to find out who these people are."

"Oh," breathed Ali. Inaya's face was frozen. Even Ibrahim, who'd risen to stand behind his parents, seemed taken aback.

"You understand why we came here now?"

"It's not me," said Ibrahim.

"I didn't say it was, and I don't think it is," Zoe told him. She caught Aaron from the corner of her eye, watching.

Ali shrugged. "They could be anyone."

Inaya held his arm. "We can't even see their faces. We might know them, we might not. But we tend not to get many youngsters in the centre."

"No?" asked Zoe.

"No." She glanced at Ibrahim. "This generation is more interested in Big Theft Auto than in their culture and religion."

CHAPTER NINETEEN

THE CLOUDS WERE GONE, replaced by a cold blue sky. Zoe shut the car door and huddled into the passenger seat, trying not to shiver as Aaron drove them away.

"I'll take the quick route back," he said.

"Will that make much difference?"

"About a minute."

There was a missed call from Tom on her phone. Before she could call him, it rang. Unknown number.

"DI Finch."

"You don't know me, but my name's Jake Frimpton and I work for *The Chronicle*."

"*The Chronicle?*"

Zoe noticed Aaron's gaze flick in her direction.

"Local paper. I know it's your first day, but I've got a story and I thought it would be only polite if I ran it past you first."

"Ran it past me first?" Zoe hadn't had this from the press before.

"It's this case. This murder. In the marina."

"How d'you know about that?"

"That's the thing, Detective Inspector... d'you mind if I call you Zoe?"

"I need to know you a little better first. The murder?"

"It's all over social media. You won't be able to keep it quiet. There are photos. Accusations. It adds up to something rather alarming."

What had he seen? Would he tell her, or was she supposed to guess?

"A woman's been murdered," Zoe said. "I would have said that's *alarming*, wouldn't you?"

"You haven't seen it, have you?"

Zoe hesitated. She glanced at Aaron, who shrugged. "No, I haven't," she said. "What photos? What accusations?"

She heard slow breathing down the line. A pause.

"I've got images of a group of men wearing what look like white robes, carrying a heavy bag, down by the marina. They're all over Twitter and Facebook. There's a bunch of anonymous accounts throwing blame around. Whoever they are, they know the victim had her throat slit. Add it all up and it looks like—"

"Looks like there's been a leak from inside the investigation," Zoe said.

Aaron braked, but continued staring at the road ahead.

"And that's what makes this newsworthy to you," she continued.

"Do you have anything to add?" There was a smile in Jake Frimpton's voice.

"Are you asking me for a comment? On the record?"

"I'm asking what you think about all this. I'm not an idiot, DI Finch. Getting the wrong information out at the wrong time can make your job difficult, and I don't want to do that."

"You don't?"

They were heading out of Whitehaven. Zoe turned as they passed the modern estate she lived on. With the sun illuminating the hills behind the red brick buildings, it looked almost beautiful.

"No. You're new here, I don't want to mess things up for you, and I don't want to stop you finding a murderer. And I don't want to be the cause of trouble in town."

"Is there often this kind of trouble?"

"We've had our share of trouble over the years, the miners'll tell you plenty of stories about that. But at the moment this feels different. Racial tension. I'm concerned about inflaming it."

"Then don't print."

"I'm only telling you what I've seen on social media. I don't think my newspaper will make much difference."

Zoe exchanged glances with Aaron. His jaw was tense.

"Listen, Mr Frimpton," she said. "I am new, and I don't know you or your paper, yet. But when people see something in print, or under the banner of a newspaper they trust, that carries more weight than social media. You know it, and I know it. So yes, I do think it'll make a difference."

"OK," he replied.

Zoe frowned and held the phone out, checking she hadn't been cut off.

"What do you mean, 'OK'? Are you saying you won't print it?"

"I am. And in return, let me buy you a drink. After work. I'd like to meet the famous DI Finch in person."

CHAPTER TWENTY

By the time Zoe had agreed to meet Jake Frimpton and ended the call, Aaron was parking his Volvo outside the station. Zoe glanced at her phone, then back up at the building. No point phoning Tom now.

"You come across this Jake Frimpton before?" she asked Aaron in the lift.

He nodded. "A couple of times. He's..." He scratched his head. "He's a journalist, and as a rule, I don't trust them. But if I had to trust one, he's the one I'd pick. If he's told you he won't run a story, he won't run it."

Zoe nodded. That was a start. But what would he expect in return?

Tom jumped up from his chair as they entered the team room.

"You've got to see this, Ma'am. It's all over social media."

I know. But Zoe waited while he showed her what he'd found.

She walked to the big screen, where he'd placed the photograph. "Whoever's taken this—"

"Was there," Aaron said. "Might have witnessed everything."

Tom was nodding, his movements jerky.

"Nina." Zoe turned to her. "Any luck with Mispers?"

"Not yet. Sorry."

"You can't find something if it's not there. Keep going for a bit. At some point we might need to run a public appeal, but we're not there yet."

There was a tapping sound. Zoe turned to see Fiona Kendrick standing outside the open door.

"Ma'am."

"Zoe." The super smiled. "Mind if we have a word?"

"Of course. Nina, carry on with what you're doing. Tom, stay on social media. Aaron, find out if there's any news on the PM or anything from forensics. OK?"

The Detective Superintendent walked fast, Zoe striding to keep pace with her as they took the stairs and rounded the corner to the larger office.

"Take a seat, please," Fiona said as she sat down behind her desk. "How are you finding your first day?"

"Good, I think. Somewhat crazy, with this murder."

"Yes." Fiona tilted her head and smiled. "I hope you're settling in. Everyone looking after you?"

"Yes," replied Zoe, not sure she expected to be *looked after*. "All fine."

"Good. Now, you'll be aware of all this speculation." The super's smile gave way to a serious expression. "We're concerned about how this has been allowed to get out."

Zoe wondered who *we* might be. "It's not internal, Ma'am. Or at least, it doesn't look like it. You've seen the photograph?"

"This one?" Fiona turned her monitor around so that it faced Zoe. The same image Tom had shown her.

"That's the one doing the rounds," Zoe said, "and it's not ours. We're working on the assumption it was taken by another witness."

"Who?"

"We intend to find out."

"Very well." Fiona nodded and returned her monitor to its usual position. "In the meantime, I understand you haven't yet established the identity of the victim."

"Yes, but it's—"

"Oh, Zoe, please don't take this as a criticism. I'm just trying to work out how and where I can be most helpful." The super smiled. "I think a press conference, tomorrow morning. We can kill two birds with one stone."

Zoe stared at her. "Ma'am?"

"Ask the public to help identify the victim, and reassure them that there isn't a racial angle."

"Yes, Ma'am. But don't you think..."

She stopped at the sight of Fiona shaking her head.

"No buts, Zoe. Press conference tomorrow morning. We can introduce you at the same time. I'll get the press office on it, and they'll liaise with you. OK?"

Zoe sighed. "Yes, Ma'am." She walked to the door.

"Very well. Off you go, and see if you can make some progress."

Zoe trudged downstairs, her stomach churning. *Will it always be like this?*

Any progress they might make was about to hit a large, Fiona Kendrick-shaped roadblock.

CHAPTER TWENTY-ONE

HALFWAY DOWN THE STAIRS, Zoe stopped and pulled out her phone.

What the hell had just happened? Did her new boss not trust her to run an investigation? Or was this just someone trying to ease her in, make things straightforward? As straightforward as they could be when your first day coincided with a brand-new murder investigation.

She stood, back against the wall, and took three slow, deep breaths.

Fiona Kendrick was fine. Perfectly pleasant. She had a new DI and a murder on the same day, of course she was going to want to be involved. And it wasn't like Zoe hadn't dealt with difficult people before. Difficult bosses. Worse than Fiona Kendrick.

She shuddered.

Far worse.

She carried on past her own office and into the team room. All three of them looked up and stared at her. She smiled, hoping she looked like she was in control.

"OK, team, change of plan. We need to prepare for a press conference in the morning."

Aaron's face twisted in confusion. Zoe raised her eyebrows.

"You were concerned it was too early," he said. "Is this the right call?"

No.

"Yes. We need to... We need to ask the public to help identify the victim, and reassure them that there isn't a racial angle. Kill two birds with one stone and stop things getting out of hand. OK?"

She looked around the room; not much confidence, but no disagreement.

"Right, Nina. We've got at least one photo we can use, but I'd like a couple more. Can you work on the ones we've got and make them useable?"

"Useable?"

"Get the blood off the image."

"What about the writing? And the tattoos?"

"Nothing with the writing. As for the tattoos, let's keep one of them off the radar too, for now. Show the rose, not the mermaid. Weed out the liars."

"OK, Ma'am. On it." Nina started tapping at her keyboard.

"Aaron, anything on the PM?"

"Won't be till tomorrow."

Zoe felt her shoulders slump. "Which means we won't have a time of death to work with, but we still have the window for the body turning up at the marina. Midnight through to four."

"Right," Aaron replied.

"OK, everyone. I'm off to meet this Jake Frimpton. I'll be heading home from there, and I don't expect you to be sticking around for long either. I'll see you tomorrow."

She turned and walked down the corridor to her own office.

The team hadn't liked the U-turn on the press conference. But then, they knew where she'd been, and how these things worked. And no one had objected.

Maybe she was beginning to build a team, after all.

CHAPTER TWENTY-TWO

THERE WAS a moment's silence while they listened to Zoe's footsteps grow quieter. When the sound had receded, Nina spoke.

"Well, that was a shit show, wasn't it?"

Aaron turned to look at her. "Now—"

"All that about the press conference. One minute it's *not yet*, it's *too early*, next minute it's *kill two birds with one stone.*"

Aaron had spent much of the last year reporting directly to Detective Superintendent Kendrick, and knew how things worked. The super always got what she wanted.

Probably not a great idea to explain that to Tom and Nina, though.

"That's not entirely fair," he said. "She had an opinion, she considered it, she changed her mind. A good copper is open to new information."

"Yeah, Nina," added Tom. "And what's with all the nicey-nice? *OK, Ma'am. On it.*"

She scowled at him. "Talking behind the boss's back already?"

"Fuck off."

Aaron was used to Tom and Nina sparring, but this was too much. "Tom—"

"And there's me thinking we were friends," Tom interrupted, staring at Nina. "Two talents, you said. What was my other one?"

"I was being kind to the needy, Tom. It's just the one talent: good hearing." She turned to Aaron. "But, Sarge, I'm not kidding. I'm sure she's great and everything, but wasn't she right the first time? It's too early for this. We'll just get the troublemakers and the nutters. We won't get anything useful."

"Nutters, Nina?"

"You know what I mean, Sarge."

He did, too. He'd taken the DI's side in public, but he knew Nina was right.

But DI Finch was the boss, and she'd been backed into a corner by the super.

"Look, she's just turned up here, she's got a murder, she's got you two to deal with, and she doesn't know anything. About the case, before you add to that, Nina. And nor does anyone else. So maybe it's not such a bad idea to get something out there."

"If you say so, Sarge." Nina didn't look convinced.

"What do you know about DI Finch?" he asked, looking from one to the other.

"Not much," said Tom. Nina shrugged.

"Right, then. Take a look at this." Aaron tapped on his phone and turned to the screen.

"Canary," he said. "Heard of it?"

Two blank faces.

Really? Didn't they watch the news?

"Organised Crime," he said, "in Birmingham. The case

was all about grooming, but the gang was into the lot: drugs, prostitution, murders, all the stuff we like to pretend doesn't happen here. Down there, it's a hundred times worse. And if that wasn't enough, there were coppers involved."

He watched them scan the text on the screen, the details of the case. Most of it, public record. Some for police eyes only.

"She took them down. Your new DI was on that case. She uncovered the crucial evidence. And then when she was given her own team, she arrested Trevor Hamm, the man running the whole thing."

"Is he the one who got busted out and killed?" asked Nina.

Tom was nodding. "Devon, wasn't it?"

"Dorset. She took down Hamm, and everyone he paid to help him or look the other way. From what I hear, they're still rooting out coppers who had the wrong idea about who they should be working for."

He cleared the screen.

"So yes, she might take some getting used to. She might do things differently. She might even get things wrong from time to time. But DI Finch is our boss, and she's a bloody good copper. So if she tells you to do something, you do it. OK?"

Tom was nodding.

Nina's nods were less emphatic. "Whatever you say, Sarge. I don't know. But she told us to go home, didn't she? See you tomorrow."

CHAPTER TWENTY-THREE

THE ANCHOR VAULTS, the pub Jake Frimpton had suggested, was almost in the centre of town. Zoe parked a few minutes' walk away and strolled past brightly painted buildings. A huge, colourful mural showed Gulliver lying on a hillside overlooking Whitehaven Marina, bound up by bow-wielding Lilliputians. She hoped the locals here were friendlier to outsiders.

The pub itself was small and white, surrounded by louder, busier establishments. Zoe checked her watch. Six pm, Saturday evening. If it wasn't busy yet, it soon would be.

Inside, it took a moment for her eyes to adjust to the gloom. At last, she saw a man standing in front of her, grinning.

"Zoe?" he asked.

She nodded. "Jake?"

"That's me." He put out a hand. She shook it and followed him to a low wooden bar.

Jake Frimpton was younger than she'd expected, clean-shaven with dark hair and thick-framed glasses. He reminded her of the Christopher Reeve version of Clark Kent.

"What are you having?" he asked, a lemonade in front of him.

"Diet Coke."

He ordered, not asking why she wasn't drinking.

She appreciated that. Explaining that her late mother's alcoholism had put her off the stuff for life became tiring.

He led her to a secluded table in the corner of the room, passing older men alone at the bar and a few couples. None of them young. Zoe made a point of looking around as she sat down.

"Nice place," she said. "I'll have to tell my partner about it."

Jake smiled and reached for his drink. "Cheers." As he raised his glass, she spotted a wedding ring.

"So," she began. "What's on your mind?"

He shrugged. "I just thought I'd introduce myself, see what we can do to help each other ou—" He stopped, seeing the look on her face. "Sorry, I didn't put that well. But there should be a proper, cooperative relationship between local police and local press. Everyone benefits. Don't you agree?"

He leaned forward, looking up at her through those Clark Kent glasses. Zoe fought a laugh.

"Is this genuine, Jake? Because if it is, I want to know more about you and how you think the relationship between press and police *should* work."

He sat back and gulped his lemonade. "Fair enough. I'm local, born here, school here, uni in Newcastle, then my dad got ill so I came back. Mum died years ago, so he's been on his own, and—"

"Newcastle?"

He nodded. "I know what you're thinking. I should have ended up in London. Or at least Manchester or Liverpool."

"You're forgetting somewhere."

"Or Birmingham, yes. Sometimes family's just more important, isn't it?"

"I suppose so," replied Zoe. Family was a tricky thing to
pin down. Her dad had died years ago and her mum had been
no parent at all. And now Nicholas was at uni. She still wasn't
sure if Carl was family. She'd find out, moving here with him.

Jake leaned in. "But the thing is, it isn't what it could be
here."

"What isn't?"

"The paper. I know it's never going to be The Wall Street
Journal, but right now it's clickbait and ads and nothing of
substance. If we can cover good stories and write them well,
people *will* read them. Then maybe the advertisers wouldn't
have all the power."

Zoe didn't really care about the local press. But she was
intrigued. "Where do I come into all this?"

"I want to be the one who does it, writes the good stories.
My boss doesn't like it, but if I can develop a working relationship with you, then I can get those stories. And you can have
someone you trust." He cocked his head. "What do you say?"

Zoe's experience of the press in Birmingham hadn't led her
to trust journalists as a rule.

But who else did she have up here?

"OK," she said. "I'll give it a try."

She ran over what they had in her head. She couldn't tell
him much. And what she did tell him would be off the record.

"We've brought some lads in for questioning," she said.
"Mal McDo—"

"Little league," he said. "Jay Whitwell and Davey Grant,
yeah?"

"Yes."

"They come up in the court reports every few months, and it's never anything serious."

"OK. What about Richard Madsen?"

His brow creased. "Not heard of that one."

"Mick Halfpenny?"

A smile. "Bit of a local character, is our Mick. He does guided walks around town from time to time, gets little features printed. Harmless enough."

"And the figures in white?"

"The ones from X?"

She frowned.

He smiled. "Twitter. I don't know who they are, but like I said, I don't like it."

"You said you didn't want to inflame things. What is there to inflame?"

"There was a punch-up last month, at one of the businesses just outside town. Nothing major, no one badly hurt, but there were a lot of people involved."

"What's that got to do with any of this?"

"It was a builders' merchant. Been around forever, but it was closing down. People blamed newcomers. Migrants. Using their own supplies, illegal supplies, smuggled, untaxed, whatever. And it might've been true; there's all kinds of stuff that goes on at the port if you believe the stories."

"The marina?"

Jake shook his head. "Port of Workington. But it didn't matter if it was true or not, people got it into their heads that migrants were to blame, and next thing there's a crowd with signs outside the builders' merchants, and another crowd calling them racist, and one thing led to another."

"This was targeting Muslims?"

"They don't care if it's Polish plumbers or Syrian refugees. Foreign means foreign."

"OK. I can see why you might not want to print something that could make it worse. Thanks."

"That's not all, though. There's the community centre, up by Shore Road."

Zoe put down her drink. The pub was getting busier. Could people hear them? "I know it."

He looked at her, surprised. "They want to expand it, turn it into a Mosque."

"I'm aware."

"This has been years in the making. Getting the land, first approval, building the community centre, getting the plans drawn up for the next stage. The planning meeting's in a couple of weeks."

"It is?" said Zoe. "They didn't mention... They didn't mention that little detail."

Their glasses were empty.

"Another lemonade?" Zoe asked.

Jake glanced at his watch "No, thanks."

Good. The bar was three-deep, and Zoe wasn't thirsty. And Carl would be waiting.

"There's something I'm surprised by," she said, tapping her empty glass.

"Yes?"

"You haven't mentioned the victim. What have you got on her?"

"Nothing. No leaks, not as far as I'm aware. We've been told to expect a press conference tomorrow. I assume that'll be where we hear something?"

Zoe nodded. The press office had called her in the car, informed her of the time. "Young woman," she told him.

"Twenties, probably. Dark hair. Nothing local on missing persons."

"Right. Could be a migrant, then."

"Could be?"

"There's... Let's just say there are more and more unfamiliar women around these days. Here, Workington, even as far down as Barrow."

"Where are they coming from?"

"Probably..." Jake shook his head. "No point in speculating, is there?" He checked his watch. "Gotta go. Good to meet you."

He stood and made for the exit, muttering greetings to a couple of the punters as he passed.

Zoe watched him, puzzled. What had he been about to say? And why had he changed his mind?

CHAPTER TWENTY-FOUR

THERE WAS no sign of Carl's car when Zoe got back. Instead, she opened the door to find Yoda standing halfway up the stairs, miaowing at her like the world was about to end.

"I'm sorry."

"Miaow."

Zoe slid past unpacked boxes into the kitchen and found a pouch of cat food in a cupboard. She squeezed it out then changed the litter. She was looking forward to the recommended two-week point, when she could let the cat out.

Jake Frimpton's half-completed sentence was bothering her. Once Yoda had finished the pouch, she put her bowl in the dishwasher. She picked up her phone, scrolled to one of the newest contacts, and dialled.

"Ma'am?" Aaron sounded puzzled. *Why are you calling me now?*

"It's OK, Aaron. No emergencies. I just wanted to pick your brains."

She could hear noises in the background. A small child. The sound of a TV stopped; he'd gone into another room.

"I met Jake Frimpton," Zoe said. She opened the fridge, in case food had magically appeared since the morning. No such luck. She grabbed an apple. It would have to do. "Interesting man. I think he could be useful."

"You'll know how difficult the press can be," Aaron replied, "but Jake means well, at least."

"He suggested our victim might be a migrant. Said there were lots of different women around the area lately. I asked him where they came from, and he clammed up. But earlier, he'd mentioned Port of Workington."

Zoe took a bite from her apple and heard the front door open and close. She went to the hall, still holding her phone to her ear.

Carl was facing away from her. Checking the front door lock? He turned, spotted her, and grinned. She smiled back, pointing to the phone, and mouthed "OK?"

"Yes," he mouthed back.

"So I wanted to ask," Zoe said into her phone, "if you know anything about people trafficking locally."

Silence. Zoe watched Carl take off his coat, walk into the kitchen and check the fridge, just like she'd done.

At last, Aaron spoke. "That would be for Organised Crime to deal with, wouldn't it?"

"Well yes, but you're my DS, so if you know anything, it would be good to hear it."

Aaron sighed. "There have been suspicions for a while. Nothing we've been able to pin down. No arrests. I don't know if there are any operations, that would be above my pay grade."

"And mine," said Zoe. Maybe she'd have to ask Fiona.

Aaron continued. "The big man over in Workington is Myron Carter. Import, export, logistics, the usual. Clean as a whistle officially, of course."

"Of course. And he operates out of the port?"

"I believe so."

"Let's pay him a visit tomorrow."

"Do we have grounds?"

"We don't need grounds for a friendly visit. He's a local employer, I'm the new DI, it's a getting-to-know-you sort of thing. Nothing wrong with that."

"No." Aaron didn't sound convinced. "I'm... May I be frank, Ma'am?"

"Of course." She took another bite from the apple.

"In the middle of a murder investigation, with the victim still unidentified, a press conference planned, and the potential for trouble in town, it doesn't seem like the best use of our time."

He could be right. "OK," Zoe said. "Let's discuss it in the morning."

Carl was in the living room, the lights low. Zoe heard the oven fan and smelled something wafting from the kitchen.

And another smell: he'd lit the fire. He'd got hold of some wood the day before and had been determined to get a blaze going in the little stove before they blew all their money on gas bills.

Zoe sat down next to him and nudged up into his arms. She breathed in the smell of him: the outdoor cold mixed with the firelighters.

"How was it?" he asked.

"I walked straight into a murder investigation."

"I heard."

"News travels fast here."

"Everyone knows about your new case. And the press conference tomorrow."

She finished off the apple and tossed the core onto a box nearby. "What about you?"

A shrug. "Fine. Nowhere near as dramatic as yours." He turned and kissed her. "Let's not talk about work."

"I just learned about an organised crime operation," she said, "which might be linked to my case. Why does this kind of thing follow me everywhere?"

Carl chuckled. "You're a DI, love. What d'you think you're going to be dealing with, drunks and pickpockets?"

"And what about you?" She saw him shut down, the smile dropping. "I mean, your colleagues. The office. I know you can't talk about work."

He shrugged. "They seem OK. Very welcoming."

"And the drive?" Carl was based in Carlisle.

"An hour. Let's hope it's not like that every day."

"It's Saturday."

"In Cumbria. It might not be like the West Midlands."

"True." Zoe heard the oven beep. "Did you bring something home?"

"Lasagne, from a Booths I drove past."

"I've heard that's posh."

Carl shrugged and hauled himself up off the sofa. "You hungry?"

Zoe thought of the cheese sandwich and the gull. "Bloody ravenous."

"Good." He pulled her up and she followed him into the kitchen.

"At least the views were good," he said as he rooted around in boxes for oven gloves.

"Views?"

"On my commute. A bit different from the A38."

Zoe smiled. The views had been a selling point for Carl.

He'd talked up the beauty of Cumbria and shown Zoe photos of lakes and fells. She'd smiled and nodded, unmoved.

"We still haven't got an ID for our body," she said. "But I spoke to a local journalist. There's some local unrest, possible racism. It could be—"

Carl put a hand on her arm. "Let's not talk about work."

She looked into his eyes. "You're right. Let's eat."

CHAPTER TWENTY-FIVE

Zoe hit the alarm clock to shut it off. It was new, a farewell gift from Connie, one of her DCs in Birmingham. She still hadn't figured out how to tone down its screeching din.

There was a cup of coffee on the bedside table, but it was cold: Carl had put it there an hour ago, before kissing her and leaving for work. It was just before seven now, earlier than Zoe needed to be up. But some time going over the case wouldn't go amiss.

She'd accessed the team inbox before going to sleep last night, along with the virtual board and everything the team had put up there. It had seemed overwhelming at midnight, so she'd gone through Nina's report instead and made some notes. Now, though, all that information was looking useful.

Zoe made herself a cup of coffee and took a spot on the sofa next to Yoda. She ran through everything they'd found, everything they'd discussed. There was nothing new, but it was good to see it in black and white.

On the *Whitehaven Chronicle* website, she found some of

Jake Frimpton's old stories. Features about local businesses, garden centres, schools. Planning applications – not the Mosque, though. Some minor crimes, but nothing that stood out. And nothing relating to organised crime or racial unrest.

On the front page of the site, she could see what Jake had been talking about: four ads to every story, headlines that bore little resemblance to the articles. No wonder he wanted to try something different.

Twenty minutes later, Zoe was showered and dressed and grabbing her *Yes Bab* mug to add to the collection in the kitchen at work. Her phone rang, and she pulled it out of her pocket to see Nicholas's name. She held it out, checking her long hair as the video call connected.

"Very smart," he said.

Zoe laughed. "You can talk."

Nicholas looked a mess, but only in the way students were supposed to. He hadn't shaved or brushed his hair, but did that matter? She knew he'd be eating well: of the two of them, he had always been the cook.

She took the phone into the living room and picked up the cat, who miaowed.

"Yoda," Nicholas said. "I miss her."

Zoe felt claws sink into her wrist and let the cat drop to the sofa. "How are you?" she asked her son.

"Fine."

"Fine?"

"Fine. I'm fine. How's Cumbria?"

She thought. "Fine too. I got a murder case."

"Already?"

"They knew I was coming."

He rolled his eyes. "Don't piss them off."

"I never piss people off."

"OK. Don't get yourself involved with any bent coppers."

Zoe hesitated. "I was never involved, Nick."

"You know that's not what I mean. Anyway, what's the new team like?"

"I think you'd like them." Zoe was grateful for the change of subject.

"I googled them. Aaron's gay. Tom's a gamer. And Nina's an Elvis impersonator."

Zoe stared at the screen. "Where did you get all that?"

"Online. I didn't hack anybody, if that's what you're trying to say. How come Nina's an Elvis impersonator? How *old* is she, anyway?"

Zoe wrinkled her nose. "Late twenties, I reckon?" She smiled. "She's got a quiff, piled up on top of her head." She stopped herself. It wasn't appropriate to gossip about her new team. Not after one day. "I heard you've seen Mo."

"Yeah. Me and Fox went round to his and Cat's for lunch yesterday."

"Fox?"

"My new person."

This was the first Zoe had heard of any *new person*, but she knew better than to push it. Nicholas's last partner had been Zaf, who'd gone off to London. Nicholas had never told her how that breakup had gone or who'd instigated it.

"Good," she said. "Cumbria's not as far as Birmingham, you know. You and Fox can come here."

"They'd like that. I think."

Zoe checked the clock on the kitchen wall, left behind by the previous owners. It was a vile thing with ornate lettering and gold embellishment, but it told the time. "I'm sorry, love. I need to be in work. Send me pictures of Mo's family, and I'll send you some of Yoda."

"Fair enough."

"And some of you and Fox, if you'd like..."

"Mum..." That familiar exasperated tone.

"Sorry." She blew him a kiss and hung up.

CHAPTER TWENTY-SIX

ZOE WANTED the shiny floor of the press room to swallow her up.

She'd been sitting beside Fiona for five minutes, and other than to introduce herself and point to the images of the victim, she'd barely spoken.

Instead, she was listening to her boss tell twenty or more journalists – TV, digital and print – the barest details of the crime, and much more about how pleased they should be to have DI Zoe Finch on the case.

Zoe hoped the local criminals were more convinced than she was.

At long last, she had a chance to tell them about the investigation. Nina had done good work on the photos and there was nothing to alarm even the most sensitive. They showed a red rose tattoo on the victim's left shoulder, but no mermaid or Arabic writing. And definitely no wound.

The super didn't let her speak for long. She was eager to reassure the press herself. "I am aware of rumours and images circulating on social media, and I'd like to remind you all that this is a serious offence which remains under investigation, and that these rumours are nothing more than that."

The room fell quiet.

"We're in the business of catching criminals," Fiona said, her voice lowering, "not pandering to trends and prejudices, and we'll follow the evidence wherever that takes us. So please, rest assured that no one in our various communities needs to draw our attention to things we're already aware of, and please also remember that wasting our time and diverting our attention are offences that can carry severe consequences."

Why use one word when twenty will do? Zoe thought. Sometimes she wished she could have brought her old boss Lesley up here with her.

"Thank you all," the super continued. "We'll be posting details on our website, together with contact information. We have time for just a handful of questions."

"We haven't been given the time and cause of death."

Fiona nodded. "We'll let you know when we have that information. But the key hours at the marina are between midnight and four am, in particular the period around two."

"DI Finch, how are you settling in?"

Zoe forced a smile. "It's early days, but my new team is very capable." She caught herself. "And I'm pleased to be working with the detective superintendent." She gestured towards Fiona, who gave her a nod.

A blogger in the back row put his hand up. "You've shown us some images, we know about this tattoo now, but is there anything else that might help identify the victim? Any distinctive markings?"

"Markings?" asked Zoe.

"Symbols, words, anything like that?"

"Let's work with what we've got," said Fiona. She straightened in her seat. "That's all we've got time for now, but please spread the word, and get in touch if you have any information that might help identify this poor woman or help us apprehend her killer."

She stood and gestured for Zoe to do the same as the audience filed out.

When the room was all but empty, the super turned on Zoe, her voice a hiss. "How did they know?"

"Same way someone had that photo," Zoe whispered. She sensed someone behind her and looked up.

"Hi, Zoe," said Jake. "Good to see you up there."

"Hi, Jake." Zoe smiled and turned to introduce him to her boss, but the super had already left the stage. "Hope you found that interesting."

"We're certainly fortunate to have you," he replied, straight-faced.

"Thank you," she said, just as her name was called from across the room: Fiona. She shrugged and went to join her boss.

"How do you know that journalist?" Fiona said as she watched Jake leave the room.

"He contacted me yesterday. Wanted to know if he should print what was doing the rounds on social media. I asked him not to, and he didn't."

"Right. Well." Fiona sniffed as the door closed on Jake and the rest of the journalists. "You know what you're doing with the press, I'm sure. But I wouldn't trust that one any more than I'd trust the rest of them."

CHAPTER TWENTY-SEVEN

Zoe entered the team room five minutes later to applause. She clutched her coffee in its Brummie mug and shrugged.

"Good performance, Ma'am," said Tom. Nina nodded. Aaron wore a grin that reminded Zoe of the one she'd just been forced to wear. All three of them were on their feet like they were applauding one of Nina's turns of *Are You Lonesome Tonight?*

"I think we got everything across we needed to," Zoe replied. "If anything comes out of all that, it won't be for a while. What have you got for me in the meantime?"

"Stella called," Aaron said. "She's drawn a blank on the fingernails, but there's foreign DNA around the markings. The writing."

"Excellent. Any matches?"

"Too early for that, but she's treating it as an urgent submission. And she's confirmed it's male DNA."

"As if there was any doubt," muttered Nina.

"There should always be doubt," Zoe told her. "Have you had any luck on Mispers?"

"Couple of possibles from not too far away. Woman missing from Lancaster for a couple of weeks. And another one from Hexham. She *did* have tattoos, but her sister didn't remember what of. Probably dead ends, but I'll follow up."

"Good. What's so interesting, Tom?"

Tom held up his phone to show her. "Calls are coming in already, Ma'am. Looks like you made an impression."

"Or the super did," she said. "Anything useful?"

"Too early to say," Tom replied.

"I doubt it," said Aaron.

"Why's that?" Zoe asked.

"I just think it'll be a waste of time." He shrugged. "And resources."

He was probably right. But that wasn't the point, not on Zoe's second day. "We won't know if we're wasting our time until we can see what we're wasting it on," she told him.

"I've had a thought for identifying the victim," said Aaron. "Trawling some of the local houses might help. Just in case."

"Houses?"

"Brothels, Ma'am."

"Yes." Zoe took a seat at the empty desk and looked up at the big screen, which was blank. "If she's come off a boat somewhere, odds are that's where she'd end up. You know some likely spots?"

He nodded.

"We'll go together. You can show me more of the delights of Whitehaven. And I still want to go to the port at some point. Follow up on this trafficking angle, see if we can have a chat with your Myron Carter."

Aaron fidgeted. "It's a long shot. The port thing. I'm not sure—"

Zoe held up a hand. Her phone was ringing. She checked the number and stood up.

"I need to take this," she said. "We'll head out in ten minutes."

She headed to her office, answering as she walked. "Dr Robertson. How can I help you?"

"It's Chris, remember? I thought you might like to join me while I carve up your corpse."

Zoe had watched more PMs than she cared to remember. She had no problem with the gore. It was the pathologists who freaked her out, the way they each developed their own brand of humour to help them deal with what they did.

"I was going to send Aaron," she told him, "but, yes. I think I'll come instead. You're at the back of the hospital, right?"

"We are. An hour OK?"

"An hour's fine." She messaged Aaron, asking him to come to her office.

He knocked on the door thirty seconds later, wearing the nervous smile she'd noticed.

"Everything OK, Aaron?" she asked as he sat down.

He nodded.

"Only you don't seem to want me anywhere near the port, even though you're the one who told me about Myron Carter. But when I suggest going to see him, you shut down. Is there something I should know?"

"It's just another distraction, that's all. We've got the immediate lines of enquiry, like Mispers and maybe the brothels, and then things like the port are part of the broader picture, I'd have said."

If he was lying, it was a convincing lie. He was right, too.

"OK. I do want to see the port at some point, though.

Meantime, change of plan. I'm going to the PM. You have a look around those brothels, see what you can find."

Aaron stood up. "Yes, Ma'am."

"Good. We'll touch base this afternoon."

CHAPTER TWENTY-EIGHT

TOUCH BASE THIS AFTERNOON, Aaron thought. What did the DI mean by that?

He was worrying about nothing. She was new, finding her feet, working with a new team in a new force. It would take time.

But he didn't like the way she kept talking about the port.

He decided to start around Workington, driving north and then out past Workington Hall Park into Stainburn. Like the rest of Cumbria, it wasn't like there were red light districts, or even bad areas. Just buildings. Houses. Streets.

He approached a house in a side street with neat front gardens. He could hear children playing outside not far away, making him think of his own daughter.

This house had been a hotel once. Still was, officially, but you wouldn't find tourists there. It wasn't in bad condition, hardly distinguishable from the places around it.

A skinny man in tracksuit bottoms opened the door. "What the fuck you want?"

"Do you know this woman?" Aaron held out their clearest photo of the victim.

The man shook his head without looking and went to shut the door.

Aaron took half a step forward. "Mind if I have a word with some of your guests?"

"Got a warrant?"

Worth a shot. Aaron shook his head and stepped back.

As he walked away, the man called, "Fucking faggot!"

Aaron tensed, waiting to defend himself.

The door slammed and there was silence. Just the gulls and the distant children.

Swallowing, he got back in the car and headed on to his next destination.

In Great Clifton, he stopped at a mouldering dirty-white semi that stood out against the cleaner houses on either side. Aaron held back, eyeing a fierce-looking Staffordshire Terrier chained up in the front garden.

When the people inside didn't come at the sound of the dog's snarls, he gave up and edged his way alongside the brick boundary with the neighbouring house.

A window opened upstairs, and a woman leaned out. "Go away!" Her accent was European, but Aaron couldn't place it beyond that.

"I just want to talk for a moment."

"Not to police," said the woman, shutting the window.

In Workington itself he had more luck, showing the photograph and managing to pass his card to a couple of the women. He'd written the DI's number on the bottom of his card and showed them a photo of her from the press conference. They might be more comfortable talking to her.

He headed back towards Whitehaven, the port receding behind him. Why was the DI so obsessed with the place?

He wished he'd never mentioned it. He'd been asking questions for months, subtly, only when he was in the area for other reasons, He'd dropped questions into conversations with colleagues in Specialist Crime and Intel, cultivating contacts, becoming someone a person might talk to. But as far as he could tell, no one knew he had an interest. No one knew what he suspected.

He was convinced there was an operation there. One that involved people trafficking, drugs, and weapons. But he had no real evidence, and so he'd kept things quiet.

And, of course, he couldn't be sure which of his colleagues to trust. There was something going on at the port, and whoever was behind it, they'd had quite a run of luck in staying off the radar.

Aaron didn't want whoever was helping Myron Carter finding out about his gentle enquiries. And he sure as hell didn't want Carter finding out about them. So, the boss suddenly showing an interest was not good news.

He tried a few more streets, a few more brothels. In most, he was told to get lost. He managed to drop off a few more cards. No one knew anything. Or if they did, they weren't telling him.

He got in his car and headed back to the station, worrying, again, about Myron Carter and the Port of Workington.

His new DI had only been here a day, and she was pushing him to take her to the port.

Was that why she was here? Was it the reason for her move? Aaron knew her reputation.

And should that make him worry even more?

CHAPTER TWENTY-NINE

THE HOSPITAL WAS TUCKED into the outskirts of a residential area of Whitehaven. Instead of the dual carriageways and concrete overpasses Zoe was used to, there was salt in the air and fells in the distance. But there were still the same rows of ambulances, the same cars driving round and round in search of a parking space.

Zoe had spent too much time in hospitals with her dad. They still made her shudder.

She parked in a small bay near the mortuary marked *Authorised Vehicles Only*. Hopefully, no one would need it. And she was authorised, to an extent.

Chris Robertson led her along a series of corridors and down the inevitable flight of stairs into the steel-slabbed world below.

"This is my lad." Robertson indicated a round-faced, harassed-looking young woman.

"I'm Melissa," the woman said. Zoe gave her a smile.

Zoe put on the apron Melissa held out for her and they

entered the post-mortem suite to find the victim ready, naked on the metal table below bright white lights.

Chris reached up to switch on the microphone above his head. He pointed to the marks on the victim's back. "These marks. Can't be sure, and Stella's taken samples to go with the DNA she managed to extract, but it looks to me like paint."

"Paint?" repeated Zoe.

"Red paint." He cleared his throat. "Moving on to external injuries, let's start with the obvious one."

He indicated the wound across the woman's throat. He pulled at the skin, parting it with his gloved hand.

"Incised wound. No significant abrasions, very little tissue bridging." He turned to Zoe. "This was inflicted by an extremely sharp knife. The movement's from her right to her left, and it looks like the knife was pressed against her throat almost as much as it was sliced across."

"So she was either dead already," said Zoe, "or she wasn't struggling."

"Exactly. Now, moving on to wounds elsewhere." He lifted the victim's arms, then let them drop, scanned her legs and her abdomen. Melissa stood behind him, recording his words and passing instruments. "There are abrasions on the fingers." He lifted a hand to show Zoe. "Nothing under the nails, but look at the ends of these two fingers."

Zoe edged closer. She could see marks. Scuffs.

"These are recent," Chris said. "The skin isn't broken, and my best guess is they were made against something soft. Something with a bit of give."

The bag. The holdall. Zoe felt her stomach lurch.

"Are you OK, Zoe? DI Finch? You went pale."

"I was just... Have you seen the footage? The CCTV that's all over town?"

He nodded. "The bag. It might mean that she was in that bag. And that she was alive at least some of the time she was in there."

Zoe swallowed. "Suffocation?"

He shook his head and pointed at an area inside the elbow. "Needle marks. Comparatively fresh." He looked at Zoe. "Cause of death."

Zoe's gaze went to the throat wound. "Really?"

The pathologist nodded. The body had already been cut, the Y-shaped incision not sewn up yet. He parted the skin and pointed to the lungs. "We'll take these out later, but can you see this?"

The area he was indicating was darker than the rest.

"Pulmonary oedema," he said. "Fluid on the lungs. She passed out, and she stopped breathing. Depending on the drug, it's possible her brain just stopped sending the message to her lungs to keep going. We'll have to wait for toxicology. But either way, there was too much fluid here for her to breathe properly. This is how she died."

"Any guess as to when?"

He frowned. "It's a broad window. I'd say probably between eight pm Friday and two am Saturday. I can't be any more precise."

Two am. The bag. The figures in white robes. That had been shortly after two.

"What about the drug? I know you said you've got to wait for toxicology, but...?"

He nodded. "Almost certainly heroin."

Good.

This wasn't Birmingham. Surely there weren't too many dealers around here. *The Port of Workington,* Zoe thought.

She'd be visiting Myron Carter if she got a chance.

CHAPTER THIRTY

AARON WAS a quarter of a mile from the station when his phone rang.

"DS Keyes."

"It's Tom, Sarge. Thought I should let you know things are starting to get a bit nasty."

"What's getting nasty?"

"The calls. Started off useless, like we expected, and now they're useless *and* racist. No one knows anything except the fact that they're sure who did it and they all want locking up, you know the story."

Aaron sighed. Hardly unexpected. "Fine. I'll be with you in a few minutes."

"There's been trouble at the community centre, too."

The lights had turned green, but instead of going straight on, Aaron spied a gap and did a U-turn.

"Go on," he said, already working out who he'd want for backup and how long it would take them to get there.

"Nothing major, Sarge. Someone's chucked a load of paint at it."

"Any violence?"

"No one hanging around, as far as we know."

No need for backup, then. "OK. Thanks, Tom. I'm on my way there now. Have you spoken to the DI?"

"I tried. I think she's at the post-mortem."

Fifteen minutes later, Aaron arrived at the community centre. He rang the DI's number: voicemail.

"I'm at the community centre, Ma'am," he said. "Someone's thrown some paint around, apparently. Just checking they're OK."

He knocked on the door. Ali opened it, his expression wary. Inaya stood a couple of paces behind him, a frying pan in her left hand.

Resourceful, if unrealistic.

"I've had a report of someone throwing paint at your building."

Ali nodded and led him to the side of the building. The paint looked as if it had just been thrown there: a splodge of green, dripping down the wall behind where Ali's Škoda was parked.

"Some of it's got on your car."

Ali nodded, his mouth tight. "Come inside."

Aaron went in and sat opposite the couple, who huddled together on the sofa and told him what had happened.

"We heard them, didn't we?" said Inaya.

Her husband nodded again.

"They drove up," she continued, "we heard them braking, shouting, swearing. Then there was that noise. Wet. I knew what it was." She looked at her husband. "And then they were gone."

"Did you see anything?" Aaron asked.

"We didn't want to get too close to the windows or doors.

We didn't even go out to see what damage they'd done until they were long gone."

"You did the right thing," he said. "I'll speak to Uniform, see if they can stop by, put you on a patrol. Just make themselves visible from time to time, so any troublemakers know we're keeping an eye out."

"Thank you," replied Inaya. "I just wish I knew where Ibby was."

Aaron frowned. "You've not heard from him?"

She shook her head. "Not since it happened. I've been calling him—"

"He's not a child, Inaya," Ali interrupted. "He can go where he likes."

"And *where he likes* is probably somewhere he can cause trouble, retaliate, get himself hurt." Inaya turned to Aaron. "He isn't answering his phone."

"He's probably still asleep," her husband said. "Or with his friends. We can't keep track of him all his life."

Inaya exhaled.

"Well," said Aaron, "if he wasn't here, he probably doesn't even know about this, does he?"

Ali nodded. "Exactly."

"But just in case, please let me know when you do hear from him. And as I say, I'll speak to Uniform and see what they can do."

Back in his car, Aaron called Inspector Keane, who was more than happy to put the community centre on a regular patrol route.

"First sweep should be in half an hour, then every eighty minutes until we hear otherwise or things kick off somewhere else. That good enough, Aaron?"

"Perfect. Thanks, Sir."

"You've heard about the break-in, haven't you?"

"Break-in?" Aaron glanced towards the community centre.

"It's nothing really. I appreciate a two-bit burglary might fall through the cracks now you've got a murder on your hands."

"Where?" asked Aaron.

"Hardware store. The one on Queen Street, opposite the churchyard."

"I know it." Aaron had driven past it the previous day with the new DI. "What's happened?"

"Not really sure yet. Broken window. Owner's a pain in the arse, so we won't be hanging around any longer than we need to."

"Right. Thanks. I'll see if we need to follow it up. And thanks for your help on the community centre."

He started his car and looked over his shoulder to reverse, but there was a car parking behind him. The DI in her Mini.

CHAPTER THIRTY-ONE

"I GOT YOUR MESSAGE," Zoe told Aaron. "Thought I'd come and check it out."

"Over here." He showed her the paint on the wall and on the Škoda.

Zoe peered at it. It wasn't much, certainly not compared to some of the things she'd seen in Birmingham. But she was glad he'd alerted Uniform.

She made for her car. "I'll drive," she told him. "You can direct me. We'll pick up yours on the way back."

"Where are we going?"

"I think it's about time we visited the Port of Workington."

His jaw clenched.

What is it with you and this place, Aaron?

On the main road to Workington, he told her what he'd achieved that morning, his tone unhappy.

"You do know I didn't expect some pimp to just pop up and say *yeah, she's one of ours?*" Zoe said.

"Yes, but—"

"Did you give any of the girls your card?"

"About eight of them. And I hope you don't mind, but I wrote your name and number on them, too. Thought it might help."

She glanced at him, making him wince as she took her eyes off the road for the briefest of moments.

"I don't mind," she said. "You've got the word out there. That's all we could have hoped for, Aaron. You did well."

"How was the post-mortem?"

"Dr Robertson says cause of death is pulmonary oedema, caused by heroin use." She swallowed, the image still fresh in her mind. "And she had marks on her fingers that make me suspect she was inside that bag for some time."

He grimaced. "Alive?"

"Most likely."

His grimace deepened. "Poor woman. When did she die?"

"Sometime between eight and two. I thought the heroin would make it easier to track. How many dealers do you have around here?"

"Not as many as we used to. But still more than you'd think."

They passed a huddle of buildings set back from the road: a church and an ancient-looking structure that stared out at them.

"What's that?" Zoe asked.

"St Bridget's. And Moresby Hall. It's a hotel."

Zoe shivered. The hotel seemed menacing, as if something was hiding behind all those windows.

She turned her attention back to the road. Aaron was tapping on his phone.

"I spoke to Inspector Keane," he said. "When I was asking him to keep an eye on the community centre. He said something about a break-in at a hardware store in town."

"Yes?"

"It's been logged. It looks like it happened the same night as the murder, got reported the following morning. No surprise it's not been followed up yet."

"Anything interesting?"

"Doesn't look like it, Ma'am." They turned left off a round-about towards Workington. "Smashed window. Owner unhelpful, apparently. We don't need to worry about it for now."

Zoe considered.

She was driving all the way out to Workington on a hunch. She'd had Aaron delivering cards to brothels on a hunch. There was nothing new from the press conference and Nina hadn't had any more luck on Mispers.

"No," she said. "It's not like we're drowning in leads. Call the station. Tell Nina and Tom to take a look."

CHAPTER THIRTY-TWO

TOM FIDGETED in the seat beside Nina, *Suspicious Minds* blaring from the car speakers. They'd already had a row about the volume.

"Something wrong?" she asked.

"What am I sitting on?" He raised himself and felt below. He waved an object at her. "What the hell is this?"

She glanced at it, then reached over, snatched it from him, and pressed it to her nose. "I think it's a Chicken McNugget."

She threw it over her shoulder, into the back seat where it would no doubt lie undiscovered for months.

"And let's not pretend you're a specimen of cleanliness and luxury yourself," she said.

He shrugged. "This is a waste of time, you know? I could be getting a lot more done back at the station."

"I know you're pissed off that the DI's dragged you away from your little computer, Tom. I think it's the first good decision she's made since she got here, but unlike you, I'm an actual copper."

He turned to her, feeling the skin of his face twitch. "What do you think I am, then?"

She shrugged. "Dunno. IT Support? Helpdesk?" She adopted a tinny voice. "'Have you tried rebooting?'"

"Fuck off, Nina. I'm as much a copper as you are."

"If you say so." They continued in silence for a moment, and she glanced in his direction again.

"Of course you are, Tom. But you've got to show a little, I dunno, a little *oomph* from time to time."

"*Oomph?*"

"Show them you want to get out and do something. Show them you want to get ahead, make something of yourself."

Make something of yourself. That was Nina's thing. It wasn't Tom's. "I just want to help people."

She scoffed, reversing into a space on Queen Street opposite the churchyard. "You're scared," she said, turning the wheel as the car bumped the kerb.

His cheek twitched again. "Scared of what, Nina?"

"I dunno. Scared of having a crack and failing at it. Same reason you haven't asked out Harriett Barnes."

"I don't—"

"You're so worried about screwing up, you don't even try to succeed. You come across as lazy, but I've seen the way you can work when you need to."

He looked at her. He didn't have to explain himself to her. "Whatever."

He climbed out of the car, reached back in to grab his backpack, and took a few deep breaths.

They were parked outside the dentist, next door to a nail bar. The churchyard opposite was deserted. In summer there would be people around, eating snacks and drinking coffee, but today it wasn't warm enough.

The hardware store was three doors down. The broken window was already boarded up. In front of the door stood a red-faced man with no hair and the thickest arms Tom had ever seen.

"Took your fuckin' time, didn't you?"

"I'm sorry, Mr—" Nina began.

"Liddell. Jackson Liddell. This is my shop and I want it open, right?"

"I understand, Mr Liddell. And I'm sorry we've taken so long. We'll be out of your hair as soon as we can. This happened the night before last, is that right?"

He nodded. "And your lot won't let me open. How am I supposed to make a living?"

"Anything taken, Sir?" she said.

Tom walked around, checking the surrounding buildings for cameras.

"Haven't really checked," the man said. "Don't think so."

"Do you mind taking a look, Sir?" Nina asked him.

"Do I..."

Tom turned to see the man advancing on Nina. She widened her stance, unfazed.

"Do I mind taking a look?" he continued. "Yes, I bloody do, you bloody—"

"I understand how annoying this is, Sir, but the sooner we can confirm this isn't related to any other enquiries, the sooner we can let you open up again."

Tom smiled to himself. Jackson Liddell would know there had been a murder. He'd know the body had been found less than a ten-minute walk from his shop.

As Liddell stomped in through his door, he approached Nina and stood beside her, looking at the broken window.

"Anything?" she asked.

"Cameras." He pointed at the estate agent, the accountant, the dentist. "Most of them probably dummies, but you never know."

Jackson Liddell was back. "Bastards nicked some paint."

"Paint?" repeated Nina. Tom stared at Liddell.

"Yeah."

"What colour?" asked Tom.

"Fuck's sake, what does that matter?"

"Do you mind checking?"

"Fuck's sake." Liddell stomped back into the shop.

Tom and Nina exchanged glances.

Paint.

Liddell emerged with a can in his hand. "Red. Same as this."

CHAPTER THIRTY-THREE

Zoe followed Aaron's directions to a narrow road with warehouses to one side and open fields on the other. They'd approached on a bridge over the Derwent, so she'd been able to get a view of the sea, but the port itself seemed elusive. Plenty of cranes. What looked like a million logs piled up in rows, in open-sided buildings, on open ground, anywhere there was room for them.

She drove past a white sign. *PRIVATE PROPERTY. NO ADMISSION EXCEPT ON BUSINESS.*

Well, this was business.

There was a gate ahead, a barrier, and a kiosk. More warning signs: *Keep Out. Caution, Heavy Plant.*

Zoe pulled up in a layby beside the fields.

"OK, what's our line?" she asked Aaron.

Silence. A woman walked past them, pulling a dog along, and through a gate into a nearby field.

"Aaron? Who should we be asking to talk to? Apart from this Myron Carter, is there anyone else we know onsite?"

He shook his head. "Sorry, Ma'am. I haven't... I'm just not that familiar with the port."

A freight train rolled past on the other side of the road, one bright red carriage after another. She hadn't realised there was a track.

"Right," she said. "Carter it is. We'll look around, introduce ourselves. Then we can head back to the station and you can start to breathe again."

"OK, Ma'am." He blinked.

Zoe smiled. "It's OK. I know you're breathing. You're not dead, are you?"

She drove to the kiosk. From there she could see more: huge gas containers, or liquid storage tanks. A woman could get lost easily enough.

A man emerged from the kiosk, hand out, a weary smile under the bright yellow helmet. He had a nose ring and a pierced eyebrow.

Beside Zoe, Aaron tensed, staring ahead. Zoe shook her head. He'd have to learn to relax.

"Can I help you?" the man asked.

"Yes." Zoe showed her ID. He didn't seem put out by it. "Is Myron Carter about?"

"I can check. Have you got an appointment?"

"No."

"OK. Wait here."

He disappeared into the kiosk and picked up a radio. Zoe couldn't hear him speak above the sound of the machinery and another train.

"I'm sorry, Miss."

"Detective Inspector."

"I'm sorry, Detective Inspector. Mr Carter's not available.

You can call and make an appointment some other time, if you want."

She'd hoped that having the police turn up might have some sort of impact. She might as well have been a lollipop lady.

The man had disappeared into his kiosk.

She turned to Aaron. "We could make them let us in."

"We could, Ma'am. But it's not like we've got any evidence this is a crime scene, is it?"

"We won't know if we can get any evidence without a better look."

She began to reverse back the way they'd come, turning in the layby. Aaron was right. She didn't have enough. And the way the port was laid out, getting a look inside would be close to impossible.

Halfway up the access road she stopped and pulled out her phone. There was a decent signal: that was something. She opened a map of the area.

"There." She handed the phone to Aaron. "I was thinking you'd need to be at sea to get a view into the port, but the other side of the river juts out."

"The south side projects further into the sea."

She raised an eyebrow. "Hope your eyesight's better than mine, Aaron."

CHAPTER THIRTY-FOUR

"OK," Tom said, ending a call with Uniform. "We need to lock it down."

Nina raised an eyebrow, reminding him how she got away with being an Elvis impersonator. "That's what I told Mr Happy over there."

Jackson Liddell was pacing outside his store, his phone pressed to his ear. Tom couldn't hear what he was saying, but didn't think it would be anything nice.

They watched in silence for a few minutes, Nina staring absently across the road, Tom huddling into his jacket. The sun had disappeared behind clouds and he was wishing he'd worn something warmer. Jackson Liddell stepped into the tattoo parlour half a dozen doors down.

"Can't we get things started?" asked Nina. "Get in there ourselves, have a poke about?"

Tom shook his head. "I asked. Stella Berry said, and I quote, *I'll string you up by your balls if you set a foot inside.*"

"So nothing stopping us, then."

They both laughed.

"How long did Stella say she'd be?" Nina asked a few minutes later.

Tom shrugged. Maybe they could take turns sitting in Nina's car. If you ignored the McNuggets chucked in the back seat, it was more comfortable than standing about on the street. Warmer, too.

"What about Minor?" Nina continued. "Shall I give him a call, see if we can hurry things along a bit?"

Tom looked at his watch. "It's been less than fifteen minutes. I know you've got a low boredom threshold, but this is ridiculous."

"Sorry, mate. I don't like wasting time."

He ignored the insinuation. The day was wearing on and there was hardly a soul about. Another five minutes, and Tom was starting to agree with Nina.

"Fuck it," she said. "Let's go in."

"You wait here, I'll sit in the car. Ten minutes, then swap."

"Why don't you sit in the car and I'll go inside and poke around?"

"Don't be ridiculous."

"I know what I'm doing, Tom."

"*Poke around*? Really?"

She glared at him.

They resumed their silent vigil. At last, Stella Berry and Caroline Deane appeared in an electric Nissan.

"Thank fuck," muttered Nina.

"What have we got?" asked Stella.

"Break-in," said Tom. "Some paint was taken, according to the owner. Red paint. Same as this."

He reached into his backpack and pulled out an evidence bag containing the can Jackson Liddell had reluctantly handed over.

"Red paint." Stella took it, exchanging glances with Caroline. "Are we thinking...?"

"We don't know what we're thinking," Nina snapped.

"We'll know more when you've had a chance to do your job," Tom said, trying to smooth the waters. He knew Nina didn't like the CSM.

"Fair enough." Stella looked at Nina. "Thanks for keeping the place clean."

"The owner boarded up the window himself," Nina said. "He's been all over the place since yesterday morning, so—"

"So we'll need to get samples from him to eliminate. You don't need to teach a grandma to suck eggs, Nina."

"Have you found anything up at the marina?" Tom asked.

Stella shook her head. "It's slow progress, and it'll be even slower now you've got us here. We can't replicate ourselves every time you find another crime scene."

CHAPTER THIRTY-FIVE

"You can head down there." Aaron pointed to a narrow road snaking out towards the headland, which was exactly where Zoe wanted to go.

But she'd spotted a lane, barely more than an alley, connecting this road with the south shore of the Derwent.

Directly opposite the Port of Workington.

She turned up the lane, found a spot under a tree, parked, and got out of the car. Aaron followed, silent.

There were two houses, both detached, both big, both reasonably well kept. As Zoe followed the narrowing lane towards the river, tarmac gave way to gravel and then to a rutted track. On either side there were half a dozen lockups, all with multiple heavy-duty padlocks.

"Who has these lockups?" she asked.

Aaron shrugged.

They turned onto the riverside path to head inland towards a marina. Zoe stopped to take in the moored-up fishing and pleasure boats and the view beyond them, across the river.

All she could see of the port were the sides of warehouses and the cranes.

A small row of terraced houses had a view of the river, but not the port.

And even if they could see the port, she wasn't about to start knocking on doors.

"Let's head back to the car," she said.

Aaron nodded and pushed out a thin breath.

As they approached the car, Zoe caught the familiar smell of marijuana. She glanced at Aaron, who'd tensed.

Six men stood leaning against a fence, smoking. Not the teenagers she'd been expecting, they were all overweight middle-aged men. Three had dogs, two had hair. They chatted as they smoked.

If these men owned the lockups, chances were they were hiding something there. More weed, possibly lots of it. Whatever it was, they wouldn't be starting trouble.

She smiled as they walked past. The men fell silent.

Back in the car, she turned onto the road leading to the southern headland. Aaron was looking at his watch.

"Somewhere you have to be, Aaron?"

He looked up. "Oh, no. Nothing important."

"It's OK, Aaron. I'm teasing you."

The road ran alongside the river and ended in a large, almost empty car park. The wind had picked up and the gulls were as fat as any Zoe had ever seen, but what struck her was the beauty.

This was the first sign of it since they'd arrived in Workington, and it took her breath away. Low grass-covered hills curved away to the south. To the north the blue sea stretched towards the more impressive hills that rose in the distance.

"What's that?" she asked Aaron.

"Scotland."

She felt her stomach clench. *Nicholas. Mo.*

Aaron continued. "Dumfries and Galloway, Kirkcud-brightshire. Lowlands. Ever been?"

Zoe shook her head.

"You should. It's quite something. And there..." He turned south, to the low hills heading down towards Whitehaven. "That's the coastal path. Decent walk, on a nice day. Do you walk?"

"Not if I can help it. City girl, me."

Something else had caught her eye. "And that?"

"It's a lighthouse."

"Smallest lighthouse I've ever seen. And where's the light?"

It was tiny, two floors at most, perched towards the end of the headland a few hundred yards away. Yellowing-grey, with letters daubed on it. Something was on the top of it, possibly a light, not switched on.

Zoe walked towards it, then turned to see the view, finally, right into the port. It was a distance, and she'd need binoculars or a good camera. But she could see more than she'd managed when she was almost inside the place.

Approaching the lighthouse, she spotted movement on the upper floor.

She quickened her pace. The letters she'd spotted read *CTC*. She'd seen those in Whitehaven Marina, carved in metal on a slipway.

Metal stairs led up to a narrow walkway around the building, which seemed to be boarded up. Zoe ran up the stairs, making the railings shake.

A figure at the top looked back towards the town, the port, and the fells behind them.

"Hello," said Zoe.

The figure turned. It was a woman in her early forties. She wore sunglasses and a headscarf, as well as dungarees with a white apron. Behind her was an easel and in her hand, a brush.

"Hello," she replied in a Home Counties accent. *Not local, then.*

"I was wondering if you could help us. I'm Detective Inspector Zoe Finch, this is my colleague Detective Sergeant Aaron Keyes." Zoe fished for her ID but the woman shook her head.

"I believe you. Olivia Bagsby. I'd shake your hand, but the paint..." She gave a deep, throaty laugh. "So what can I do for you, Officers?"

"Do you come up here often?"

"Are you chatting me up, DI Finch?"

"I—"

"I'm joking, don't worry. And yes. I'm renting a place down there." She waved towards the south shore. "I come here to paint when there's good weather. You get a beautiful view of the fells beyond the town. Sometimes it's clear and you can see every little crag, sometimes it's hazy and there's just an impression of height, of land in the sky. Either way, it's worth capturing."

Zoe thought of her former colleague Connie, her Art Historian brother Zaf. Nicholas's ex. "Been here long?" she asked.

"Five months. The lease is up next month, but I've asked if I can extend it."

Zoe looked at the easel. Olivia had painted a foreground of sharp, straight lines disappearing into a misty backdrop of hill and cloud.

"Is that the port?" she asked.

"Yes. It's fun to paint that, too. I was planning on looking at the sea and the fells, not the usual tired old Lake District stuff. Something more edgy."

"Edgy?" Zoe wasn't sure what the woman meant.

"Yeah. Like, this place, it's an edge, isn't it? Edge of the country, a line between the land and the sea. And then, with the hills, there's all that vertical edge, the edge between land and sky. But also, it's different from places like Penrith and the Lakes, isn't it?"

Was it? Zoe nodded, as Olivia Bagsby continued.

"It's not twee. I like it." She smiled. "I come before dawn, up here, and I paint real life. The port, the comings and goings, all the dirty business of trade. And behind it, the town, waking, and behind that the fells, which, well, they are magnificent, aren't they?"

"So you paint the port often?"

The woman nodded. "Oh yes. Day, night, sometimes I even come down with a telephoto lens so I can get the detail and fill it in later."

Zoe felt a shiver run through her. "Have you ever seen anything unusual going on there?"

Olivia frowned. "I don't really know what's normal at a port and what isn't, I'm afraid."

"What about people? Coming in, probably at night, that sort of thing?"

"Oh, yes. Definitely that."

Zoe waited.

"When I come for the sunrise I sometimes set up an hour or two earlier, and there's often boats coming in and out at night, lots of people coming off them, moving about. I've seen a minibus, too."

"A minibus?"

"People get off a boat – I couldn't see their faces, but I think they were women, from the way they stood and walked. So they get off, and they walk along one of those... walkways, in a line, all very organised. Although, I have seen one or two stumble and you wouldn't want to fall in, it's cold in there. And then they disappear, behind all the warehouses and everything. But later, still before sunrise, a minibus leaves the place. So I think they must be on it, those women."

Zoe waited for Olivia to finish. There could be a lot here. Particularly when it came to that telephoto lens.

"Do you mind giving me your contact details, Olivia? I'd love to pop round at some point and, er..."

"See your work," said Aaron.

Olivia beamed. "Certainly." She pulled a card from the pocket of her dungarees. *Olivia Bagsby, Artist*, with a phone number and email address.

Walking away, another question occurred to Zoe. She turned.

"Can you tell me, while you've been living here, have you heard anything about a man named Myron Carter?"

Olivia blinked. "No."

Zoe watched as a shadow crossed the woman's face.

"No," she repeated. "I don't think so. Goodbye, Officers."

She turned away, suddenly unfriendly.

CHAPTER THIRTY-SIX

"You go back," Nina said. "Do your thing. I'll stay here."

Tom turned to her, surprised. She'd hardly made a secret of the fact she didn't like Stella Berry.

"You sure?" he asked.

"You go digging online. You'll find some vital piece of evidence and then we can all go home."

"You just want all the glory when they find another body in this place." He gestured towards the hardware store, where the single thread of police tape had been replaced by a more serious-looking cordon. "Or a signed confession."

Nina shrugged. She liked to be at the heart of things, but she wasn't sure this was it. It was a logical use of resources; Tom would achieve more than her back at the station, while she'd be more likely to notice something out here in the real world.

"Take my car." She threw him the keys and he caught them one-handed.

"You sure?"

"Get out of here before I change my mind. And you'll have to come and pick me up later, right?"

"Course. And I promise not to add to the McDonald's collection in the back seat."

She watched him pull out into the still-quiet street, drive past and turn right at the end, disappearing from view. She probably didn't need to be here any more than he did: the cordon would keep troublemakers out, and she wasn't going to offer a lot to Stella and Caroline.

But she hadn't seen Jackson Liddell leave the tattoo parlour, and he was one troublemaker who might not be deterred by tape.

And she was the most senior officer at the crime scene. The fact that she was the only officer here was beside the point. She was in charge of a crime scene that might be connected to a murder, and that didn't happen to detective constables every day. Not detective constables in Whitehaven, at least.

Ten minutes later, she popped her head under the tape and through the open door. "Any luck?"

"Yes." Stella Berry was looking at her phone. She turned it around so Nina could see the screen: Facebook.

"My ex has just been dumped by his latest tart. This is shaping up to be an excellent day. Wouldn't you agree, Caroline?"

Caroline said nothing. Nina backed out of the shop and took up her position outside.

After another fifteen minutes she'd had enough. She marched over to the tattoo parlour, yanked the door open, and walked in.

A young woman sat behind a table in the corner of the tiny reception area, chewing gum and staring at her nails.

"Can I help you?" she asked, not looking up.

"Where's Liddell?" asked Nina. "Jackson Liddell."

The woman looked up at her.

"From the hardware store. I saw him come in here."

"Oh, him. He buggered off ages ago. Said he might not be able to stop the fucking police tearing his shop up, but no one was gonna make him watch while they did it."

"Right. Thank you."

Nina sighed. She'd have to track him down, get prints, DNA, details of what he'd been wearing.

She retreated to the hardware store.

"Any joy?" she asked Stella.

"Not yet." Stella didn't look up. "Plenty of digging around to do before we give up, eh, Caroline?"

Caroline said nothing.

Stella looked up at Nina. "Go back to the station. Me and Caroline are probably wasting our time here. No need for you to as well."

"Thanks," Nina replied. "But Tom's taken the car and he's coming to pick me up later. You're stuck with me."

"Knock yourself out," replied Stella. "But outside the shop, please. Don't want to have to eliminate your blood from the evidence too."

CHAPTER THIRTY-SEVEN

"So what do you think?" Zoe asked. She and Aaron were back in her car, heading back to Whitehaven.

"I don't know, Ma'am. I think—"

"You know what, Aaron, I don't think this whole *Ma'am* thing is working out. Shall we try boss instead?"

"Sure. Boss."

"But Ma'am in front of Tom and Nina. No, that's going to be too complicated, isn't it? Right. Boss for everyone."

"Boss. I'm not sure about Olivia Bagsby, though."

"You don't believe her?"

"I don't think she's lying, boss. I just doubt she's got anything useful."

"I guess we'll see. Any news from Tom or Nina?"

He checked his phone. "Nothing. Nina's still at the scene with the CSIs. Tom's gone back to the station."

"Right. What's this *CTC*, then?"

He frowned. "They have bike races here, sometimes. Coast to coast, all the way over to Sunderland or wherever. Shorter ones, too."

Zoe nodded. "So, tell me about the port, then."

He turned to her, a question on his face.

"I just want to get a handle on the scale of it," she said, "how busy it is, what happens there."

"Right." He nodded. "Well, the commercial dock has around half a dozen berths, and it can accommodate vessels up to, well, over a hundred metres long and probably twenty metres beam."

"Berth? Beam? In English please, Aaron."

"Six or seven ships, boss. Big ships. It's rarely full though, has a few hundred movements a year. You've seen the rail connections, the warehouses, and open storage. There's a lot of liquid and dry bulk goods go through there."

"I saw a lot of logs."

"Forest products, they call it. And then there's the project stuff. There's a lot of offshore wind farms in this area, and they run maintenance and operations from the Port of Workington. So that keeps them busy."

"But would any of that account for a bunch of women coming in late at night and leaving in a minibus?"

"If they did, boss."

"So you don't believe her?"

"I don't think it's possible to be that accurate. You've seen how far away the port is from the lighthouse. Even she said she couldn't see their faces. Seems a bit thin to me."

"Maybe." Zoe fell silent as they joined the main road south. She'd have to head to the community centre, where Aaron had left his car. "You seem to know quite a lot about this place, for someone who doesn't think it's worth looking into."

He shrugged. "I just... I'm just interested in, well, it's a major local employer, isn't it?"

"Is it?"

"Yes. It's the kind of thing I think we should know about."

"And nothing to do with your Myron Carter and what he might or might not have been up to?"

"No, Ma'am. Boss."

Zoe breathed out, resisting the urge to slam on the brakes.

"I don't believe you," she said.

Silence.

"I don't believe this is just general interest," she continued. "You've been looking into this place, haven't you?"

Nothing.

"You suspect there's something serious going on here but you've kept it to yourself. Am I right?"

"Yes."

"But I don't think it's a good idea to rush into anything, boss." Aaron's voice was low. "I don't think it's connected with our current case—"

"Why not? No one seems to know who our victim is, which makes it possible she's been trafficked here. If anyone's doing any trafficking, this is the obvious place, isn't it?"

"I... I suppose so."

He looked so uncomfortable, Zoe almost felt sorry for him.

"But I still think that's a lot of ifs, boss. When we've got this Richard Madsen character right in front of us."

"Madsen was with the others. We'll look into him, but I reckon he's a dead end. I want to focus on the victim, and if that means the port, that's where we should be looking."

"I don't know, boss." Another pause. "I don't think it's a good idea for people to know I'm interested in the port."

"Why not?"

No answer.

"No," she said. "Don't tell me. You think Carter's connected, don't you? You don't know who you can trust."

"Yes," he said finally. "He could have anyone in his pocket. And with respect, boss, you should know about this sort of thing."

"What are you trying to say, Aaron?" Zoe kept her voice flat.

"Well... you've been through it, haven't you? Force CID."

She wasn't sure how to respond.

"So really, boss," he continued, "you should understand why I've been reluctant to talk to you."

"Hang on." She braked, a little harder than she'd intended. The driver behind hooted. "Are you suggesting that *I'm* one of the people you can't trust? That, because there was corruption in Force CID, I must be somehow implicated?"

"No, boss." He sounded panicked.

Good.

"It's not that," he said. "But the safest thing's been to talk to nobody."

Zoe turned towards town, down a street with a terraced hill on one side. It was easy to navigate without a thousand side roads and one-way systems and the whole place being torn up and rebuilt every week. And not a million other cars on them. She pulled up outside the community centre just as a patrol car eased by, a constable peering out of the window.

"Come on," she said. "Let's get back to the station." She walked with him to his Volvo, spotting a child seat in the back as the interior lights came on.

"It's OK, Aaron," she said, before he shut the door. "I'm not bent, but you don't know that, and if all you do know is that people I worked with *were* bent, then I suppose I get it. But you've told me now."

"What have I told you?" He sounded surprised.

"You've told me you suspect Carter, you think he has

contacts inside, you're worried about the port. That's good. That's a sign of trust."

CHAPTER THIRTY-EIGHT

The interior of Nina's car might have been a health hazard, but she had been right about Tom's priorities. He smiled as he entered the team room.

Home.

He'd done his time on the beat. He'd broken up pub fights, been punched and spat at, and now he didn't have to do all that. They could laugh all they wanted at him, sat behind a computer, but he didn't care. That was how Tom Willis solved crimes.

Tom Willis, Crime Solver. It had a ring to it.

There was a message on the team inbox: Mick Halfpenny, claiming to have information.

Tom would call back when he had time, but there was every chance that wouldn't be until they'd solved the case. Mick had seemed like a nice chap and was only trying to help. But like most of the public, his idea of help was worse than no help at all.

And they'd been busy. Forty-eight calls following the DI's press conference. More than half of them the work of idiots, pranksters, or lunatics, but that still left around twenty for Tom to sift through.

After the first five, he was wishing he was still outside the hardware store with Nina.

One was drunk. Another had called from Bournemouth about a different crime in a different county. Two claimed to have committed the offence themselves, but had got the most basic details wrong. The fifth was just a high-pitched voice repeating, "I know who did it," accompanied by giggling.

He went to the kitchen and made a coffee. He drank it with a chocolate digestive, feet up on his desk.

The sixth call was a deep-voiced man announcing that he could solve any crime in any location through his psychic powers, but only if the price was right. The seventh was a drunken woman struggling to speak properly, saying she couldn't find her friend.

Halfway through number seven, he heard the door open behind him. He turned to see the sarge enter with the DI. The sarge looked bothered by something, in a way he hadn't been for a while.

Tom put the phone down.

"Right, Tom," said the DI. "What have you got for me?"

He hoped she wasn't expecting much.

CHAPTER THIRTY-NINE

"Recap time," said the DI. She gave Aaron a smile which he returned, his mind racing.

They were in the team room still, with Nina on speaker-phone outside the hardware store. Tom had told them about the call from Mick Halfpenny, which Aaron wasn't inclined to take seriously. Nina had talked them through what they'd found at the scene.

"The missing can of paint," Aaron said. "What with the post-mortem results—"

"The sarge and I have spent the afternoon looking into the Port of Workington," the DI interrupted.

Aaron's heart sank.

"Nothing specific." She was looking at him. He looked down at his shoes.

"Checking up on whether our victim might have come through there," she continued. "We spoke to a potential witness, but we haven't got anything concrete so we're parking that for now. Anything from the public yet, Tom?"

"Not really, Ma'am."

"It's boss now."

"Sorry?"

"Call me boss. I've gone right off Ma'am."

"OK, boss." Tom glanced at Aaron, who shrugged. "So far it's just the usual drunks and time-wasters."

"Well, it was worth a shot," the boss said. "The press conference still has to go out on the evening bulletins, and there'll be people who won't see it online until they're home from work. So all is not lost. So, moving on to the men in robes. Anything?"

"I don't know, boss," began Tom. "I haven't been looking at that." His cheeks reddened.

"Of course," the DI said. "We know what the design is and that it could be from anywhere. And we know half the town has seen a picture of them dragging a bag around. Which reminds me, the victim had abrasions on her fingers. From rubbing against a soft material like the inside of a bag."

We already know this, Aaron thought.

"Which leaves us with your friends, Nina: Mal and the rest of them. We don't know enough about Richard Madsen."

"Not my friends," Nina said.

"Nothing new on Madsen, boss," said Tom. "I'm drawing a blank on him."

"You admitting defeat?" asked Nina. Tom gave a sigh, and nodded.

Nina stood, lifted the cover from the back of her chair, and draped it over Tom's. He leaned forward a look of disgust on his face.

"OK," said the boss. "What is that thing?"

"Has no one explained?" asked Aaron.

"No," she replied. She didn't look particularly thrilled by the whole thing. More like it was something she had to find out, whether she wanted to or not. She was right, thought Aaron.

"It's an antimacassar," said Nina.

"A what?" asked the DI.

"An antimacassar. You use them to keep the back of chairs clean."

"You do what when?" asked the DI.

"From Victorian times," Nina explained. "My mum made this one. Even sewed the pattern on." She lifted it off Tom's chair and held it up, displaying the gull and the fish. "Mum thought – well, with the hair." Nina gestured at her own quiff. "The oil. She thought it would ruin the furniture."

"And why is it here?" asked the boss.

"It's what we use, when we make a bet," Aaron stepped in. "Whoever loses, they have to – well, it's theirs. Until someone else loses a bet. Tom couldn't find Madsen, he lost the bet. He's got the antimacassar now."

"And I'm thrilled by it," added Tom, looking anything but.

The DI pursed her lips. "OK. Let's move on. It's time to head home for the evening. Start again tomorrow with fresh heads, oily or otherwise. Here's our priorities for the morning. Nina, I want you checking out the crime scenes again, the hardware store and the marina. Keep an eye on things, liaise with Stella."

"Fine by me, boss."

"Good. Tom, you call Mick back, finish up with the public calls, and see if we can get anywhere with the men in white. If you've got any thoughts on them, feel free to share them."

"Sorry, boss. I'm clueless."

She sighed. "Now, Aaron. You're not going to like this, but I want you back at the port tomorrow."

She was watching him. He nodded. He'd do what she wanted, find nothing, and come back. *Fine.*

"See if you can talk to Olivia Bagsby again," she said. "Look at her photos. And if that gets us nowhere, we can continue the hunt for Richard Madsen. I'll speak to the super, see if we can get any help from Organised Crime."

Aaron felt sick. "Boss?"

"Yes, Aaron?"

"You're going to speak to the super about the port?"

"We've got an unidentified murder victim. It'd be strange not to think about people trafficking, and even stranger if we didn't think about the port. There's no way round it. So yes, I need to talk to her about that."

Aaron allowed himself to relax. She was telling him that not speaking to the super would be even more suspicious than speaking to her. And she was implying that she wouldn't mention his suspicions.

The three of them trooped down the stairs.

"Pint?" asked Tom as they headed out of the building and into the car park. "I've got to pick up Nina, but after that?"

"Why not?" Aaron replied. He wanted to catch up with Nina and Tom. "Boss, a quick drink?"

He watched her think it over, then smile and shake her head.

"Sorry, guys. I'm exhausted. But thanks for the offer. Maybe another time, yeah?"

Probably for the best, thought Aaron. It would be good to talk to the team without the new boss listening to every word.

CHAPTER FORTY

"IT's NOT HERE," shouted Carl from upstairs.

Zoe lay on the sofa, eyes closed, trying to remember where she'd seen the glass bowl Carl was looking for.

It had gone in a box, she knew that. Which meant it was almost certainly still in a box, upstairs.

This didn't narrow things down.

"Give me a hand?" he said, standing next to her now.

All she wanted to do was lie down, close her eyes, eat something, and sleep.

"OK." She dragged herself to her feet. "Let's do this."

"We should have done it before we started work," he said, as she trudged up the stairs behind him. "It's a nightmare up here and I don't have time to sort it all out now."

"Don't look at me," she said. "It's not like I'm sat at home all day doing nothing."

"Yeah." He went into Nicholas's room and started looking through boxes. "Yeah, I know. Come on, let's see if we can find the toaster while we're at it. I'm fed up waiting for the grill to warm up every time I want a slice of toast."

Zoe bent down to the nearest box.

"Not that one. Books and a bit of posh crockery."

She opened the next one. Why couldn't she just go and lie down? Why couldn't they just find things when they needed them?

They'd tried that. It hadn't worked.

"How's your case?" asked Carl, head down at the other side of the room.

"Might have some leads, might all be dead ends. Think we'll have to pull on them before we know."

"Nothing concrete?"

Zoe straightened up and pushed the box to the side with her foot. *Why does Carl have so many photo frames?*

"Zoe?"

"Sorry, miles away. Yeah, nothing concrete."

"Anything I can do to help?"

"I bloody hope not."

He looked up. "What d'you mean?"

"Nothing. Sorry."

"Zoe, what do you mean?"

"Well, if you get involved, it's hardly a good sign, is it?"

"I just wanted to find out about your day. What, you think PSD are going to step in?"

She pulled an eggcup out of a box and turned it in her hands, trying to find it interesting.

"Zoe?"

"I don't know, Carl. It's just... It feels like I can't get away from any of it. Randle. Bryn Jackson. It's followed me up here like I knew it would."

"What have people been saying?"

"They know more than I'm comfortable with. They've heard of me."

He stood in front of her, concern on his face. He took the eggcup and put it back in the box. He reached out to touch her cheek, leaned in, and kissed her lips. The touch was so light she could barely feel it.

"They've heard of you because you're a brilliant copper, Zoe." He stepped back and looked into her eyes. "They've heard about Canary. About Hamm. *Everybody's* heard about Hamm. Your reputation is that you get to the bottom of serious crimes and you put away the people who commit them."

She smiled. He was right.

Yes. He was right. She was almost sure of it.

CHAPTER FORTY-ONE

THE DAY STARTED WELL.

Carl rose early, found the toaster, and brought her coffee and toast. The coffee was excellent – she'd taught him well – and she surprised herself by being hungry, wolfing it so quickly that Carl had brought her another two slices.

She managed the drive in under sixteen minutes to find the car park still almost empty. She went straight to Fiona's office, expecting to find the super either busy or out. But the super was in, available, and willing to help.

And so far, no one had mentioned Birmingham, her past, or police corruption.

"So I think," she said to Fiona, "it would be helpful if I could speak to someone who knows what's going on around the port, if anything is."

Fiona nodded, making notes in a little book on her desk.

Zoe hadn't mentioned Myron Carter. She didn't feel comfortable saying it out loud. Maybe Aaron's nervousness was contagious.

"That's fine." Fiona stood up. Zoe's cue to leave.

"So you'll give me someone's details, Ma'am?"

"Fiona when it's just the two of us, remember? And I'll do better than that." They were at the door, somehow.

Fiona opened it. "Ralph Streeting. DI within Specialist Crime and Intel. We don't have a unit for organised crime up here, we've never really needed one. But that falls under Ralph's remit. I'll set up a chat with him today if I can."

"Thank you."

"You're welcome. And don't forget to let me know if you need anything. It must be tough getting a murder so soon. I'm right on the end of the phone."

The super ushered Zoe out and into the corridor. Zoe walked towards the team room, feeling like she'd been stage-managed.

CHAPTER FORTY-TWO

The day started badly.

Nina woke with a hangover. Tom's suggested pint had become three, and then she'd been reminded that it was karaoke night at Buck's.

Who'd been there? Definitely Tom. Not Aaron, who'd disappeared pleading family commitments. It didn't matter. She'd done her turn, drunk cocktails, and walked home.

At least she'd remembered to set the alarm early. Walking home meant she'd have to walk back into town.

She walked, trying to make the most of it. The open air, the breeze, the smell of the sea, the fact that it was downhill most of the way. But she could only smell the chips, beer, and cocktails, and her legs didn't care about the fact it was downhill.

And there was something new, too. Something worse.

She spotted the first one on a lamppost on Scotch Street. Black background, white text, block capitals. *FREE THE NORTH.*

A band? A political movement? Maybe just some weird performance art things.

But then she found another one on Duke Street: *WE WILL NOT BE ENSLAVED*.

Further down the road, its meaning became clear. *THE NORTH IS WHITE*, followed by, *THEIR WAYS ARE NOT OUR WAYS*, *WHITEHAVEN FOR THE WHITES*, and finally, *FIGHT THE ISLAMISATION OF YOUR HOMELAND*.

Nina's feet suddenly felt even heavier.

She turned onto Queen Street and glanced at a closed-down nail bar whose frontage had been filled with posters for club nights and gigs.

There were five new posters. Black background, white text, block capitals. The same messages she'd seen on the lampposts.

Nina hurried to the hardware store. Caroline Deane was there, no sign of Stella Berry. Jackson Liddell stood outside the shop, right next to the cordon, complaining.

"About fucking time," he said as he saw her. "I'm losing money."

"I'm sorry, Sir. I can give you a compensation form, if you want."

She knew he wouldn't take it. Proving earnings meant paying tax.

"I don't want your fucking forms," he told her. "I just want to open my shop."

She looked back at him, forcing herself to retain a calm expression. *Arsehole.*

He retreated across the road, loitering at the entrance to the churchyard while she entered the shop and stood on the forensic plates.

"Morning."

Caroline looked up. "You look rough."

"Any luck?"

"Not yet."

"I'll be outside. Might pop over to the marina. Give me a shout if anything turns up. If he gives you any trouble and I'm not here, call me, OK?"

Caroline nodded and Nina stepped outside. Liddell stared at her, but stuck to the other side of the street. She took a deep, long breath, closed her eyes, and forced herself to relax.

"You!" came a voice.

Ignore it.

"Yeah, you! I'm talking to you!"

Nina opened her eyes.

A man was walking towards her. Not a man really: in his teens or early twenties. But unlike Jay and his mates, this man wore one of those robes.

"I want to talk to you." He stood in front of her, trying to intimidate her.

"Ibrahim?" she asked, unintimidated.

"Yeah. How d'you know?" He frowned. "You seen all this?"

He waved in the direction of the lampposts.

"I've seen it," she replied.

"What're you gonna do about it?"

He was so close she could smell the sweat on him.

She shrugged. "We'll get it removed. I'll call it in later. Got other priorities right now." She jerked her finger towards the cordon outside the shop.

"You know this is your fault, right?"

Nina took a step back. "How d'you figure that?"

"Your lot leaked stuff, now everyone thinks this is a Muslim crime. I mean, it's not like they need an excuse to blame us, but all this stuff, it's obvious they'll take it out on us, isn't it?"

"Too fucking right," came a shout from across the road.

Nina felt her shoulders drop.

"What?" Ibrahim turned to face Liddell, his voice calm but clear.

"I said, too fucking right." Liddell crossed the road, looking at Nina. "Why do I have to be the one who gets his place shut down? Why don't you give this lot the same shit you're giving me?"

Nina felt herself tense. She could handle these two. But she wasn't about to get herself hurt by breaking up a fight between a racist moron and a dumb, angry kid.

"Everyone knows they did it." Liddell turned towards Ibrahim and folded his arms.

"Easy," said Nina. "Easy." She pointed at Liddell. "You get back. Over. There." She kept her eyes locked on Liddell's.

Liddell took a step back, turned, and crossed the road.

Thank fuck for that.

Nina turned to Ibrahim. "We're working as hard as we can to sort this out. To find out who actually did it. Don't you want us to do that?"

"Well, yeah."

"Then go home and let me get on with my job, OK?"

He turned and started to walk back the way he'd come. She watched him stop outside the tattoo parlour and turn back to her. "You'd better sort this."

She nodded. *Job done.*

Nina stepped back, leaned against the wall of the dentist, and realised she was starving. There was a café here. There were half a dozen places she could get chicken within a thirty-second walk.

The thought of chicken made her feel sick.

"Detective Constable?" said a small voice.

Nina looked round to find Caroline Deane in the shop door, looking serious.

"Nina. Call me Nina."

Caroline nodded. "Nina, then. I think you'll want to see this."

CHAPTER FORTY-THREE

Zoe was alongside Moresby Hall again, driving north. It was busier than on the previous day, but quiet enough for her to take her eyes off the road for a moment.

Her phone rang. She glanced towards it, then jerked the wheel back and swore to herself.

"DI Finch," she said.

"Zoe. It's Stella Berry. Are you at the station?"

"I'm in the car."

"You nearby?"

"Not far." She was on her way to Workington to meet Aaron. Stella didn't need to know that. "Why?"

"We've had a call. Something's been found."

Zoe indicated and pulled in at a right turn, little more than a track. "What d'you mean?"

"Member of the public found a knife on the rocks on North Shore. You know where that is?"

North Shore. She'd been there with Aaron. Twice. That was where the community centre was.

"Yes," she said. "What sort of knife? You think...?"

"The knife that cut her throat? Can't rule it out. It's sharp enough – bloody sharp, in fact."

"Right." Zoe turned the car round in the road. Aaron could handle the port by himself.

"It's not a common knife," Stella said. "Imported, I think. Expensive."

"Not the sort of thing you'd just chuck away on the rocks."

"Exactly."

"I'll meet you there." Zoe turned her attention back to the road.

"Come straight to the lab. I'm taking it in for analysis. Uniform have put a cordon round where it was found. I doubt there's anything else there, but we'll have a proper root around when we get a chance. Meanwhile, I want a good look at this knife. Because there's something else, and I think you'll like it."

"What kind of something else?"

"Prints, DI Finch. There are prints on the knife."

Zoe hit the gas, hard. "I'm on my way."

CHAPTER FORTY-FOUR

Aaron put down his phone and turned to PC Harriett Barnes. They were parked in Harriett's response car, in the layby just outside the port.

"The DI's heading back to Whitehaven," he told her. "They've found a knife."

"Oh."

He liked that about Harriett: she was enthusiastic, happy to express her surprise. She'd only been on the job a few months. He hoped the novelty would take its time to fade.

"So, should we go back too?" she asked.

"No. Let's take a look around."

A different man was at the kiosk this morning, thin, with red hair poking out from under his hard hat. Aaron felt himself relax.

He produced his ID and waved back towards the response car. "Can we take a look inside?"

The man retreated into his kiosk. To make a call, no doubt.

"Wait up," shouted Aaron. The man stopped and came back out. "We won't be long, mate. Just want a quick look."

The man ran his tongue across his lower lip, before nodding and lifting the barrier.

We're in.

But Aaron didn't know what he was looking for, wouldn't even know if he found it. He could ask questions, difficult questions about minibuses and night movements and that sort of thing.

But he wouldn't catch them like that. Better to play it softly.

They parked the car between two trucks and picked their way to the nearest warehouse. It was enormous, filled with boxes and shipping containers. No one approached them, but no one kept away.

They tried the warehouse next door, a fenced-off area around the liquid bulk storage, the area around the piled-up logs and the pickups that raced around them. They got the same reaction everywhere.

"This is pointless," he said. "Let's get out of here."

On the south side, the men outside the lockups were still hanging around with their dogs, but this time there was no smell of marijuana. They stared at him and Harriett, especially Harriet.

The two of them walked alongside the riverbank and tried the address Olivia Bagsby had given them: one of those smart, balconied houses overlooking the river. Aaron knew nothing about art, but Olivia Bagsby had money.

No answer. He tried the house on the left, but there was no one there either. The door on the other side opened onto its chain before he knocked and a woman in her seventies eyed him suspiciously.

"DS Aaron Keyes, Cumbria Police. This is PC Harriett Barnes."

"What do you want?" snapped the woman.

"I was wondering if you'd seen anything of your neighbour. Olivia Bagsby." Aaron pointed to the house.

"Not lately. Silly hippy, that one."

"And can you—"

But the door was already shut.

Pointless. All pointless. He wished the DI had been with him to see how pointless it was.

"Let's head back to the station," he said.

His phone rang a few minutes into the drive.

"Tom, everything OK?"

"Yes, Sarge. But I've got someone on the line. She wants to speak to a senior officer."

"Put her through."

There was a click, then another voice, anxious and high-pitched. "Hello? Hello?"

"This is Detective Sergeant Aaron Keyes. Cumbria Police. Who am I talking to?"

"Elaine."

"How can I help you, Elaine?"

"I've got information for you."

Aaron straightened up. It was probably nothing, but this woman sounded nervous, not mad. "What sort of information?"

"I can't tell you now. I'm at work."

"Where's that?"

"Whitehaven."

"No, I mean—"

"You don't need to know any more than that. I can meet you, though. You know the Alphabet Café?"

Aaron knew it: out on the St Bees Road, most of the way along the headland. "I do."

"I'll see you there in an hour." She hung up.

Aaron called Tom back. "Tom, did you get anything from that woman before you put her through?"

"No, Sarge. Sorry. I couldn't see the number she was calling from either."

Aaron looked to his side. Harriett Barnes, hands at ten-to-two, all her attention on the road.

"Why did you put her through to me instead of the DI?"

A pause.

"Tom?"

"I'm sorry, Sarge."

"I know it's a big change, and that's..."

He tailed off, aware of Harriett right next to him. She didn't need to know about Tom's challenges with anything new.

"It's not just that, Sarge," Tom said. "I think I might have screwed up."

"What do you mean?"

"There was another call. Yesterday. Remember when you came in with the boss and I said there wasn't much on the public calls?"

"Yes." Aaron moved the phone to his left hand, further from Harriett.

"There was one that might actually be something. I forgot about it till the other woman called. I'll play it for you now, Sarge."

Aaron listened as another female voice came on the phone. She sounded confused, possibly drunk, he thought, but then realised she was struggling with the language.

Her accent was European, possibly. Maybe Middle Eastern?

The woman couldn't find her friend. That was innocuous

enough, people often couldn't find their friends, but there was more.

"We come here together, in boat," she said. Then more about how she couldn't find her friend. No names: not her, not the friend. And then, "I not see her after Friday in the morning."

Tom came back on the line. "You hear it, Sarge?"

"Yes." He clutched the phone. "How the hell could you forget this, Tom?"

"I'm sorry, Sarge. I hadn't heard the bit about the boat. Or the Friday reference. Just that she couldn't find her friend."

"For crying out loud, Tom."

Tom should have listened to the rest of the call, flagged it, called the DI before he called Aaron.

But that wasn't why Aaron was annoyed.

Aaron was annoyed because of those three words: *In boat together.*

It might not mean the port. But the moment the DI heard it, she'd think of Workington.

"OK, Tom," he said. "We'll sort this out between us. And we'll talk about adjusting later, the two of us. I've got another lead to follow up first. But the DI's going to have to hear this call, OK?"

"OK, Sarge."

"Good. Don't worry. We'll deal with it."

CHAPTER FORTY-FIVE

THE CSI LAB was on an industrial estate a stone's throw from the West Cumberland Hospital, but that wasn't why Zoe couldn't have missed it.

It consisted of four huge shipping containers, meeting in the centre like a giant metal cross. Each one was painted a different colour – blue, red, yellow and green – and each had the words *CUMBRIA POLICE* stencilled on one side and *CSI* on the other.

Inside a pale, unsmiling young man behind a reception desk asked for her credentials, examined them, then spoke quietly into the phone on his desk. He raised a finger and asked her to wait.

Zoe slumped into a sofa, wondering if she'd be offered coffee, then looked up to see Stella Berry striding through the glass doors.

"DI Finch."

"Zoe."

"Of course. Thanks for coming. I think you'll find this interesting."

After the excitement of the exterior and the reception area, the lab itself was disappointingly normal: white walls, benches containing inexplicable scientific equipment and bagged-up forensic suits on shelves.

On one of the benches was the knife.

Zoe hadn't seen anything that shape before. Like a cleaver but with a longer blade. She stood over it, Stella hovering behind her.

"It's OK, Stella. I'm not going to touch it."

Stella took a step back. "Sorry. Anyway, it's a US import."

"US?"

"Carnegie-Beller Instruments. Specialist knife. You can get one online, but it would set you back a few hundred quid."

Zoe heard footsteps and turned to see a man enter. Stella walked to him and they conferred.

"You'll like this," Stella told her. "Results on the writing. The letters on the body."

"Yes?"

"Red paint. A perfect match for the can your DC gave us, the same sort that was nicked from the hardware shop."

Zoe nodded, hiding a smile. Suspicions were all very well, but nothing beat a solid lead. Someone had stolen a can of paint from the hardware store on Queen Street, and they'd used that paint to write on a dead body.

Zoe brought her phone out and snapped a handful of photos. "Do you have the prints?"

"Over here." Stella waved at a laptop.

"Could you send them to Tom?"

Zoe called Tom while Stella bent over the laptop. She asked him to run the prints.

"Yes, boss." He sounded flat.

"This is good news," she said, irritated. "It might be a breakthrough."

"Sorry, boss. I know it is. I'll get right on it."

Zoe turned to Stella, who stood over the knife. "Could this be a religious slaughter knife?"

Stella took a moment. "We shouldn't jump to conclusions."

"I'm not jumping to conclusions. I'm asking you a specific technical question about a weapon that was used on a murder victim. Could it be a slaughter knife?"

"It could be used for Kosher or Halal slaughter. It's sharp enough, and it's the right sort of blade. But there's nothing to say that's what it *has* been used as, or that's what it was purchased for, just because it *could* be—"

"Stella, you don't need to tiptoe around this. I understand that you think I should be careful."

"I just think it's all a little too convenient."

"I know. But I've got to follow the evidence, and so far, that gives me men wearing Islamic robes, an Arabic word written on the body, and a weapon that might be a religious slaughter knife found yards away from the community centre. Which reminds me, any news on the scene?"

"We haven't had a chance to examine it yet. I've got some photos if you want to see them, the knife in place and the surrounding rocks." Stella passed her phone to Zoe.

Zoe spent a moment flicking through the photos. "Could it have washed up there?"

Stella shook her head. "Too high up. If someone tried to throw it out to sea and misjudged it might have landed there, though."

Zoe's phone was ringing: Tom.

"Anything on those prints?"

"No match, boss. Sorry." He still sounded flat.

"You've checked against the lads Nina and Aaron brought in the other day?"

"Sort of. The three that Nina knew are on the system already. Nothing there."

"What about the other one? Madsen?"

"We don't have his prints, boss. Nina and the sarge didn't arrest them."

Zoe sighed. "Tom, you can *ask* people for their prints, even if they're not under arrest. They don't have to give them, but that doesn't stop you asking."

"It wasn't—"

"It wasn't you. It was Nina and Aaron."

"That's not what I was saying, boss. It didn't seem like there was any point at the time. I think that's what the sarge reckoned, anyway."

"If you take a bunch of innocent lads and tell them you'd like their prints to rule them out of a murder investigation, either they'll say yes, and you've got the prints, or you know they've got something to hide."

"That's not what—"

"I know that's not what they teach you in training." She sighed. "But now at least I know why you haven't been able to find anything out about Madsen. All you've got is his name, right?"

"Right, boss."

"I'll be back in soon," Zoe said. "Call Nina. Tell her to go and pick up Madsen. I want to see him for myself."

She ended the call, shaking her head.

Mo would have known what to do. Connie and Rhodri would have got prints out of those lads before they'd even realised they'd given them.

But she had to give her new team some time.

CHAPTER FORTY-SIX

"So what am I looking at?"

Nina stood on a plate just inside the hardware store, next to the broken window, bending down. There were instruments there, things with lenses she couldn't name, tiny little tape measures next to even tinier fragments of glass.

None of it made sense.

"Here." Caroline bent and pointed towards one of the tape measures and the fragments of glass beside it. "On the glass. There."

Nina screwed up her face.

There was something protruding from the glass. A line.

Caroline pointed to another fragment, a couple of inches away. "There's more here." She indicated a larger piece of glass, closer to the wall. "But this one's the clearest."

Now Nina knew what she was looking at. "Fibres."

Caroline nodded. "It's most likely they come from the owner, left there when he boarded the window up. But they could be from an item of clothing that snagged on the broken glass. Here, take a closer look. You can see the colour."

Nina leaned forward. "Orange."

Caroline nodded. "Very bright. Distinctive. If it doesn't come from the owner, then..."

Nine straightened up. Bright orange fibres. Distinctive. Which would make the clothing they'd come from much easier to track down.

But she knew what came first. *Liddell.*

"Just going to have a little word." She backed out of the shop. Jackson Liddell was still across the road, staring, arms crossed.

"Mr Liddell," Nina said. "We're going to need your help. We've found fibres around the broken window, possibly from whoever broke in. We need to check they aren't from anything of your—"

"If you think I'm letting you bastards put bits of me in your files, you're dumber than you look."

"We just need fibres from any orange clothes you might have. It'll speed up the investigation."

"So what?"

"Well, it means you might be able to open the shop within the next couple of days."

"Or?"

She shrugged. "Don't know. Could be weeks."

"Fibres, you say."

"Anything with orange in it."

He blinked. "I'll head home." He scowled at her but turned and walked away.

"Thanks," she called after him. "One of our CSIs will join you." Thank God she'd taken his home address.

Nina looked back at the shop, and Caroline inside. Caroline was small. Liddell was large, and angry. She'd call Uniform, get Roddy Chen to go along as well.

She was being useful, at last. Which had brought back her appetite.

Fried chicken. The places along here were starting to open up for lunch.

Nine was heading back to the shop to let Caroline know she was taking a quick break, when her phone rang.

"Tom, everything OK?" she asked.

"Not really," he said. "DI wants your blood."

Nina froze. "What? What's wrong?"

"You didn't get Madsen's prints. Now they've found a knife, they've got prints off it, and they've got nothing to match them with. She's not happy, Nina."

"Hang on." She stood there, thinking back to what had happened with Madsen. A car hooted, and she realised she was standing in the middle of the road.

She stepped out of the way with a wave. "We didn't arrest them. We couldn't—"

"Boss says you could have just asked. Look, don't worry about it. I'm on your side and I reckon I'm in more trouble than you are, anyway. She wants you to bring Madsen back in. Get his prints. I've sent you the contact details he gave us."

"OK, Tom. Cheers."

The chicken would have to wait.

CHAPTER FORTY-SEVEN

AARON DROVE AWAY from Whitehaven Police Station where Harriett had dropped him. He was probably wasting his time, coming out here to St Bees. But he wanted to know what the mysterious Elaine wanted. Maybe she was connected to the woman who'd lost her friend. Maybe she was the same woman.

His phone rang: Nina.

"I can't find him, Sarge." Nina sounded out of breath. "I've been there, and he wasn't around. They've never heard of him."

"Slow down, Nina," he told her. "Can't find who?"

"Madsen. We didn't get his prints. The DI wants me to track him down and get hold of them. I had an address, but no one there's heard of him."

"You tried the other lads?"

"I tried Davey and Jay's place, but they say they haven't seen him since we dropped them all back in Whitehaven." She paused for breath. "I don't know what to do, Sarge. I reckon I'm in the shit this time."

"Slow down. Give me a minute."

It wasn't her fault. But now there was a knife, and Madsen had given them a false address.

The DI was going to think they were idiots. But it was his mistake, his responsibility.

"You're not in the shit, Nina. I'll take care of it. As for Madsen, we'll keep digging. Maybe speak to your friends again, see if they've got any idea where else he might be."

"They're not my friends, Sarge. And I tried that, anyway. They haven't got a clue."

"OK." He took a breath. "Leave it with me."

He couldn't think of anything, but maybe a change of scenery and some food would help.

The Alphabet Café, half a mile from St Bees, wasn't Aaron's sort of place. The windows reflected the yellow of the oilseed rape in the fields opposite, and the lower-case letters stencilled on them did nothing to hide the layers of grease. But there was something about that greasy spoon smell that made him hungry.

As he approached the counter, torn between bacon and sausage, he spotted a woman sitting alone at a table in the corner, her hair wrapped in a scarf. She was staring at him.

He mouthed, "Elaine?"

She gave a tiny nod. On the table, her hands were trembling.

He approached the table and pulled out a chair. She nodded again, and he sat. She was in her early thirties, maybe younger. She looked even more nervous close-up. Tired, too.

She gazed down at the table. She had a mug of tea, half empty.

"I'm Detective—"

She held out a hand. "You're DS Keyes. I recognise your voice from the phone."

Her accent was local. *So, not the woman looking for her friend.*

"And you're Elaine?"

"Not really," she said. "But it's not me I want to talk about." She glanced at her watch. "It's my boyfriend."

"OK."

A domestic?

"He's one of the men you brought in the other day. He'd been out with his new mates. Young lads."

"Hang on, is his name Richard? Richard Madsen?"

She shook her head. Aaron felt his body slump.

"Morton. Rob Morton."

Aaron frowned. The name wasn't familiar.

"So what do you want to tell me about him?"

"He's been behaving oddly. Disappearing in the middle of the night. I wake up and he's not there, and he shows up again six hours later like that's normal."

"Right. And where has he been?"

She drained the last of her tea. "Dunno. He says *out*. That's it, just *out*. I don't want to push him, you know."

Aaron knew. "And where do *you* think he's been?"

"Dunno. But after what happened to that poor lass..."

"You think he might have had something to do with that?"

She shrugged. "He was picked up by the police. I thought you might know him."

Aaron narrowed his eyes. "When?"

"Saturday. He wasn't arrested or anything. Just wanted a word, apparently. I had to come and pick him up from his mate's in Corkickle."

In Corkickle. Aaron felt his heart rate pick up. It wasn't like Corkickle was tiny. But still...

"Can you show me a photo?"

"Yeah."

She lifted a bag from under her seat and pulled out a phone. She tapped for a moment before handing it to him.

Aaron stared at it.

He tried not to smile.

"That's him," she said.

That's him, alright.

He was looking at a photograph of the man who'd called himself Richard Madsen.

CHAPTER FORTY-EIGHT

"Aaron," Zoe said as she picked up the phone. "Tell me you've got good news."

She was still in the lab. Stella had been showing her more photos from the three scenes her team was now looking into.

"Maybe, boss. I've got something, anyway."

"OK. I've got stuff I want to share with the team too. Can you hook everyone up?"

"Hang on a minute."

A minute later, they were all on the line, the four of them in four different locations. Zoe's phone was on the table beside the knife, on speaker so that Stella could listen in.

"Right," Zoe said. "So we've got the ID of our victim still to determine. Madsen, wherever the hell he is. The shop break-in and the red paint. And then there's the racist graffiti."

Was it all linked? Were her team chasing too many leads?

No.

"What have you got, folks?" she said. 'Anything?"

"Yes, boss," Aaron said, "I want you to hear this call to the information line. Tom, can you play it?"

Zoe listened as an unnamed woman spoke about her missing friend.

"Thoughts?" she asked.

Silence.

"Come on, folks. I know what I think. I want to know what you think."

Aaron's voice came on. "I think it's her. I mean, she doesn't mention tattoos, but there's no reason she would. The timing matches. And then there's the thing about the boat." His voice tightened on the last sentence.

"OK. And is it any use?" she asked.

"Not really. I mean, if she calls again, great. But as it stands, there isn't much we can follow up."

"Anyone disagree?"

Another silence.

"Good," said Zoe. "I'm with you, Aaron. I think it's her, and I think it's useless, for now, at least. It doesn't tell us who she is, and it doesn't tell us who killed her. If it was the only thing we had, I'd be all over it, but thankfully it isn't. When did this come in?"

More silence.

After a moment, Tom cleared his throat. "I'm sorry, boss. It came in yesterday. I'd only heard the first bit before you came in, so I thought it was just a drunk woman on a night out. I forgot about it till today, and then—"

"You forgot about it?" Zoe asked.

"It didn't seem like much at the time, she hadn't mentioned the boat or Friday or anything—"

"She *had* mentioned them, Tom. You..." She stopped herself.

"Yes, boss."

"Nina, have you got Richard Madsen yet?"

"No, boss, it looks like—"

"Have any of you got anything useful at all?"

"I think I have," said Aaron.

"Fire away." Zoe glanced at Stella, who was standing at a bench two along, eating an apple. *Great.*

"I just spoke to a woman who's worried about her boyfriend. He's been going out at odd hours, in the night, not telling her what he's doing. His name's Rob Morton. But she showed me a photo, and it's Richard Madsen."

Zoe clenched a fist. *At last. Progress.* "So you've got his real name *and* his real address?"

"Yes, boss."

"Excellent. OK. Nina, tell me what's happening at the hardware store."

"Well, there was a bit of a to-do between the owner, Jackson Liddell, and Ibrahim Bashir. I managed to break it up."

"Good."

"And we found fibres. Orange, looks like fleece or similar. I managed to persuade Liddell to let us check it against his clothes."

"That sounds encouraging."

"Thanks, boss. Caroline's on her way over to you with the evidence, and then she'll be going to Liddell's house to take samples. Inspector Keane's sending Roddy Chen over to keep her company, in case Liddell gets out of hand."

"He sounds a real charmer," said Zoe. "Right. Good work there. Anything else?"

Nina jumped in. "It's probably not directly related, but I've seen a bunch of posters around town. Whitehaven for the whites, that sort of thing. They're new, and given the way things are already..."

"I've seen them too," Aaron said. "Definitely new, boss."

Zoe nodded. "OK. Like you say, Nina, not directly related, but I don't like the way this could feed off what's already happening. Aaron, can you let Inspector Keane know about this? I want to make sure he's ready."

"On it, boss."

"Right." She felt calmer. There had been screw-ups, but they might be back on track. "Aaron, I want you to go and pick up Madsen or Morton or whatever his name is. He's given us a false name and address, which gives us a reason to bring him in. Get his prints this time."

Awkward silence.

"We've got the knife, by the looks of it," she continued. "And it's got prints on it. It's just possible we could have this wrapped up by the end of the day. I've got Stella here with me, and she'll be working with her team on these fibres as soon as they get here, right?"

Stella was standing next to her. "If we're lucky, there'll be DNA on it. If not, we still might be able to figure out what it's from."

Zoe smiled. "Excellent. I'm going back to the station. Nina, I want you to take a look at the spot the knife was found, in the unlikely event there's CCTV. Then I want you to head over here and help Stella out."

"I don't need any help," said Stella.

Zoe ignored her. She wanted someone in her team there, pushing for this to get done. So far, Stella had agreed to treat most of their evidence as urgent submissions. Zoe wanted that to continue.

"That's OK, Stella. I'd like Nina here anyway."

"What about me?" asked Tom.

"Get online. Find out what the fibres came from. See if you can beat Stella's people to it. Oh, and Tom?"

"Yes, boss?"

"If you do find anything, do me a favour and write it down, will you?"

CHAPTER FORTY-NINE

ZOE FORCED BACK her frustration as she sat in traffic.

It was hardly heavy traffic. Hardly what she'd sat in all those years driving through Birmingham. But she wanted to be there when Aaron brought in Rob Morton. Assuming Morton was at home, he'd be back in half an hour.

She should still beat him.

As she passed the hospital, her phone rang.

"DI Finch."

"Zoe. Tell me what I've been hearing isn't true."

She glanced down at the display. *Check, next time.* "Ma'am?"

"Fiona, please, Zoe. Remember?"

"Yes, sorry. What do you mean?"

"Well, Zoe, I'm not the kind of boss who'll tell you how to do your job, but I've been hearing things that concern me a little."

Zoe joined a short queue for a roundabout. Could she end the call and pretend the signal had dropped?

No. It was good enough everywhere she'd been so far, and Fiona would know that.

She tapped her fingers on the wheel. "What things?"

"Well, I gather you have three crime scenes, three lines of inquiry, you still don't know who the victim was, and you're no closer to finding out who killed her. Is that right?"

The marina, the hardware store, the rocks where the knife was found. Three scenes, yes. But when it came to lines of inquiry, there was Morton, the men in white, the community centre, the port.

More than three.

"There *are* three scenes, but we can't help the geography. We've got a body in one place, a knife in another, and it looks like whoever killed her broke into a hardware store during the night. They're all important leads."

"This isn't Birmingham, Zoe. We don't have the resources to manage all of this."

Zoe pulled out onto the roundabout, thinking. This was nonsense. But was it political nonsense designed to put her in her place, or nonsense that Fiona actually believed?

And even if it was nonsense, it could be true. Zoe had three scenes, all of which needed to be examined. Fiona had one team of CSIs at her disposal and limited access to Uniform. That might mean Zoe couldn't examine three scenes.

"They're all important," she repeated. "This is a murder inquiry. Three scenes is good going, to be honest. I've had more than seven before."

"And you had a bomb on a plane and all the rest, Zoe. This is one body in the middle of the night in the marina. No one knows who she is. It's sad, of course, but it's hardly the fucking IRA, is it?"

Zoe's foot slid off the accelerator. She righted herself, cursing.

"You're going to have to choose, DI Finch."

"We're bringing in a potential suspect shortly," she said. "We've got prints off the knife. It's possible—"

"I know what's possible, Zoe. If your suspect happens to match the knife, brilliant. If not, let him go and focus on any DNA you can get from that hardware store and the body."

"Let him go?"

"Interview him, get what you can, but don't waste time. I shouldn't have to tell you this."

"But he's given us a false name, he's misled the police, he's—"

"I know what he's done. He's a waste of time. He'll get a slap on the wrist and told to behave himself."

"And if the prints match? Or he admits something in interview?"

"He won't. Now get your priorities straight. Are we clear?"

"Yes. And if—"

But the line was dead.

CHAPTER FIFTY

THE CAR PARK at the Hub was as quiet as ever. Zoe couldn't imagine that happening at a Birmingham nick.

She sat in the car, staring at the distant fells, then at the concrete and steel and glass. She let her gaze drift upwards to Fiona's office.

At least the super wasn't at the window. Zoe felt like the woman was watching her every move.

She slammed her hand against the wheel, jumping when the horn sounded. She looked around: no one near. If she'd hit her horn back in Brum, at Rose Road, all the times she'd sat in the car thinking or talking to Mo, the car would have been surrounded within thirty seconds.

She missed Nicholas. Yes, he'd been away for ages already, but she'd been in Birmingham. *Home*. She'd been surrounded by people she knew. Even when Mo had gone, there'd been Connie and Rhodri. Even the insufferable DCI Frank Dawson.

She ran her fingers over the steering wheel and looked back up at the building. Why was her new super being so obstructive? This wasn't a burglary or a fight in a pub. It wasn't the sort of thing that happened every day up here. Zoe had checked.

Aaron would know, but she couldn't ask him. Not yet.

She could talk it over with Carl, but he wouldn't know any more than she did. The same went for Mo.

There was one person who might be able to help.

Zoe dialled, and smiled as her old boss picked up on the second ring.

"Zoe. I was just thinking about you."

"Were you?" Zoe could hear chewing. An afternoon snack or a late lunch – a chocolate bar, maybe. A cream tea.

DCI Lesley Clarke, Zoe's old boss, had always had a knack for figuring out when something was up. When Zoe had known that Lesley's own boss was corrupt, it had been all she could do to keep it from her.

"What's up, Zoe?"

"Oh, the usual. Dead body, obstructive boss."

She laughed. "Don't tell me Frank's followed you all the way up there?"

"I wish."

"That bad?"

"I'm probably over-reacting."

"Try me."

"I found myself in the middle of a murder case on my first day. We've got three crime scenes and a bunch of leads. And my new super wants me to rein things in and use fewer resources. Or that's what she's saying."

"So you want me to tell you why your boss is being a bitch?" Lesley asked.

"I wouldn't go that far."

"Good. Because I can't. What you really want to know is what to do about it, right?"

Zoe considered. "I suppose so. What would you have done?"

"Me?" Lesley sounded surprised. "I *always* follow procedure, Zoe. You know that."

Zoe sighed. "Yes, but... The investigation's taking me in one direction and the super's taking me somewhere else. So which way am I supposed to go?"

"You've handled worse than this. It's hardly David Randle, is it?" A pause. "Is it?"

Zoe swallowed. "No, it's nothing like that."

"Good. So do what you need to do. You're more than capable of figuring it out."

"Yeah," replied Zoe. Lesley wasn't going to tell her what to do.

But that was OK, Zoe told herself as she said goodbye and emerged from the car.

Lesley was right. Zoe had been through enough difficult situations with enough difficult bosses to handle this one.

She'd just have to trust her instincts.

CHAPTER FIFTY-ONE

AARON PRESSED Rob Morton's doorbell, half expecting to hear the sound of the back door opening and the man legging it out the back. He hadn't got backup in the end: everyone was busy.

They were often busy, these days.

"Mr Morton?" he called, bending to the letterbox.

Nothing. He called again. He checked his watch. *Damn.*

The door opened. Morton was dressed, at least: jeans and a T-shirt. Unshaven, and with dark circles below his eyes.

"Mr Morton," repeated Aaron.

The man nodded.

Good.

"I am Detective Sergeant Aaron Keyes."

"I know that."

Also good.

"I'm arresting you on suspicion of wasting police time by giving false information contrary to section 5 of the Criminal Law Act."

Morton took a step back, but didn't try to shut the door or

run. Aaron completed the caution and cuffed him, attaching the cuffs to a kitchen door handle.

"Mind if I take a look inside?" he asked.

"Whatever," replied Morton.

Downstairs was a kitchen, with a small table and a portable TV sitting on a stack of boxes. Upstairs, a single bedroom and a bathroom. There was mould around the shower, but otherwise the place was in decent condition. But it was very, very empty.

Aaron descended the stairs and went into the kitchen to find Morton on the floor, tugging half-heartedly at the cuffs. "Lived here long?" he asked.

Morton shrugged.

Aaron put in a call to the station, asking for someone to keep an eye on the place. He doubted there'd be anything of value in there, either financially or as evidence, but better safe than sorry.

On the drive to the station, Morton gazed out of the window in silence. There was no fear on his face, no sign he hadn't done this before. Plenty of times, maybe.

At the custody suite, PS Clive 'Ilkley' Moor looked at him. "Rob Morton?"

"No," Morton replied.

Moor looked up. "What do you mean?"

"You're gonna find out soon enough. Might as well get it over and done with. My name's not Rob Morton."

"Richard Madsen, then?" asked Aaron.

A shake of the head. "Ryan Mulcaster."

"Really?"

A nod. Ilkley watched, impassive.

Upstairs in the team room, Aaron watched as Tom ran the new name on the system. He felt his mouth dry up as the results filled the screen.

"It's him alright." Tom pointed at the photo.

Ryan Mulcaster was a sex offender. His record showed a number of non-violent offences against sex workers across the north-east. Recording without consent. There were no outstanding warrants, but he'd only been released from prison three weeks earlier, out on licence a year into a two-year sentence for voyeurism.

"Check the conditions please, Tom," said Aaron.

Tom had already brought them up in a second window. The two of them read through in silence.

"Shall I call?" asked Tom.

Aaron nodded and sat down at his desk, his limbs heavy. He looked through Mulcaster's record again while Tom spoke into his phone.

"He's in breach," said Tom, a few minutes later. "He's moved out of the area without getting approval for his new address. But he's been reporting back to his officer, so they had no idea."

"Explains why he was disappearing in the middle of the night, at least."

Tom nodded. Aaron left him to look through Mulcaster's record while he returned to the custody suite.

It was busier, a handful of Uniforms checking in a group of men who looked like they'd been in a drunken fight. Aaron pushed past them and explained Mulcaster's background to Sergeant Moor.

"Want him in the dungeon, then?" Moor asked.

"The dungeon?"

The dungeon was a cell all on its own, at the bottom of a staircase behind the custody suite, a remnant from whatever had been here before the police station had been built. Part of a cellar, small, dark, and isolated. It was no longer deemed suitable for any suspect, no matter how heinous their crime.

"I don't think so," Aaron replied.

Ilkley grunted. Had he been joking?

"It'll probably come out, all this," Aaron said. "So keep an eye on him. I don't care what he's done. He can't come out of this in worse condition than he went in. OK?"

"Fair enough," replied Ilkley. Aaron could hear whispering behind him.

He turned to see two uniformed PCs staring back at him, alongside DS Tracy Giller-Jones. She had a nasty smile on her face. Tracy often had a nasty smile on her face.

He pushed through them on his way out.

"Looking after your own, is it, Aaron?" came a voice.

He turned. "What was that?"

He walked back to the group. "What was that, Tel?"

"Nothing, Sir." Cummings didn't meet his eye.

But Aaron knew what he'd heard.

He turned to the other constables, each of them looking away. DS Giller-Jones continued to smile. He turned and walked away, the words ringing in his ears.

CHAPTER FIFTY-TWO

Z OE ENTERED the team room to find Tom there on his own.

"Alright, boss." He gave her a nod then looked back at his screen.

"All OK, Tom?" she asked.

"Yes, boss." He didn't meet her eye. She glanced behind him, at the cover on his chair. The antimacassar, Nina had called it.

The gull's beak was bigger than the rest of the bird, and the fish trapped in that beak looked as if it was laughing. Mrs Kapoor might have many qualities, Zoe thought, but she was no artist. She resolved not to get drawn into the team bets.

She turned as the door opened behind her. Aaron, his face downcast.

"You OK, Aaron?" she asked.

He stopped dead and gave a tiny nod. Something flickered across his face.

"Yes, boss. We've got him, by the way. Morton. Only that's not his name. Has Tom told you?"

"No." Zoe glanced at Tom. What was up with him?

"Ryan Mulcaster," Aaron said. "Sex offender. Just out of prison three weeks ago on licence."

"What's the offence?"

"Voyeurism. Two-year sentence," said Tom.

Zoe looked at him. "You've checked him out on the system?"

A nod. "He's in breach of his conditions, moving out of the area. They didn't know cos he's been reporting back to his officer."

"He's in the cells," said Aaron. "I told Sergeant Moor to keep an eye on him."

"Good."

"Not put him in the dungeon, then?" asked Tom.

Zoe turned to him. "The dungeon?"

"It's a joke," Aaron said. "Ilkley wouldn't put him in there. But we don't like sex offenders up here, boss."

"You think we did in Birmingham?"

She thought it through, then realised.

"He's got a record, then? He's on the system?"

"Yes, boss," Aaron replied. "And no. The prints don't match the knife."

Shit. Fiona had been right.

"It doesn't put him in the clear though, does it?" she said.

Aaron and Tom both looked at her.

"He might have worn gloves. Or he might not have been working alone. We need to push him, Aaron."

Aaron smiled. *Good*.

"I want the two of you interviewing him," she said. "You arrested him, yes?"

"Yes, boss," said Aaron.

"Any idea what he's doing about a lawyer?"

"I'll have a word with Ilkley."

"Press him on the night of the murder. I want every minute accounted for. I don't care how drunk he claims he was. What about the house?"

"Don't think he's been there long, boss. Shouldn't take long to go through it."

Zoe sighed. "Stella's going to chew my ear off when I tell her I've got yet another potential crime scene." She looked up. "Aaron, go and sort out the brief. I'll call Stella."

Aaron nodded and left the team room. Zoe pulled out her phone, but before she could dial Stella, it rang.

Number withheld. She didn't have time for this.

"DI Finch."

"Hello, is that the policewoman from television?"

All I need. She sighed and aimed for the red button to end it.

"My friend is still missing from Friday."

Zoe stopped herself. She recognised that voice, that accent.

"I'm sorry?" she said.

"My friend." A pause. "She is still not back."

"Who are you?" Zoe asked. "Who is she?"

Another pause.

"I am sure it is the woman you are looking for."

CHAPTER FIFTY-THREE

THE SITE where they'd found the knife was a bust. An office overlooked it, and there was even a balcony. But speaking with the site manager, Nina discovered that the balcony doors hadn't been unlocked since a suicide attempt three years ago, and there were no windows or CCTV pointing the right way.

So she headed for the lab, as requested. She knew what was expected of her: hover, and make sure Stella and her team were working on their evidence. Be annoying, if necessary.

Nina was good at being annoying.

Stella was flustered by her presence, kept looking at her and sighing. At one point she stopped work and said, "You don't need to stay here and keep an eye on me, Nina."

Nina just shrugged.

Truth be told, she was enjoying herself. Nina had never liked Stella Berry. And now she got to stand around asking the same questions over and over again, and it was working.

Stella and her junior colleague, Huz, had already isolated some DNA from the fibres they'd recovered from the hardware store.

"Look at this." She beckoned Nina over to a screen, her mouth a straight line. "This is the sample under nearly a million times magnification."

It was just lines to Nina. She nodded. Huz winked at her. He knew.

"It's been stained and rinsed," Stella said, "and it'll take a while to get a really good picture, but for now I can tell you it's male."

"What?"

"Male. From a man. A male human. Fart a lot, forget things, you know?"

Nina forced a laugh.

"And the DNA from the body, from around the paint, that was male too."

"Is it the same person?"

Stella shrugged. "Too early to tell. Something else, though. Over here." She pointed to another screen.

Nina approached it. "This is them. The fibres."

"Congratulations, NIna. Your eyes are in full working order."

Nina looked up. This was the Stella Berry she was more familiar with. Huz had already walked away.

"Here's the cross-section." Stella tapped an icon on the screen and an almost-circular shape appeared. "See the central dark section?"

Nina peered in. The circle had dozens of smaller shapes within it, squashed up against each other. In the middle of it all was a darker section, about a tenth the diameter of the whole thing.

She nodded.

"The medulla," Stella said. "That wasn't in most of the strands, but we did find it in a few. Most of them weren't so coarse."

"What is it?"

"Lambswool. Natural fibre. Orange and white. I can't be a hundred per cent certain, but... well, look at this."

She led Nina to another screen. It showed a picture of an orange and white jumper in the distinctive argyle diamond pattern. Nina grimaced. *Hideous.*

"You think this is it?" she asked.

Stella nodded. "This or something very similar. Pringle used to make this, they don't anymore but they'll have sold enough over the years. I'm almost certain that the fibre in the hardware store came from that jumper. Given the store's layout, I'd bet it came from whoever broke in."

Nina looked at the jumper. No way Liddell would own one of these.

"This is brilliant. Thanks, Stella."

Stella stepped back in surprise.

"Just gonna call Tom." Nina walked to the other end of the room. He answered after a few rings.

"I've got something for you," she said.

"That's good."

"Stella's pretty sure she knows where the fibres came from. An argyle jumper, historically made by Pringle." She glanced over at the screen. "I'll send you a link. It's hideous. I mean, even you wouldn't wear it."

"Right," he replied.

She frowned. "You OK, Tom?"

"Yeah," he said. His voice was flat. "Fine."

"What's up?"

"Nothing."

She could hear a voice in the background. The DI?

"What's going on, Tom?"

"DI's on the phone, Nina."

Was he in the boss's office, getting a bollocking?

"It's an orange and white argyle jumper, Tom. Think it would suit the DI?"

Nina smirked, imagining the jumper clashing with the boss's red hair. Tom forced a laugh. What was with him?

Nina sighed. Tom was her friend and he was struggling with the new DI. She'd have to keep an eye on him.

CHAPTER FIFTY-FOUR

"Can you tell me your name?" Zoe asked.

"It is her," replied the woman on the other end of the line.

"Can you—"

"I called the number from the television and I said it then, I said I not see her from Friday, but then I thought, how will you know it is real, how will you know it is me?"

The woman paused.

Zoe asked again: "Can you tell me your name?" She could hear Tom muttering into his phone behind her.

"No," replied the woman. "I saw policeman with cards, he speak to some of the other girls. I ask for card and it has name Zoe Finch." She pronounced the *ch* hard. Wherever this woman was from, she wasn't local. "You are Zoe Finch?" she asked.

"I am."

"I want to speak to a woman. I not tell you my name. I tell you only what I think you should know. We come here three weeks, through port."

"Which port?"

"We come from Romania, Daria and me."

"Daria is your friend, the woman you think—"

"I tell you only what I think you should know. Not safe. We come from Bârlad. And Daria, she disappear on Friday."

"How do I know you're telling the truth?"

A pause.

Zoe waited.

"Mermaid."

"Sorry?" Zoe asked.

"Mermaid. You show rose, you do not show mermaid. But Daria is my friend, I know about mermaid. I am right?"

"Where are you now?"

"It is not safe."

"I can come and find you. We can keep you safe, wherever you are."

"It is not safe."

"Are you in Whitehaven?" Zoe clicked her fingers, and Tom turned to her. She put her hand over the phone and spoke quietly. "If a woman had been trafficked to the area, where would she be?"

"It is Daria, it is, the mermaid, I am right, yes?" said the woman.

"Please, just tell me where you are," Zoe replied. She listened to Tom fire off a list of places, repeating them to the woman. "Workington? Barrow? Millom? Are you in White-haven somewhere? Are you in Stainburn?"

"It is her?"

"Moresby Parks? Sandwith?"

"She has mermaid, yes? By her foot?"

"Yes," replied Zoe. She clenched a fist. She shouldn't have said that.

"No," said the woman. "Oh, oh no."

"Listen," tried Zoe.

"Oh, oh no. My friend. Oh no. Oh, oh no."

"You can come in, to the station, come here, or we can send a car to you. We'll look after you."

"Oh no. Oh, oh no."

"Do you know the name Myron Carter?" Zoe asked.

A pause. "Myron Carter?"

"Yes," said Zoe. "Do you know him?"

The line went dead.

CHAPTER FIFTY-FIVE

When Aaron reached the custody suite Tel Cummings had gone, along with the rest of the constables. There was no sign of Tracy Giller-Jones, either.

He breathed a long sigh of relief.

"Any sign of Mulcaster's brief?" he asked Ilkley, who shook his head. Aaron was wondering what he could do to hurry things along when his phone rang.

The DI.

"Boss," he said. "Brief's not here yet. I—"

"I've just had a call from the victim's friend," the DI said. "The one Tom forgot about. It's her, Aaron. She knew about the mermaid. And she mentioned the port again. I think she'd heard of Myron Carter, too."

Aaron walked to the other end of the room, not wanting Ilkley to overhear.

"You talked about Myron Carter?" He knew the tension was audible in his voice.

"I mentioned him. She repeated the name, clearly. Like she'd heard it before. Then she hung up."

"Did she give you her name, location, anything else?"

"No. She was scared. She gave her friend's name and where they'd come from, so we need to follow that up. And I want to find a way of tracking her down."

"Right."

Myron Carter, again. Aaron wished he'd never mentioned the man to his new boss.

Half the county was probably asking the other half if they knew who Myron Carter was by now, and if Carter himself had any sense, he'd be burying anything and anyone that could lay a glove on him.

Had Aaron put anyone in danger?

"You and Tom do the interview," the boss continued. "I'll send him down."

"OK. But he won't talk to us without his brief."

A sigh. "I'm coming down, see if I can do anything to hurry things up. We can't hold him forever." She hung up.

Aaron looked at the phone and turned back to Ilkley. The custody sergeant gazed back at him.

He wasn't sure what the DI thought she could do to *hurry things up*, but it was unlikely to work.

CHAPTER FIFTY-SIX

"She's gone," said Tom, on the other end of the phone.

"Who's gone?" asked Nina.

"The DI. She had a call from that woman, the one who called yesterday. And now she's down with the sarge trying to talk to Mulcaster."

"Who's Mulcaster?"

"Morton."

"Morton?"

"Richard Madsen."

"Hang on, Tom." Nina turned to check the room. Just Stella, busy fiddling with a slide. "Rewind a minute. The woman called back?"

"Yeah."

"Well, that's good, isn't it?"

"It doesn't change the fact that I screwed up and could have set the whole investigation back."

"Everyone makes mistakes, Tom. Even I've made a few."

Tom didn't laugh. "I don't think the DI reckons much of me."

Nina laughed herself. "She doesn't think much of any of us. '*Have any of you got anything useful at all?*'" She tried for her best Birmingham accent, and it got a snort out of Tom.

"I know you think I'm lazy," he said.

Nina sighed. She looked around the room again, then at her watch.

"No—" she started to object, but he was still talking.

"I know you think I don't really care and I'm not the sort of person that makes DI by the time they're thirty, and you don't understand it, but that doesn't stop me loving this job."

"You're a good copper, Tom."

"I know my way around a computer, but when it comes to finding stuff out on the street, or even just remembering someone's made a bloody phone call..."

Nina had never heard Tom like this. "You've got this all wrong, you know?"

"How?"

"There are four of us in this team. The DI's in charge. She's got to deal with Detective Superintendent Kendrick, but we're shielded from that. The buck stops with her, not with us. She said that right at the start, remember?"

Tom grunted.

"That CCTV, you got that before the investigation had even kicked off. You'd cultivated a useful contact, and knew when to use it. Textbook CID."

Another grunt.

"And then you screwed up," said Nina. "So did I, so did the sarge, and ours was worse. You didn't listen to a phone call that was recorded and accessible any time we needed it. We lost a man who'd given us a false name and address and might turn out to be the killer. Now we've got the phone call and the man, but we've been lucky."

"I just can't stop thinking—"

"You think the DI never made a mistake when she was a DC?"

"I dunno."

"Listen, you're getting hung up on the negatives instead of treating it like an opportunity to learn. Just make sure you listen to every call in future and make a note of anything interesting."

"I'll be doing that, alright."

"Right then. Job done. OK?"

"OK. Thanks, Nina."

CHAPTER FIFTY-SEVEN

Zoe burst into the team room, Aaron a few paces behind. Tom was still there, putting the phone down, his body tense.

"Got to wait for Mulcaster's bloody lawyer," she said.

Aaron passed her and sat down. *Did he just smile?*

Tom nodded. "Just been talking to Nina."

"Any news?"

"They've figured out where the fibre came from. The stuff they picked up from the glass in the hardware store. Orange and white argyle jumper."

Zoe smiled. "That's brilliant. Can't be too many of them about."

Another nod. "And they've got DNA from it. No details yet except they know it's male. Same with the DNA from the body. Around the paint."

"This is really good," she said. "Really good. You OK, Tom?"

"Yeah, boss." His fists were balled on the desk. "Fine."

She frowned. "Nina's still at the lab?"

"Yes."

Zoe dialled Nina. "Are you with Stella?" she asked.

"Yep, boss."

"Can you ask her to take a look at Mulcaster's house? The sarge tells me it shouldn't take too long."

There was a shuffling noise, a hiss, and a couple of bangs from down the line before Stella's voice replaced Nina's.

"Are you an expert on forensic searches, DI Finch?" she asked.

"No, but—"

"We've got the hardware store and the marina. We're nearly finished at both of them, but I've got Caroline with your Eric Liddell—"

"Jackson Liddell."

"Who?"

"Jackson Liddell," Zoe said. "Eric Liddell was the Scottish one from *Chariots Of Fire*."

"Whoever he is, Caroline's dealing with him, then we've got to check the rocks where the knife was found, not that that'll get us anywhere. It may have escaped your attention, but there are other crimes and other police officers in Cumbria, and they need our help as much as you do, Zoe."

Zoe bit back the urge to ask if those other crimes were murders. "OK. Get to it when you can."

Stella grunted and hung up.

Zoe turned to Aaron and Tom. "We've got a name and a place of origin. Let's see if we can find out a little more about our victim, shall we?"

"I'm on Google," said Tom. "Bârlad, where her mate says she's from, it's a city in Romania. I've checked the name too. Daria's very common, sorry."

"OK. Well, we'll just need to speak to other agencies. See if there's a record of her."

Tom nodded and picked up his phone.

Zoe glanced at Aaron, then retreated to her office. She needed a moment alone.

She sat back in her chair, running through the day in her mind and trying to work out what had gone right and what had gone wrong. Five minutes later, Tom knocked on the door.

"No Romanian citizen named Daria has entered the country in the last four weeks, or not legally." He paused. "I didn't expect her to have come in legally, though."

"Nor me." Zoe gave him a smile. He was working hard, trying to impress her. "I need to speak to Organised Crime."

Fiona had told her she'd be setting up a call, but there'd been nothing.

She stood up. "Time for a word with the super."

CHAPTER FIFTY-EIGHT

NINA HAD PLANNED to go straight from the lab to the station. Her plan was to avoid the town centre, get there in twenty minutes. The hangover was history, she'd eaten, she could do a bit of work and go home. The easy thing.

But instead, she'd taken a drive through town to see those posters again.

They were still there. And there were more of them. But the posters weren't the problem.

The people were the problem.

A handful of small groups, some just two or three men, some as many as six or seven.

All men, all in blue jeans and dark hoodies. And she didn't recognise more than a handful of them.

They were all walking in the same direction. North.

It became more obvious as she headed down North Shore Road; apart from a few cars coming the other way, there was no one else there. Just these men. Nina had counted more than thirty of them, in total.

In Whitehaven, thirty was as close as you got to a mob.

They were gathering outside the community centre. Eight when she arrived, six more once she'd parked and called for backup, another three by the time she'd steeled herself to get out of the car, walk over to the door with her head high, ignoring the shouts and whistles, and announce her presence.

"If there's anyone in there, this is Detective Constable Kapoor from Cumbria CID. I'd be grateful if you let me in."

Grateful if you let me in. Nina didn't usually speak like that.

A man opened the door a few seconds later and let her in. He closed it quickly. A woman was inside with him, her expression agitated.

"Ali and Inaya?" she asked.

They nodded. She showed them her ID.

"What do they want?" asked Inaya.

Nina shrugged. "I think they're just a mob. Nine times out of ten they just want to shout a bit. But you need to be ready."

"Ready?" asked Ali, his jaw set.

"Ready to leave."

He shook his head. "We're not going anywhere."

His wife turned to him. "Don't be stupid. If the constable says we have to go, we'll go."

"I am not being driven out of this place by a bunch of racist thugs," her husband told her.

Nina hesitated. She sympathised. But she knew how these things worked, from a policing point of view.

"Mr Bashir," she said.

"Ali."

"Ali. I understand you don't want these men to feel like they've won. And I've called for backup, so I'm hopeful that won't happen. But you need to be prepared, in case they get violent. I can't let you stay here if it becomes dangerous. So please, can the two of you gather together what you need, and be ready to go if it's necessary?"

The man was about to speak, but his wife put a hand on his arm and steered him away. She glanced back at Nina and nodded.

Nina opened the door a crack and looked out. A response car was parked beside hers. *Good.*

There were more than twenty men in the little car park. *Not so good.*

She opened the door, stepped out, and shut it behind her. The crowd fell silent.

Nina glanced into the response car. One man, one woman. They got out, looking wary.

Here goes. Nina strode to the middle of the car park.

"What's up, guys?" she said. "Pubs all kicked you out?"

No response other than a couple of titters and continued grumbling.

"Seriously," she said. "What are you doing here?"

"Look it up," shouted one man. They'd pulled their hoods up, but she could still recognise a few of them.

"Look what up?"

"You figure it out," shouted another.

Nina pulled out her phone, searched *Whitehaven*. Nothing. Added *Community Centre*. Added *Islamic*, then *Muslim*.

Just some planning applications. That wasn't what this was about. She opened Twitter and ran the same searches.

It took her seconds to find it.

Muslim gang terrorising our town.

Muslims murdering innocent girls.

There were photos: the same group wearing white, the community centre. Two of the body, one from the press conference, and another definitely not from the press conference. It included the writing. That word.

Shit.

There was a video, too. Nina walked towards the response car so she could hear it. A man wearing a balaclava was addressing the camera.

"They call us kafir," he said in a local accent. "They murder our women."

She turned to the two anxious-looking constables. "We need more backup."

"We'll try," replied the woman. "I don't think there's much available."

The two constables got back in the car and Nina turned to face the crowd.

"Oh look," someone shouted. "It's the brown Elvis."

A smattering of laughter.

"Give us *In The Ghetto*, love," shouted someone else. More laughter.

Nina stared at them. Some of the voices were familiar. More shouts, more insults. Some witty, others less so.

"Even the filth have gone brown," someone called out. "This country's gone to the dogs."

Nina moved without even realising she'd done it. She stood in front of him, jabbing a finger in his face. Rage and contempt coursed through her.

"I see you're still the same loser you always were, Pete Cunningham," she said. Shouted. "Do your mates here know you were still pissing yourself in high school?"

He lunged at her, but she'd anticipated it and stepped

back. She watched him go down face first, too slow, drunk, or stupid to put his hands out.

Be professional, she told herself. *Sod professional.*

She did nothing as he hit the ground.

CHAPTER FIFTY-NINE

"Come in!"

Zoe pushed open the door to find Fiona behind her desk. Opposite her was a tall man, radiating size and power. He half-turned towards Zoe.

"Zoe. I was just going to call you. This is Detective Inspector Ralph Streeting. Ralph, this is our newest and most glamorous recruit, DI Zoe Finch."

Streeting stood up. He brushed down his suit and took a step towards Zoe, hand outstretched.

Something about him set her nerves on edge. Something she couldn't place but that reminded her of her old boss, David Randle. She shook his hand, resisting an urge to wipe hers on her jeans.

"The infamous Zoe Finch," he said in a higher voice than she'd expected. "The woman who wrung the canary's neck."

"Sorry?"

"Canary. That was you, wasn't it?"

"Not just me."

Infamous. Was that supposed to be a compliment?

"Take a seat, both of you," said Fiona. "Zoe, we're in luck. Ralph's based out of Carlisle and Workington, but fortune's brought him here today."

"Just visiting." Streeting smiled.

How convenient, thought Zoe.

"Ralph, I've already mentioned that Zoe's interested in some areas that might fit within your domain. She wanted to speak to someone in Organised Crime, I told her your Specialist Crime and Intel area was probably best."

Streeting cocked his head. Zoe couldn't fathom his expression. What was it that made her distrust him?

She sure as hell wasn't going to mention Myron Carter.

"How are you finding our northern climes, Zoe?" asked Streeting. "Not too cold and wet for you, I hope."

"Birmingham wasn't exactly the Bahamas." She ignored his laugh. "It's fine. I'm going to like it very much."

Streeting rocked back and forth on his chair, his eyes sparkling. "Then you must come to the auction."

"Auction?"

"The charity auction. It's an annual thing, at the White-haven Golf Club. All the money raised goes to a bunch of local charities. It's on Thursday. You *must* come. I absolutely insist."

"Well, I..." Zoe glanced at the super, who seemed disinterested. "I don't have tickets or anything, I'm not—"

The super jerked to life. "Ralph, you're quite right. Zoe, I'll sort out tickets. One? Two? Two. All the local names will be there. It's the perfect way to introduce yourself to Whitehaven. I'll send you the details."

"Thank you." Zoe forced a smile.

Carl would hate this.

CHAPTER SIXTY

THE MALE CONSTABLE APPROACHED NINA. Behind her, the mob was reacting to what she'd just done.

She hadn't laid a finger on Pete Cunningham, but they wouldn't see it that way.

The PC drew level with her. "Get in the car," he hissed.

"Why?" she said.

"Let us handle this, will you?" his female colleague said.

Nina looked around. The crowd was more than thirty-strong and beginning to spread out a little. "You think you can?" she asked the two PCs.

"We don't have much choice," the man said. "I've spoken to Inspector Keane. He says there's no one available." He thrust his phone into Nina's hand. "Go."

"But—" Nina began.

The noise was growing. Random shouts, aggressive.

Nina would have preferred a nice, solid chant. She'd seen it with football mobs, political demos, the crowds that formed almost spontaneously when a gig got cancelled or the train station got shut. Those kinds of crowds, she knew how to calm. Those, she could sympathise with.

This lot, she couldn't.

She ran to the response car, closed the door. She put the male PC's phone to her ear. "This is Detective Constable Nina Kapoor." She had to raise her voice. "We've got a situation here."

"Inspector Keane is well aware of the situation. Gregor's spoken to him and he's doing everything he can, but he doesn't have the numbers."

"Well, what—" Nina began, just as the sirens sounded.

The crowd moved to one side as not one but two vans screeched into the car park.

The driver's door to the first one opened. Inspector Keane jumped down and ran to the rear door. He shouted, "Mobilise!"

The driver of the other van climbed down and followed suit.

The crowd had seen enough. Within seconds, they were gone. Every last one, streaming towards the town centre.

Keane hadn't even had to open the rear door.

Nina got out of the response car. Keane approached her, a huge grin on his face.

"Nina."

"Good to see you, Sir," she said. "And thanks."

"It worked?"

The male PC – Gregor, she now knew – was grinning back at his boss.

"Looks like it, Sir."

"That's a relief, son. Been a while since I had to get my hands dirty."

"*Mobilise!*" The female PC laughed. Keane joined in. "Nice touch, Sir."

Nina looked at the vans, the rear doors. No one was coming out.

"Oh," she said.

"Oh indeed, Nina. Sometimes we've got numbers, sometimes we've got vehicles. All you can do is pretend and cross your fingers."

The vans were empty. Two police officers had turned up and dispersed a mob of nearly forty angry thugs.

"And if they hadn't fallen for it?"

Keane swung his baton around in a circle. He winked at her.

"I abhor violence, Nina. But needs must when the devil drives."

CHAPTER SIXTY-ONE

"DI Streeting," Zoe began.

"Ralph, please."

She ignored him. "We've got a murder victim, and we've finally figured out who she is, but we're no closer to knowing how she got where she did and who killed her."

"You've got an ID?" asked the super.

"Sorry, Ma'am. It's just happened, and we're still checking it out. But it looks like she's a Romanian woman by the name of Daria. We think she's been in the country about three weeks, and that she entered via the Port of Workington, but we might be wrong." She took a breath. "And we think she died from a heroin overdose, administered by someone else."

"So you've got drugs," said Streeting, "and people trafficking. I can help you on both of them."

Zoe turned to him, surprised. She'd expected to have to work harder than that. "Thank you."

"Not a problem. I can give you some names, street-level stuff, not the top."

"Right." Zoe looked from Streeting to Fiona, who was

leaning over her desk, hands clasped together. Street-level wasn't what she was after, but it would do for now. "Will I have your officers working with me on this?"

Streeting exchanged a look with the super. "When I say I can give you names, I mean for information purposes only. For digging around the system, that sort of thing. But my officers will follow up any organised crime elements, and that includes the names I'm talking about here."

"But how am I supposed to get information from these people if I can't talk to them?" Zoe asked.

"You're Zoe Finch." Streeting gave her a thin smile. "I'm sure you can manage it." The smile dropped. "But I don't want your team anywhere near my targets."

"How do I know who your targets are?"

"Good point. You might have to run names past the detective superintendent here. Or directly through me."

Zoe took a breath. "How am I supposed to run an investigation like that?"

Streeting shrugged.

"OK," Zoe said. "How about the port?"

"That's my territory, Zoe." The smile again, but his eyes were cold.

"What about witnesses? Just say we need to speak to people who might have seen what was going on over there?"

Streeting shook his head. "Keep your people away from the port, please. I—"

Fiona's phone rang. She raised a finger and spoke quietly, forcing Zoe and Streeting into an uncomfortable silence.

"Thank you." Fiona ended the call and looked up at Zoe.

"DI Finch, I've just been informed that there's been a disturbance at the Islamic community centre in Whitehaven."

"I'm sorry, Ma'am. I don't know anything about it."

Streeting held up his own phone. "Have you seen this?" He placed it on Fiona's desk, angled to make it difficult for Zoe to see.

Zoe walked around the desk to stand behind the super.

Streeting's phone showed a video embedded within a tweet. He tapped it to start playing.

In the middle of the shot was the community centre. The camera panned around the buildings, a small crowd. There were shouts. Taunts. The words weren't clear. Then a jumble of shapes parted to show a woman jabbing her hands towards someone in the crowd.

Zoe's heart sank. *Nina.*

More shapes. More shouts, and people running. The shot switched from the sky to the ground; the camera must have fallen. It was picked up and focused on Nina, walking away. It turned to show the man she'd been pointing at.

The man was being helped to his feet by another two men.

And there was blood running down his face.

CHAPTER SIXTY-TWO

NINA'S PHONE rang as she was saying goodbye to Ali and Inaya. She saw the boss's name on the display and picked up immediately.

"What the hell is going on out there?" the DI asked,.

"What do you mean?"

"I mean, I've just been in a meeting with the super and she's not best pleased that one of her detectives is picking fights with an angry mob."

Ali and Inaya were still thanking her. Nina turned and smiled at them as she walked away.

"Where are you?" asked the DI.

"I'm leaving the community centre. I was checking Ali and Inaya were OK."

"They're probably more OK than you are, Nina. What on earth were you thinking?"

Nina got into her car. The Bluetooth connected as soon as she had the key in the ignition. "I was just talking. Trying to calm things down."

"That's not what it looked like from here."

"Looked like?"

"There's a video, Nina. You're on Twitter."

"Shit."

"It looks like you're confronting them, making it worse. Someone got hurt, Nina."

"I was... I was trying to calm things down." She heard doors opening, the boss walking around the building. "Really. I think it might have been worse if I hadn't."

"Seems unlikely. You called Uniform in, right?"

"Yes, boss. I really... It might not look good, but the fact is I spotted a problem, anticipated it getting out of hand, called for backup, and kept things from spilling over while I waited for them to show up."

"And someone got a bloody nose." The DI's tone had softened. "I guess he's unlikely to file a formal complaint, whoever he is. Are you heading into the office?"

"Yes, boss."

"OK," said the DI. "I'll see you in the team room. It's been a long day, and it isn't over yet."

CHAPTER SIXTY-THREE

ZOE WAS TIRED.

And now she had to walk to the team room.

OK, so it wasn't far. But it wasn't right outside her office like she was used to.

She stood up and shook her legs out. Before she'd got any further, the door opened.

"She's here," Aaron said.

"She?"

"Clarissa Bexley. Mulcaster's lawyer."

"About time. You know her?"

Aaron nodded. "She's a bit of an ogre."

Zoe laughed. "What do you mean?"

"She's a hard case. She's good at her job and she doesn't care who she insults or hurts while she's doing it."

"Sounds reasonable to me."

A shrug. "She's not popular, boss. I don't know who hates her more: us, CPS, or the other defence lawyers."

Zoe stared at him. "In that case, you and I will have to do the interview."

He nodded. "I already told Tom."

"You did?"

"He was... disappointed."

She smiled. *Disappointed* was good. It was better than *relieved*. "He'll have his chance."

"He will."

"Lead me to the ogre, then."

Five minutes later, they were face-to-face with the mythical creature herself. Clarissa Bexley stood in the corridor, leafing through her notes. She was a tall woman in her early fifties, with stylish thick-rimmed glasses and neat shoulder-length blonde hair.

She didn't look like an ogre to Zoe.

"Tea," she said to Aaron in a deep voice as she spotted him. "Two sugars, and I don't want the bag in there when you bring it. I don't want the bag in there for more than ten seconds, young man."

Aaron glanced at Zoe, then disappeared to fetch tea. Zoe looked at him as he returned, puzzled.

"Thank you, young man."

Zoe bit her lip. *Young man*: was this equal-opportunity patronising behaviour, or something else?

"Aaron," she muttered. "You don't—"

"I've spoken to my client," Clarissa interrupted. "We'll go in, shall we?" She gave Zoe a look of disdain.

You're not dismissing me like that. Zoe stepped forward and offered her hand.

"Zoe Finch. I'm the DI running the case."

Clarissa Bexley squinted at her. "I know who you are."

Zoe swallowed and went through to the interview room, Aaron leading the way.

Mulcaster was already behind the table, unshaven and

tired. He was smaller and less significant than Zoe had expected. But small, insignificant men could murder as easily as bigger, louder ones.

Clarissa Bexley took a seat and tapped a pen on the desk as they ran through the formalities. As soon as the names had been stated, she sat straight. "I think we can all agree this is nonsense."

"I'm not sure I follow," Zoe said.

Bexley took a long sip from her tea and grimaced. She turned to Aaron. "Too strong. Did you press the bag against the side of the cup?"

Aaron said nothing, not meeting her eye.

Clarissa frowned and returned her gaze to Zoe. "My client already has an alibi, as you well know."

"It's not exactly—"

"I hadn't finished, DI Finch. My client has an alibi, and he's been complying with the terms of his release in all major respects. So the important question here isn't one you'll be asking, but rather, why precisely you've seen fit to drag him in here and, I understand, to tear apart his property without his consent."

"We don't need his consent when we're investigating a murder." Zoe leaned forward. "And Mr Mulcaster's alibi isn't strong. He was seen drinking in various clubs and bars, and there's CCTV to corroborate that, which we're more than happy to share with you. But you'll see that much of the evening isn't covered at all. The centre of Whitehaven is a small area. There's more than enough time for your client to have travelled to the marina, committed a serious offence, and then returned."

Clarissa Bexley stared at her, then turned and looked at Mulcaster. Had her lip curled?

"As for the release conditions," Zoe said, "moving to another area without seeking approval could be seen as a serious infringement."

"Poppycock!" Bexley replied. From the corner of her eye, Zoe saw Aaron raise an eyebrow. "He forgot. That's all. Other than this minor technical infringement, you've got nothing on my client and, what's more, he's been subject to threatening behaviour at the hands of the police in this very station, and is considering filing a complaint."

The dungeon. Zoe sat back and waited, refusing to give Clarissa oxygen.

The lawyer said nothing.

Zoe looked at Mulcaster. "Mr Mulcaster, you've wasted police time by providing false information. During a murder investigation. Why did you do that?"

"It's a minor offence," huffed Bexley. "Slap on the wrist."

Zoe looked at her. She was right: nine times out of ten, something like that would be dismissed.

"The thing is," Zoe said to Mulcaster, "we can chat all day about misleading the police and not getting permission to change your permanent address and all those things, but we all know why you're really here, and that's because we'd like to talk to you about murder."

She took a photograph from a folder and pushed it across the table. It was one of the original shots, the wound prominent and stark against the pale skin. She watched Mulcaster's eyes slide over it, stop, watched him shift back as far as he could. He took a moment to collect himself and then looked again.

"I didn't do it."

"You know he didn't do it," said Bexley. "It was a racially motivated murder and my client has no interest in that sort of thing. What's more, I understand you've recovered the weapon that inflicted this wound," she gestured towards the photograph, "and taken prints, and if those prints matched my client's, you'd have charged him. So why are you wasting everybody's time?"

Zoe frowned. Yes, they'd recovered prints, but that was confidential. And why had Bexley said *the weapon that inflicted this wound*, not *the murder weapon*?

Someone had been talking. But Zoe wasn't about to say that to Mulcaster and his brief.

"Racially motivated murder, you say," Zoe said. "Is it not just as likely that your client, having committed the murder, and then seen a group of men in Islamic dress, took the opportunity to disguise what he'd done and implicate them to cover his own back?"

Bexley snorted. "Let's put our cards on the table, shall we? You think my client is guilty because he has a record as a sex offender. But is there any evidence whatsoever that this murder was sexually motivated?"

Mulcaster winced.

Zoe held the lawyer's gaze. "We have reason to believe the victim was a sex worker, which is the vulnerable group your client has targeted in the past."

The lawyer sat back, eyebrows raised.

Zoe took a breath. She didn't know if this was wise or not. But...

"Mr Mulcaster," she said, "are you familiar with the name Myron Carter?"

Aaron pulled in a sharp breath. Mulcaster looked back at Zoe. He blinked slowly.

Maybe he was a good actor. Maybe he'd never heard the name.

But Clarissa Bexley clearly had. She leaned forward, mouth open, lips working like she was struggling to speak.

"What does any of this have to do with Mr Carter?" she asked at last.

Zoe hesitated.

"Mr Carter," Clarissa said, "is a respected member of the community who has contributed hugely to the area. I very much doubt he will tolerate having his name traduced by association with all this..." She waved at the photograph on the table.

Zoe swallowed. She didn't have anything else to present to Mulcaster and his lawyer.

"We're still running some final tests," she told Bexley, beginning to wind up the interview. "We've extracted DNA from a number of locations, and we'll be seeing whether they match your client's. If they do, Mr Mulcaster, you can expect to see a lot more of me and my colleagues."

CHAPTER SIXTY-FOUR

FOR ONCE, Zoe was glad her office wasn't part of the team room. After an hour with Clarissa Bexley, she needed time alone. So, she wasn't pleased to find Fiona Kendrick sitting behind her desk.

"Zoe." Fiona stood up. "Sorry for waiting here, but we need to talk. Come with me."

Zoe sighed and followed the super upstairs to her office. She took a seat.

Fiona wasted no time. "Drop the organised crime angle, Zoe."

"I think we need to know—"

Fiona raised a hand. "You've got a suspect. Charge him."

"We don't have enough evidence," replied Zoe. *And you thought he was a waste of time.*

"Then get it," Fiona said. "Look." She raised a finger for each of her points. "He's from out of town. He's lied to us. He's a sex offender. He has a history of offences against sex workers. And he's breached his parole conditions. It's obvious, isn't it?"

"But his prints don't match. That all leads in the right direction, but it's circumstantial."

What would Lesley do?

She wouldn't focus on this. She wouldn't ignore it either, wouldn't just release Mulcaster, would wait to see what the DNA told them. But she wouldn't drop everything else.

"Yes." Fiona gave Zoe one of her patronising smiles. "It *is* circumstantial. And you, by all accounts, are a good DI, so if anyone can find evidence that *isn't* circumstantial, you can."

Zoe shook her head. "We need to find out more about the victim."

"You've got her name. It's classic, Zoe. It's sad, but it's classic. She's the typical victim of a sexual predator whose offending has followed the usual pattern, stepping up when the opportunity arises. You know what that sort of man's like. They find women who won't be missed. Exactly like your Darla."

"Daria," Zoe corrected.

"Daria."

Had someone been leaning on Fiona? Had Ralph Streeting put pressure on her?

Zoe tried to put herself in the super's shoes. She supposed it was obvious. So much easier to blame the murder of a foreign victim on an out-of-towner with a record. Easier to treat it as an isolated incident and draw a line under it. Much easier than exploring racial tensions and the possibility of organised crime closer to home.

But *easy* wasn't the same as *right*.

She thought of Mulcaster looking at the photo. He'd been shocked. He hadn't faked that.

"It's getting late." Fiona looked past Zoe at the clock. "You've got less than twenty hours to get the evidence if you want to charge him. Get yourself home and think about the best way to go about it."

Zoe stood up. She was being dismissed.

"Oh, and we'll be running another press conference later."

Zoe clenched a fist. "OK, Ma'am."

"Fiona, remember?" A smile. "After all that nonsense by the Mosque, I'd like to get the message out there. Calm tensions."

"It's a community centre. Not a Mosque."

"Very well." Fiona held the smile, but it was tense. "Anyway, I won't be needing you for this one. I think a local voice is probably best. But if you could send me a photo of the knife, that might be useful."

"Of course. Goodnight, ma... Fiona."

"Goodnight, Zoe. I've emailed you the details for the charity auction on Thursday. It's formal dress."

Formal dress. Zoe's heart sank as she trudged downstairs.

She might have something appropriate. But finding which box it was in would be harder than solving the murder.

CHAPTER SIXTY-FIVE

Zoe walked into the team room to find Aaron sitting on his desk, telling the team about the interview.

"Right, you lot," she said. "It's been a long day, and I'd like it to be over shortly. Nina."

"Yes, boss." Nina looked nervous. *No bad thing.*

"I'll back you up on what happened at the community centre," Zoe said. "You messed up, but you were there and you got the backup. There's a lot more to congratulate you on than there is to rip you a new one."

"Thanks, boss." A smile, less nervous.

"Tom. Any developments?"

"We've heard back about the CCTV on Queen Street, around the hardware store. All dummies." He paused. "And there's one other thing..." He looked away.

"Yes?"

"I was going to get back in touch with Mick Halfpenny. He called the other day, said he had some information."

"Rings a bell. So what was it?"

"I don't know, boss. It's just..."

"You forgot, didn't you?"

He nodded. Zoe felt her nerves jangle. *Why bring it up?*

"We've got bigger fish to fry," she said. "It's a learning experience. Like you and your fighting, Nina. Make a note, don't do it again. Everyone go home. I'll see you tomorrow."

Tom and Nina poured out of the door, a flurry of coats and chatter. Zoe smiled as she watched them leave.

Aaron watched them too.

"Not heading home, Aaron?"

"Just wanted a quick catch-up. Are you OK, boss?"

"Of course. I'm fine." She lifted her chin. He didn't need to know the truth.

"Are you sure?"

Zoe looked at him. He was her DS. Maybe she could talk to him. Not about everything. But a little.

She walked to Tom's chair and turned it so she was facing Aaron.

"I'm not happy with the way this investigation's going. And no, I don't mean the mistakes. But we're still no closer to getting answers. The super wants me to charge Mulcaster."

Aaron opened his mouth so wide she almost laughed.

"That was my reaction too, although I managed to be subtler about it than you. She doesn't—" Zoe stopped herself.

"She doesn't what, boss?"

"I'm not sure I should be discussing this with you."

He laughed. "You probably shouldn't, but I think you'll be happier if you do."

He was right. She would.

"The super wants me to charge Mulcaster, and an hour earlier she was telling me to let him go. And the worst of it is, I can see why, from her point of view. Forget the port, forget the Islamic angle, just blame it on an outsider. It's tempting. But it doesn't answer the other questions. Where did she come from? What were the men in white doing there? And how did Bexley know about the knife, and the prints?"

Aaron nodded at each point.

"I can see it from her angle," he said. "I can see the pressure to charge, too. It would dilute the tension."

"I'm all for diluting the tension, Aaron. But I won't charge the wrong person just because it's convenient. Look, I shouldn't be keeping you here. Don't you have a family to get back to?"

"I'm a detective, boss. It's part of the job. And anyway..." He furrowed his brow. "Anyway, my husband works freelance. He'll be with our little girl."

Zoe nodded. "It can't be easy," she said.

"What?" He watched her.

"Being in a same-sex marriage with a young child when you're in this job. I brought up Nicholas by myself and that was hard enough, but I know how people can be."

"You'd be surprised, boss."

"Really?"

"Cumbria isn't as backward as you'd imagine. We even have Cumbria Pride. Not that it's my scene. But it's nice to know it's there."

"That's great." The watchful look was fading. "Some places are better than others, I suppose."

He pulled at the skin on his fingernails. "When I came out it was like an alien had landed. But that was a long time ago, in a tiny place you won't have heard of. Probably full of rainbow flags these days. Brings in the tourists."

Zoe laughed. "Good to know. Maybe I'll tell my son to move here after he's finished university."

An eyebrow went up. "He's...?"

Zoe nodded.

They left the office together, sharing details of their lives and families. At last, Zoe was feeling like she could open up to someone.

It wasn't Mo – it would never be Mo – but suddenly the prospect of coming back tomorrow didn't feel so bad.

CHAPTER SIXTY-SIX

ZOE WAS RELIEVED to see Carl's car as she turned into their road. Chatting to Aaron was good, but there were things she wasn't ready to talk to him about yet.

She'd tried calling Olivia Bagsby on her way home, but it had rung out. Fourteen times, with no voicemail. She'd sighed and hung up. She wouldn't be speaking to Olivia Bagsby tonight.

Carl had coffee waiting, and had dug out enough pots and pans to cook steaks for them both. He worked in the kitchen while Zoe leaned on the counter, sipping her coffee and telling him about her day. She saw his shoulders slump when she mentioned the charity auction, but he put on a brave face. It was all for a good cause. And they might just enjoy it.

He had his back to her when she moved on to the more interesting elements of her meeting with Fiona and Ralph Streeting. When he turned back to face her, his face was hard.

"Do you want my advice?" he asked.

Zoe shrugged.

"OK. Well, I think it's wise to tread carefully in a new job.

Don't alienate your colleagues. Especially your boss." He gave her a smile that didn't fool anyone.

"I'm not trying to alienate anyone, Carl. I'm just trying to do my job. If that means following the evidence, regardless of whose feet I might be treading on, well..."

Carl had finished with the salad, and the steaks were resting. He stood behind her, hands on her shoulders.

"You're probably right. And as it happens, I've come across your DI Streeting myself."

"You have?"

"He's based in Carlisle. We always end up working with these specialist teams. I didn't think much of him either." Carl spun her around to face him. "He's one of those who likes to think he's king of his domain. Best steer clear. You've met the type often enough."

"Sounds like PSD."

"No—" He stopped himself. "Yeah. That's fair."

While they ate, she talked about the team. About all the mistakes they'd made in the space of two short days. About Aaron, and the conversation they'd just had. About Tom, who'd stood there and announced that he was guilty of a small error just as they were about to leave for the evening, and her suspicion that he'd done it to shield Nina.

"Loyalty." Carl nodded. "It's a good sign."

"As long as they stop wasting my time. But I like the way they look out for each other."

"If you want a good team, you need good people. This lot sounds like good people."

Zoe considered. "I think so."

· · ·

After they'd loaded the dishwasher, Carl led Zoe into the living room and revealed another surprise: he'd managed to get the TV working.

"You're a bloody genius." She kissed him.

"Just a TV."

"It's civilisation." She caught his look. "You know what I mean."

He said nothing, but pulled her in next to him and waited for her to fire the remote.

"Shit," she said as the TV came on. Fiona was on.

The press conference. Of course.

The super was appealing for calm, just as she'd said she would. In the background was a picture of the body, the same one they'd used at the last press conference. The hotline number scrolled across the bottom of the screen.

"And I'll just hand over to Detective Inspector Markin to wrap up," said Fiona.

"Markin?" Zoe sat on the edge of the sofa. "Alan Markin?"

"Isn't this your case?" asked Carl.

"Markin?" repeated Zoe. "Yes. He's got nothing to do with it. The super said she wanted a local voice. But Markin?"

"Thank you," said Markin, onscreen. "As the detective superintendent said, we've made an arrest in this case and we're hoping to bring you further updates in due course."

"Made an arrest?" Zoe felt her heart rate picking up. "He doesn't even know the guy's name. And there won't be any updates, because he didn't do it."

Markin continued. "In the meantime, we're aware of speculation online and on social media, and we'd urge you not to encourage or participate in it. There's been an incident tonight which might have been serious had it not been for the quick thinking of our officers—"

"It was Nina!" shouted Zoe. "It wasn't his bloody team!"

Carl put a hand on her lap and she slumped back, her mouth wide. *Bastard.*

"In the meantime," said Markin, "we do have one further development we'd like to share with you."

Zoe frowned as the background changed: the photograph of the victim was replaced by one of the knife.

The photograph Zoe had sent Fiona, just before she'd left.

"We believe this weapon was involved in the crime. It was recovered on North Shore earlier today. If it looks in any way familiar to you, I'd urge you to contact the number above."

He pointed up. "As you can see, it's an extremely sharp knife, the sort of thing that's used as a ritual implement in certain circumstances," he said.

Zoe turned to Carl, dumbstruck. She returned to the TV.

"Please contact us should you have any relevant information, and I'd repeat my warning to remain calm and not to engage in speculation or rumour-mongering. We'll be taking no questions."

CHAPTER SIXTY-SEVEN

Zoe didn't like being up this early.

The house was silent, Carl asleep upstairs. Markin's comments had put Zoe in a bad mood, leaving her tossing and turning for hours. She'd woken at five, the unfamiliar noises and the fact that she was missing Nicholas conspiring against her. Not to mention Markin.

At last, she gave up and slid downstairs, brewing coffee and hoping its warmth would soothe her.

Might as well do something useful, she realised when she'd finished it.

She left a note for Carl and headed out into the dawn. The roads were quiet but the sunrise was spectacular, and she struggled to keep her attention on the road. Her gaze kept shifting to her right, to the hills and the layers of cloud gleaming red and gold. To her left, the sea was hidden behind mist so thick there could be more mountains there for all she knew.

In Workington, she parked on the south shore, close to the

lockups. It was too early for anyone to wonder where she was; the office wouldn't start to perk up for hours.

She wouldn't visit the port itself. Just someone who happened to live on the other side of the Derwent. Streeting would never know. And Aaron didn't need to know now, not in advance.

She'd expected to see no one, but two of them were there again, the overweight, middle-aged men hanging about by the waterside. No weed this time, or nothing she could smell. They were chatting as she approached, pointing across the river towards the port. They fell silent when they saw her, and watched her walking away, saying nothing.

She dialled Olivia Bagsby for the third time that morning. The early hour might explain the woman not picking up, but it didn't explain the message she got: *The number you have dialled has not been recognised.*

Zoe approached the house, checked the windows – no movement – and peered through the downstairs windows. The house was empty. Surfaces clear.

Olivia was an artist; she'd have supplies. And all the other things everyone had: keys on the table, pens, books, shoes. But looking through the two windows on the ground floor, Zoe could see nothing.

The house to the left was just as empty, but Aaron had mentioned a woman in the house on the other side. Zoe knocked, and the woman opened the door on the chain.

Zoe gave her a smile and held up her ID.

"Can you tell me if you've seen your next-door neighbour in the last day or so? Olivia?"

"Dunno, don't care." The woman grunted and closed the door.

Zoe glanced back at the house, half-hoping Olivia might appear, then walked around to Stanley Street, the road behind Olivia's. The houses were taller here, had probably been grand once.

At the first door she tried, a man dressed in a vest and ripped boxers opened the door. He blinked at her, hungover.

She held up her ID. "DI Zoe Finch, Cumbria Police. Don't suppose you've seen Olivia around recently? The artist who lives down by the shore." She pointed.

He laughed. "Cleared out, in't she? Sunday night, it were. Night before last."

"Cleared out?"

"Piled all 'er stuff into 'er car and buggered off. Good riddance. Only been 'ere a few months and thought she were queen of the bloody town. Knew she wouldn't stay long. That sort never does."

"Can you describe her car?"

"Red." He screwed up his face in concentration. "No, blue. No, you know what, I dunno what colour it was."

"Do you know why she left, then?"

"Not a clue." He yawned. "S'pose her tenancy was over. Like mine will be if I can't sort out the rent soon."

Zoe smiled. "Thank you."

Sunday night, he'd said. By the look of him, he hadn't been sober since long before Sunday night, but he'd been precise: Sunday night, night before last.

Zoe returned to her car. The men outside the lockup were gone. The mist was lifting and she could see movement across the water: a crane swinging, the sound of vehicles.

She and Aaron had seen Olivia Bagsby on Sunday. They'd spoken to her, not far from this spot. She'd told them what she'd seen. She'd told them her lease wasn't up for another month, that she'd be renewing it.

She hadn't sounded like someone who was planning on packing up and leaving.

CHAPTER SIXTY-EIGHT

At half past seven, the station was almost deserted.

Aaron had had a long night, up with his daughter Annabel who was poorly. He'd finally left Serge in charge, yawning all the way to work.

The team room was empty. No sign of the DI. But half past seven wasn't too early to call.

She answered after a couple of rings.

"Any news, boss?" he asked. "Any developments?"

"Did you see the press conference?"

"Yes." From his point of view, the press conference had been a disaster.

"I'm not happy about it, Aaron," said the DI.

He grinned. "Don't blame you. Are you on your way in?"

"Yep," she replied. "Be about half an hour."

"I thought..." He stopped himself. She lived closer than that, but it was none of his business. "I thought we need to focus on Mulcaster. What with the timing."

"Agreed. See you shortly."

He dialled again.

"Morning, Nina," he said. "I've spoken to the boss."

"Do you never sleep?" She yawned.

"I want you to stop at the hardware store on your way in, see if they're finished, then we can cross it off the list."

"It's not on my way in, Sarge."

He frowned. Nina was good at her job, but she sometimes forgot about the chain of command. "Plan a different route, then."

His phone was ringing before he'd had the chance to put it down. Front desk.

"Sarge, there's someone here to see you."

"Who is it?"

"Says his name's Mick Halfpenny. Wants to talk to someone involved in the murder investigation. He mentioned Tom Willis, but he's not in yet."

And won't be for a while, knowing Tom.

"OK. Can you put him in four, give him a cup of tea, and tell him I'll be along shortly?"

Interview room four was the nicest. The chairs were upholstered and the table sat straight. Aaron made his own tea then stood outside watching Mick Halfpenny through the camera. From what Tom had told him, Aaron would have picked this man out of a line-up. Especially with those glasses.

Mick Halfpenny sat back in his chair, arms folded, tea steaming on the table in front of him. Almost like he owned the place.

As Aaron entered, Mick stood up, almost knocking over his chair, and thrust out a hand. He gestured to the chairs like he was the host.

"Sit down, please," Aaron said. "What can I help you with?"

"I was just wondering if there was anything *I* could do to help."

"Help?"

Mick cleared his throat. "I don't like to push myself forward, but I am something of an expert on Whitehaven. Not just the history, but the geography, as it were. I did call, the other day, you know? I was expecting a call back."

He peered at Aaron over the tops of his glasses. Aaron resisted a roll of the eyes. *Something of an expert on Whitehaven.*

"And as I mentioned to your colleague, I was out and about that night. When the local warehouse is running I can't sleep, so I've taken to examining some of the historic sites by night. You get a different sense of them in the dark. It feels more real, sometimes. More honest."

"I can imagine."

Aaron could imagine nothing of the sort. He was just trying to work out how to get rid of the man.

Mick leaned in. "And did you ever find that group of men, the ones in the white clothes?"

"I'm sorry, Sir. Between you and me, we've drawn a complete blank. But if you have any new information yourself?"

Aaron stood up. Mick Halfpenny stayed in his chair, taking sips from his plastic cup of tea.

"I'm afraid I'll have to head back, Sir," Aaron said. "It's a busy time."

"Oh, oh yes, I'm terribly sorry, Detective Sergeant. After this tragedy, and then that terrible business last night." Mick stood up.

"Last night?"

"That crowd. Marching through the town. Most

unsavoury." He looked away. "But I'm sure you have it all in hand. Please, don't hesitate to contact me if you'd like any help."

Aaron climbed back up to the team room, lamenting the wasted fifteen minutes. But he had the feeling that, with Mick Halfpenny, it could have been a lot worse.

CHAPTER SIXTY-NINE

Nina was outside the hardware store, on the phone to Caroline Deane. The place was deserted, the tape still up. No Uniform, no CSI. No sign of Jackson Liddell, thank God.

"You're finished here, then?" she asked.

"Yep," replied Caroline.

"So we can open it up?"

"Yep."

Nina pulled down the tape, then phoned Jackson Liddell, who didn't answer. *Thank God.* She left him a voicemail: the police were finished, the tape was down, he could come back and open up.

Back in her car, she made a snap decision. Woodhouse wasn't on her way, but then, the hardware store hadn't been on her way either. If she was going to waste time, maybe she'd waste some more and have something to show for it.

The route took her right through town. More of those posters and stickers had been put up. But that wasn't what bothered her.

What bothered her was the people. It wasn't nine in the

morning, and they were already gathering. Groups of three, four, as many as six. Street corners. Holding cans of lager, cider, unidentifiable bottles.

Last night had been bad enough. This looked worse.

Roddy Chen was standing outside Mulcaster's house looking like one of those statues they put outside a tomb. No one would be getting in without Roddy's say-so. Nina asked him if anything had been found. He shook his head and she found herself imagining a conversation between him and Caroline Deane.

Inside, the house was like no one had ever lived there. Yes, there was a TV propped up on some boxes, but even that felt like the work of a squatter or someone passing through. Nina went back outside and asked Roddy if much had been taken away by the CSIs.

"Toothbrush," he replied.

"That's all?"

"Yeah."

She dialled the DI as she set out from Woodhouse.

"On your way in, Nina?"

"Yes. Sarge asked me to check out the hardware store. They've finished there, which'll take pressure off Stella's team. But there's a lot of people about."

"People?"

"Same as last night. They're already up and drinking. Small groups, but it's weird. I've never seen anything like it here."

"Thanks for letting me know. I'll tell Inspector Keane."

"And then I thought I'd check out Mulcaster's place," Nina said. "Make sure there wasn't something obvious we missed."

A pause.

"And was there?"

"No, boss. It's very clean. Hardly anything there. I'm leaving now."

"Right." Another pause. "Well done, Nina. I know you didn't find what you were looking for, but you've been proactive."

Nina smiled as she ended the call. But being proactive was the obvious stuff. That was the stuff she knew she was good at, and she hoped the DI knew it too.

It was the other side that she had to work on. The judgement calls. The fine decisions.

The not getting into fights with racist mobs.

It was a learning process, she reckoned. She'd get there in the end.

CHAPTER SEVENTY

ZOE DROVE TOWARD THE OFFICE, heading inland. There were more cars than she'd seen since moving up and she found herself stuck at forty in a sixty zone. *Calm down*, she told herself. *It'll only add two minutes to your drive.*

Her phone rang again.

"DI Finch."

"Zoe. It's Stella. You in the office?"

"On the way. Have you got news for me?"

"We've got some preliminary results. The fibres aren't new. They're from something that's been worn for years. But the DNA on them doesn't match what we got from Mulcaster. Nor does the sample we took from the body."

"Shit." Zoe wasn't looking forward to telling Fiona.

"There is some good news, though," Stella continued.

"Yes?"

"The fibre DNA didn't match Liddell, either. It wasn't his, and it wasn't contaminated by him. Which means..."

"Which means whoever it belongs to, chances are they

broke into the store, they stole that can of paint, and they wrote on the body."

"Exactly. And our early results suggest that the fibre DNA could well be from the same person as the body DNA."

"This *is* good news."

"I think so. We're not quite ready to check against the full database, but we should be there soon enough. But Zoe?" Stella sounded serious.

"What's up?"

"This means Mulcaster's probably in the clear, right?"

"Yes."

"So do you really need us to go through his house? We've been in to get his toothbrush, and I know it doesn't look like there's much there, but if we go through it top to bottom it'll take a day or two, and that's... Well, it wasn't him, was it?"

Zoe considered.

"Fair enough. You've saved yourself a job. You can forget Mulcaster."

"Thanks, Zoe."

She was only ten minutes away from the station now, but called Aaron to give him the bad news.

"So it's definitely not Mulcaster, then," he said.

"I think, painful as it is, we're going to have to let him go."

"Want me to get that started?"

"Please. Get rid of him. We won't charge him for now, but we've always got the section five charge if we need to bring him in again. I'll tell the super when I'm in."

The traffic cleared, and Zoe was doing sixty again. She sighed. For once, she wouldn't have minded a delay.

CHAPTER SEVENTY-ONE

Tom liked the office quiet. It meant he could focus. And this morning he was focusing on an internet search.

Bârlad. That was what the DI's mysterious caller had said. Daria, from Bârlad.

The town had a police station. He tracked it down and found a Twitter account. He tweeted the station from the little-used CID account; he'd delete it later if he had to, but he didn't think he'd done anything wrong.

He sat back and waited, then smiled as his PC pinged. The CID account, with its little grey tick, had been authentic enough for them to respond.

He was already following the station. He opened up Google Translate and sent them another tweet. *Follow me so we can DM.*

The local detective in charge of Mispers was called Constantin. They exchanged email addresses and Tom explained who he was looking for.

Tom's phone rang.

"Tom, it is Constantin."

Tom smiled, impressed. "Hi, Constantin."

"You think you have found a missing person from Bârlad?" The man's voice was smooth, his words fast and even. *At least he won't need me to speak his language.*

"I can send you a photo. But we've got a name, too." Tom fired off an email with the photos of the body.

"The tattoos," said Constantin. "It is her."

"Her?"

"Daria Petrescu. She left home three, no, nearly four weeks ago, with her friend Elena. Nobody has seen or heard from them since. Her family. Oh."

Silence.

"Constantin?"

"Sorry. Her family. They were sure she would be fine. They thought she would be home soon. Thank you, Tom. I will have to tell them."

CHAPTER SEVENTY-TWO

ZOE ENTERED the team room to find an air of muted celebration. Tom leaned against his desk with a smug grin on his face and Aaron stood opposite, nodding. Nina wasn't around.

"Solved it, have you?" she asked.

"Solved what, boss?" replied Tom.

"The murder. Found our killer?"

"No, boss. But I've confirmed the victim's ID. Her name's Daria Petrescu. I spoke to a detective in her hometown and he corroborated it."

"Impressive."

"Thanks." His grin dropped. "The bad news is there's nowhere local that stocks that horrible orange jumper."

Zoe nodded. Something else to follow up on. "Meanwhile," she told them, "it looks like there's more trouble on the way."

"Trouble?" asked Aaron.

"Nina called. She's seen more groups gathering. Drinking." Zoe checked her watch. "At nine am. We need to let Inspector

Keane know. And Tom, can you do some digging into where this is all coming from?"

Tom grunted an affirmative.

Zoe turned to Aaron. "Can I borrow you for a minute?"

He shrugged and followed her to her office. Once inside, she told him what she'd learned about Olivia Bagsby. The worry on his face intensified.

"It's OK, Aaron," she said. "I didn't broadcast my presence and I didn't mention your name. I only spoke to a couple of neighbours. But it looks like our artist has disappeared."

"Where's she gone?"

"That's what I want you to find out. See if you can trace her car. DVLA, rental places. If we know what she was driving we might be able to track her down. I'm also coming round to your way of thinking on this whole Port of Workington thing."

"What's that?"

"We're not supposed to be sticking our noses in there. If someone tells me not to stick my nose in somewhere, I stick it as far in as it'll go. But quietly. You're right about that. So just you, no one else on the team, OK?"

"OK, boss."

"Good," she said. "Anything else I need to know about?"

"Mick Halfpenny was in, earlier."

"Who?"

"The historian. The one who spoke to Tom the other day. He was waffling on about historical sites, how much he knows about the town. He wants to help."

Zoe rolled her eyes. "I know the type."

"I got rid of him."

"Good." Zoe bit her lower lip. "Is Nina OK? After what happened last night?"

Aaron looked surprised. "She's probably in now. You want me to have a chat with her?"

"Might be worth doing."

They returned to the team room: still no sign of Nina.

"Has Nina been in yet, Tom?" Aaron asked.

"I haven't seen her, Sarge."

Aaron looked at Zoe. "She called me from the car park, not long before you showed up, boss."

Zoe frowned. "I'll call her."

She went back to her office and dialled. Nothing.

Nina was in the building. But where?

Zoe didn't know the building all that well yet, so she tried searching logically. Five minutes later, she heard a woman sobbing in a cubicle in the toilets.

"Nina?" she asked.

"Yes. Sorry."

Zoe leaned against the sinks, waiting.

Nina emerged a minute later, drying her eyes. "Sorry, boss. Ready to get back to work." She moved towards the door.

Zoe stepped in front of her. "You're not fine, Nina. Want to tell me what's wrong?"

Nina shook her head. "It's fine."

Zoe lowered her voice. "Tell me. You're not in trouble."

Nina gave her a wary look. "It's the super, boss." She glanced towards the door.

Zoe clenched a fist. "What happened?"

"I got into a lift. She got in after me." Nina drew in a shaky breath. "I should have taken the stairs."

"What happened?"

Nina eyed Zoe. She blinked.

"You can tell me," Zoe said. "I'm not going to go running to her."

Nina nodded. "She laid into me." She rubbed her face. "She told me I was a disgrace and that my actions were a stain on the reputation of the force. And then the lift got to our floor and she just waited for me to get out without saying another word. I'm sorry, boss. I just needed a minute. It won't happen again."

Zoe looked her in the eye. "Give yourself five minutes. Then come straight to my office, please. We need to straighten this out."

Zoe went via the team room and asked Aaron to come with her. In her office, she explained what had happened.

"I'm beyond furious," she told him.

"It's not her fault, boss. I mean, I know she messed up, but she did good work last night. And this morning."

"It's not Nina I'm furious with. It's the super."

"Oh."

"I've half a mind to go up there and tell her that if she wants to insult my team, she should come through me."

"Oh. Right."

She watched him. He'd done that thing she'd noticed, head tilted, hands playing with each other, a frown creeping across his face.

Aaron Keyes knew Fiona Kendrick better than she did and was clearly terrified by the prospect of her taking the super on.

He wasn't going to say it out loud, but he was warning her. And she was listening.

A knock on the door. Nina entered.

"Sit down, Nina."

Nina sat, looking up at Aaron and Zoe, her expression wary.

Zoe gave her a smile. "Nina. I just wanted you to hear it from me, in front of your DS. You're doing a great job. It's not my place to disagree with the super, but I can only assume she's commenting on the basis of incomplete information, and I want to assure you that I don't share her views."

Nina bit her lip. "Thank you, boss."

"Good. You take your lunch break now, give yourself a breather. And tell Tom, I want the two of you working together when you get back, following up this trouble. It was your intel, after all."

"Thanks," repeated Nina as she left.

Zoe's phone rang before Aaron could follow her. She gestured for him to stay as she answered; she'd seen who was on the line.

"Dr Robertson," she said. "Good to hear from you."

"You too, Zoe. Toxicology's back. The full report should be in your inbox shortly, but it boils down to I was right."

"You were right?"

"Heroin. Nothing unusual about it, purity or source. Just a lot of it. Enough to kill her quickly and, I think, relatively painlessly."

"Thanks, Chris. That was quick work."

"I fast-tracked it. Sent it down to Hutton, where the serious scientists hang out."

"Don't let Stella hear you say that."

Chris Robertson laughed. Zoe turned to Aaron.

"You go and look after the team. I've got to track down an angry detective superintendent and make her even angrier. Wish me luck."

CHAPTER SEVENTY-THREE

FIONA SAT behind her desk wearing the sweet smile that was starting to make Zoe uneasy.

"Zoe. Good afternoon. I'm hoping you've come with good news."

Was it afternoon, already? Zoe felt like the day was running away with her. She'd taken the stairs one step at a time, giving herself time to calm down. She needed to be careful.

She took a breath. "I'm sorry, Fiona. About last night. I know things got out of hand, but that's my responsibility. My team. I've told them the buck stops with me, and I can't pretend it doesn't when things go wrong."

Fiona nodded. "That's refreshing, Zoe. A lot of people might say they're willing to take responsibility for their team's actions, but not many of them would walk in here and stand in front of me and do it."

"I—" Zoe began.

"And I have to say, having looked over the logs from last night, I'm not sure things *did* go wrong. Nina Kapoor's precipitate behaviour may have made it a little worse, but there's no doubt that her presence of mind made it a lot better."

Zoe hadn't been expecting that.

"So," the super continued, "in the spirit of apology, I owe Nina one. Please do pass it on."

Zoe stared at her. "Thank you," she managed to say. "I do have a couple of items to update you on, though."

"Take a seat."

Zoe had considered telling the super about Olivia Bagsby, but that would mean admitting she was looking into the port. And she had enough bad news to impart.

"There might be more trouble on the way."

"Trouble?"

"Groups gathering in town. Drinking. Something like last night. Inspector Keane already knows."

"Thank you," Fiona said. "Forewarned is forearmed. But I wouldn't worry too much. This isn't Birmingham. They don't riot and burn the place down just because they're a little unhappy. And Zoe?"

"Yes?"

"If you can see your way to solving this crime, the trouble-makers won't have anything left to be unhappy about, will they?"

"Yes, Ma'am."

"Is there anything else?"

"Yes. Ryan Mulcaster. His prints don't match those on the knife, and his DNA doesn't match anything we have. He's been released without charge."

"I'm sorry?"

"We released him," Zoe said. "No match on prints, DNA, no evidence he had anything to do with it. We can't charge him."

"You shouldn't have done that."

"I think—"

"I think you'd better leave."

"I—"

"Please." There was no smile this time.

Zoe turned to the door. "I'm not going to charge an innocent man just because it's convenient," she muttered.

"I heard that, Detective Inspector."

Zoe turned back.

"I heard what you just said," the super said. "About not charging an innocent man just because it's convenient. Is that what you think I wanted you to do? Think carefully before you answer, DI Finch."

"No, Ma'am." Zoe's gaze was fixed on the floor.

"No. Good. You may leave."

CHAPTER SEVENTY-FOUR

"What are we looking for?" asked Nina as she entered the team room. She'd taken half an hour sitting in her car, catching her breath. She wasn't used to lunch breaks in the middle of an investigation.

She could get used to this new DI.

Tom looked up. "White rabbits."

"White rabbits?" Nina had no idea what he was talking about, but then her brain was still in a fog.

"Sign that something's weird. Just a clue, really. Shouldn't be hard with this lot. They're not exactly subtle. You find a white rabbit and you follow it and before long you've got, I dunno, a whole warren of them."

"Why's that a white rabbit, though? What's weird about white rabbits?"

"Nothing. Waistcoats. You wouldn't get it."

Nina looked at him. If she asked what he was talking about, they'd be here all day. And she knew where to start.

She repeated her Twitter searches from the previous evening and it took less than a minute to find her first white rabbit. From there, she tracked the warren: a host of anonymous accounts, almost all of them new, and almost all following each other and hardly anyone else.

There was a common motif. Users were encouraging *the people* to protest *the Islamisation of England* and the focal point for their rage was Whitehaven Islamic Community Centre. It all seemed to be coming from a seemingly local account, also new, called *Knights of Whitehaven*. That one had posted a video of the man in the balaclava, which had been shared by the others.

The man in the balaclava held up a photograph of the knife as he spoke. "I'm citing the police here," he said. "They're the ones saying this, not me. This is a ritual weapon."

Implement. Not that there was much difference.

"And if it was a ritual weapon, that means it was a ritual killing, and none of us is safe."

Nina felt her skin run cold.

But there was worse.

The photograph the man held up wasn't one of theirs. It looked like it had been taken with a flash. The background looked like rocks. The same rocks where the knife had been found.

"Oh fuck," said Tom.

Nina looked up, wondering if he'd seen the same thing.

"Come and look at this."

Nina stood behind him and looked at his screen. He had more anonymous accounts on-screen, retweeting a blog – also anonymous – with an *exclusive* from *confidential sources.*

"They've given his bloody name," whispered Nina.

"And his photo," added Tom.

Ryan Mulcaster. Named, photographed, his crimes listed.

Nina read it out. "*This is Ryan Mulcaster. Ryan Mulcaster, the notorious sex offender, picked up and almost immediately released by police, and now free to go on murdering innocent women on the streets of Whitehaven."*

"Oh fuck," said Tom.

The DI walked in. Nina looked up, then at Tom.

"You go first," she said.

CHAPTER SEVENTY-FIVE

ZOE STARED at Nina's screen, and then at Tom's. She listened as they explained what they'd seen to her, but it was all there, onscreen.

Damn.

She needed to speak to the super. Again.

She hurried to her office and picked up the phone. She wasn't ready for another face-to-face.

"I hope you're not calling with more bad news, DI Finch."

"I'm afraid I am." Zoe pulled at her shirt, straightening it and trying to feel more confident. "Someone took a photo of the knife before we found it. They're using it on social media, it's been taken with a flash, isn't one of ours."

"This sounds a lot like the photo of the men in white that was doing the rounds the other day, DI Finch. Have you considered it might be the same person behind it?"

"Yes, Ma'am. And there's another thing." She gripped the phone tighter. "They know about Ryan Mulcaster. About his release, and his history."

"I'm very disappointed, DI Finch." A pause. "I'll speak to

Uniform about contingency planning for tonight. And I suppose they can warn Mulcaster. If he wants to come in, we'll have to offer protection."

"I know," replied Zoe, praying that he wouldn't. Would he be safer in the station, or not?

"Meanwhile," said the super, "I want this murder cleared up. And I don't care if you have to be politically incorrect to do it." She hung up.

Aaron knocked and walked in as Zoe was putting the phone down.

"More bad news?" she asked. "Sorry." She didn't want to come across like the super.

"Sort of."

He passed her his phone, open at Olivia Bagsby's website. Zoe scrolled through. The artwork wasn't her thing, but she could see why some people might like it. It was bold, with big splashes of colour.

"That doesn't look like bad news," she said.

"Click through to her Instagram."

Zoe clicked the link and scrolled through the images: photos of the river, shots of her artwork. The feed had been added to several times each day.

Until Sunday morning. Since then, nothing at all.

"I sent her messages," Aaron said. "I used her social media accounts, and the email address."

"And?"

"Nothing. DVLA and rental companies don't have anything either."

Zoe shook her head. "Either Olivia Bagsby doesn't want to be found..."

"Or someone doesn't want us to find her."

CHAPTER SEVENTY-SIX

"Sorry about last night," Zoe said to Carl. They were on the sofa, her head resting on his shoulder and her eyes closed.

"Me too," he said.

"You don't have anything to be sorry for."

He shrugged.

She turned to him. He returned her smile.

"The curry's late," she said.

"It's Whitehaven, love. Not Birmingham."

Zoe sighed. "I got a proper dressing down from the super today. We released someone she thought was guilty, then someone leaked his identity online. Someone else has got photos of our murder weapon, and they're trying to encourage people to, I don't know, rise up against their supposed Muslim overlords, whoever they might be."

"Sounds tough." Carl's gaze kept darting past her, to the TV and the News.

"And the team. I can't figure them out. They keep making stupid mistakes like not getting prints or forgetting phone calls, or starting fights—"

He turned to her. "Starting fights?"

Zoe lay down, her head on his legs. "My Sikh Elvis-loving DC managed to start a fight with an angry racist mob. You couldn't make it up. But then they do good work. It was her who tracked that racist mob in the first place. My other DC's got a positive ID on the victim. My DS is supportive, even if he seems terrified of the super. And I'm spending half my time looking over my shoulder, making sure Ralph bloody Streeting isn't watching me. How am I supposed to do my job?"

She sat up and looked at him.

He shrugged. "I can't help you there."

She wrinkled her nose. "I didn't expect an actual answer. But now you've almost given one, perhaps you can tell me what you mean?"

He looked at the screen.

"Carl?"

"You've got to be able to handle your own colleagues," he said.

Zoe watched him. He was being odd. But he'd just started a new job himself. And she couldn't even ask him about it.

The bell rang a minute later: the curry, only a few minutes late. They sat and ate in near silence, avoiding each other's gaze, commenting on the food and the TV and nothing else. Zoe wanted to confront Carl, but was too tired.

Half an hour later, her phone buzzed: Nicholas, on WhatsApp video.

She positioned the phone so Carl wasn't in the shot.

"Hey."

"Hey. You eating curry?" He was sitting on a bed, a wall of photos behind him.

"Yes. Why?"

"Taste of India?"

Zoe smiled, glancing at Carl. "Er, yes."

Nicholas pulled a sympathetic face. "I'll understand if you need to get off the call to be sick."

"What?" Zoe looked up at Carl, who was heading into the kitchen with their plates.

"Everyone knows the best takeaway curry in town comes from Akash," Nicholas said.

"Everybody in Stirling knows the best takeaway in White-haven comes from Akash?" Zoe asked.

Nicholas laughed. "I've been doing my research, yeah? Nothing wrong with that."

"No." Zoe felt warmth spread through her. "There's nothing wrong with it at all. I've been thinking about the Christmas holid—"

"That's miles off, Mum." Nicholas looked to one side. "I've got to go. See ya."

The screen went blank.

Zoe slumped back in her chair as Carl sat down with two mugs of coffee.

"Thanks," she said.

"So Nick's a connoisseur of Cumbria curry houses, is he?"

"Seems so." She chuckled, and he stroked her hand and flashed her a grin.

The TV was still on. They watched in silence, the mood less tense, until the local news came on.

A report from outside the community centre.

Zoe let go of Carl's hand and sat forwards. "Shit."

There was a crowd there. Dozens of them, hoodies and drunken shouts, just like the previous night.

"Is this from yesterday, or is it live?" asked Carl.

"I don't know."

"... second night of violence in the town centre..." said the reporter.

"Live," said Zoe, her voice thin.

It looked like a bigger crowd, with more joining every minute. There was a police presence. Inspector Keane and his team had been warned in advance this time. But no one had expected quite this many of them.

Her phone rang. Nina.

"Boss, have you seen this?"

"I'm watching now."

"Think we should go down there?"

"No," Zoe snapped. "Uniform's on the scene. There's nothing we can do that they can't."

"Oh," said Nina.

"Oh?" echoed Zoe.

"It's just..."

"Just what, Nina?"

"It's just, well, I'm here at the moment."

"Where, precisely?"

"I'm inside with Ali and Inaya. I wanted to make sure they were OK."

Brilliant. Just brilliant.

"OK," Zoe said. "Just keep out of sight and keep out of trouble, Nina. I don't want to see you on TV."

"Got it, boss."

Carl was looking at her, concern written all over his face, and even though the situation was clearly a lot worse than it had been, the fact that he seemed to care made her feel a lot better than she had done.

"It's OK," she said. "She's not going to make the same mistake twice." She put an arm around him.

She heard the bang and pulled away from Carl with a jolt.

It had come from the TV. "Sounded like a petrol bomb," the reporter was saying. There were people running about, shouting, the sounds of sirens, the edges of flames.

Nina answered on the first ring.

"It's OK, boss. I got them out before it happened. They're in my car with me now."

Zoe could hear a voice in the background: Inaya. "Hello, DI Finch."

"Are they OK?" she asked Nina.

"They're fine. A bit shaken up, but unhurt."

"What about you?"

"Tickety-boo."

"And the community centre?"

"I don't think it was much of an explosion. We're not dealing with the IRA here, boss. We'll have to wait till daylight to see."

"Did you see who did it?"

"Too many people. Too much chaos. Morris's guys might have something on the bodycams, but I doubt it. It was like a zoo out there."

"They've dispersed," said Carl. "They ran at the first bang."

He pointed at the screen. Only the firefighters and police were left.

"Cowards," said Nina.

"Stay calm," Zoe told her. "Take Ali and Inaya home."

"Will do."

"And don't do anything stupid, yes?"

"I won't." Nina hung up.

"You sure that was wise?" asked Carl.

"What?" Zoe looked at him.

"The way you talked to her. She did well."

"She went somewhere she shouldn't have, and put herself in harm's way."

He shrugged. "It's your team. I'm going to bed."

CHAPTER SEVENTY-SEVEN

THE NEXT MORNING, everyone was on edge. Aaron and the boss had left Nina and Tom sniping at each other from behind their screens, both reluctant to focus on what the DI wanted them to work on.

Which was to get to the bottom of what had happened last night.

"Stay here," she told them. "Use your brains and your computers. Don't leave the building."

She turned to Aaron. "Come on. You're taking me to the community centre."

There were no crowds on the street, but the boss looked like she was trying to peer around every corner before he turned it. Her lip curled at every red light, her head shook when someone in front had the nerve to indicate right and wait for a break in the traffic.

"Can you speed things up a bit?" she said, eventually.

"It's not like you haven't been in the car with me before," he replied, and they lapsed into silence. Had he gone too far? No. The new DI valued straight talking more than politeness.

After he pulled into the car park, she turned to him.

"I'm sorry. It's not for me to tell you how to drive."

He nodded. "We're all on edge."

She raised an eyebrow but said nothing.

Ali and Inaya were standing outside, surveying the damage. A part of the main wall had been badly burned, four windows were shattered, and there was roof material on the ground. But Ali was smiling.

"It's not that bad," he said. "It's really not that bad."

Aaron wondered if he was trying to convince himself more than anyone else.

Inaya shrugged as she approached them. "At least no one was hurt. DC Kapoor saved our lives, you know?"

The boss smiled. "I don't know about saving your lives, but she did well."

They were summoned inside for the usual tea and sweet coffee.

"We'll do what we can to find the culprits," the DI told them. "But you know our resources are limited."

"We do," said Ali.

The DI put down her coffee. "I was wondering, though, why you didn't mention the planning application to me."

Ali frowned. Inaya looked lost.

Zoe continued. "You said you were looking to expand eventually, turn this place into a Mosque, but I didn't realise you meant so soon. It's coming up, isn't it? The application hearing?"

"Well, yes. It's the week after next. I didn't think you would find it particularly interesting, DI Finch," said Ali. "It's my Mosque, and even I don't find it interesting." He smiled.

Aaron waited for more. Why hadn't the DI said anything about this?

"The other day," she continued, "you told us there wasn't much of an Islamic presence here. So why go to all this trouble?"

Inaya licked her lips. "From that baseball film. Build it and they will come? It is the same with religion, with Noah and his Ark, it will be the same with our Masjid."

Aaron leaned forward, ready to correct her, then thought better of it.

"Meanwhile," continued Inaya, "we heard about that poor man getting injured."

The DI looked at Aaron. He shrugged.

"What man?" asked Zoe. "We didn't hear about anyone getting hurt here last night."

Aaron put down his cup. It couldn't be...

Inaya shook her head. "Not here. In the town. There was a lot of trouble. I hope he is OK."

The DI turned to Aaron and tilted her head.

Mulcaster?

He looked into the boss's eyes. She was tilting her head, towards the door.

He needed to find out what it was they were talking about.

He turned to Ali and Inaya. "I'm so sorry,. I need to go."

CHAPTER SEVENTY-EIGHT

Zoe drank her coffee as fast as she could. Either it had improved, or the sense of urgency was dulling her taste buds.

Aaron was in the car when she reached Inaya and Ali's door, talking on the phone. Hopefully he was checking if the man attacked had been their former suspect.

"Detective Inspector," Inaya asked as Zoe was about to walk away, "have you had any luck tracking down those youngsters in white? I suppose that's where all this started."

Zoe turned to her. "Sorry. I don't know if it would make things better or worse, to be honest. But we'll keep you informed. And as I said, we'll do what we can to bring in whoever did this." She gestured at the wall. The writing.

Inaya nodded.

Zoe made her way to the car and slid in next to Aaron. "Any news?"

"It's Mulcaster. And it's not good."

"Damn."

She looked back at the house, thinking over what Inaya had just asked her. "Hang on."

She jumped out of the car and ran back to the centre, leaving Aaron confused behind her. She hammered on the door.

Inaya opened it within seconds.

"Youngsters," Zoe panted. "Why did you say 'youngsters'? The group in white. We've got no idea what age they are. How do you know?"

The woman frowned. "Come in."

Zoe followed her inside. She could hear Aaron catching up behind her.

"Do you have that photograph?" Inaya asked. "Of the group? The youngsters?"

Youngsters. That word, again. Zoe pulled out her phone and found the photo. She passed it to Inaya.

"There," said Inaya. She pointed at one of the figures. At their feet. "And there." Again, someone's feet.

"What am I looking at?" Zoe asked. Aaron was leaning over, trying to see.

"Those. They are trainers, yes?"

"Well, I don't know." Zoe looked at Aaron, who shrugged. "I suppose they might be, but anyone can wear trainers, can't they?"

Inaya shook her head. "Not this sort. Look at the shape of them."

Zoe leaned in and examined the image. The soles were enormous. It was like they were wearing lifts. And there were lines running vertically down in a distinctive pattern she didn't recognise.

"What are they?" she asked.

"I only know," replied Inaya, "because Ibby has been going on about these things for weeks. He showed me pictures. As if I care what he spends his money on."

"So you know what they are?"

"Zeps, they are called. I don't know the manufacturer, I only know the name. Zeps. Teenagers. They know nothing, but they're so sure they know everything."

Zoe thanked her. For all the morning's bad news, she had a renewed sense of focus. She was smiling as she and Aaron walked back to the car. When they reached it, she looked over the roof at him.

Aaron was grinning too.

CHAPTER SEVENTY-NINE

Nina was walking along the corridor to the team room when she heard a familiar voice call her name.

She froze.

"Nina," the voice repeated.

Nina turned round, trying not to look terrified.

The super raised an eyebrow. "What are you doing, skulking out here?"

"Just using the Ladies, Ma'am."

The eyebrow dropped. "Hmm. Where's DI Finch?"

Nina exhaled. She knew the answer to that. "At the community centre Ma'am, with Sergeant Keyes."

"For Christ's sake."

Nina braced herself.

"Your team," the super continued, "is hardly covering itself in glory. But—"

Nina felt herself pick up a little. "Yes, Ma'am?"

"But I have some congratulations to pass on."

"To who, Ma'am?"

"To whom, Nina. To you, of course. The article?"

"I'm sorry, Ma'am. I don't know—"

The super smiled. Nina had seen Fiona Kendrick's smile before, and it wasn't something she relished. For a short time, and before she'd found out about it and brought it to an end, the super's nickname had been *The Crocodile*.

But this didn't look like a crocodile smile. It looked real.

The super pulled out her phone and passed it to Nina.

It was open on a *Whitehaven Chronicle* article. The headline was *Hero Cop Saves Couple From Burning Mosque*.

Nina scanned it. It was under Jake Frimpton's by-line. There were a couple of minor inaccuracies, such as the fact that it wasn't a Mosque, yet, and she wasn't sure she'd really saved anyone.

But.

She looked up to see the super staring at her, hand outstretched, the smile already turning.

"Sorry, Ma'am." She handed back the phone.

"I've had Assistant Chief Constable Carghillie on the phone this morning, offering me congratulations on the basis of this article. He asked me to pass them on to you."

"Thank you, Ma'am." Nina suppressed a grin. Little Joe, as the six-foot-six ACC Joseph Carghillie was known, was something of a legend in the force.

"Anyway, Nina. Back to work. I'll be talking to your DI."

"Thanks, Ma'am."

"Not about you. About this Mulcaster business. Appalling."

Nina watched the super walk away.

CHAPTER EIGHTY

"You're handling this investigation like an amateur, DI Finch."

Zoe sat in the passenger sea of Aaron's car, listening to Fiona shout at the other end of the phone.

"Ma'am, I—" she said.

"No, DI Finch. I explicitly told you it was a bad idea to release the man. And now he's been attacked."

Aaron had filled her in on the details after they'd left the community centre, or at least on what Nina had been able to tell him while she'd been inside. A section of the mob had broken off from the march towards North Shore Road to divert two miles south and drag Mulcaster out of his kitchen, where he'd been heating a can of soup.

He'd been left lying in the street with a *PREVRET* sign around his neck and a head injury. He was now in a ward in West Cumberland, unconscious. No one seemed to know if or when he'd be conscious again.

"With respect, Ma'am," Zoe said when she finally got a word in, "if there was a leak, then it didn't come from my team.

It was my team that found out about the leak. I told you about it, and you informed Uniform, who passed it on to Mulcaster. He could have sought protection if he'd wanted it. We're not to blame here."

Silence. Zoe exchanged glances with Aaron. Any attempt she'd been making at maintaining a professional distance was shot to pieces now.

"Not directly, Detective Inspector, no." Fiona's voice was icy. "But if you'd wrapped this case up..."

Zoe sighed, listening to the super tell her how different things would be if she'd found Daria Petrescu's killer by now. It seemed that all the woes of the town were to be laid at Zoe's feet.

But Zoe wasn't listening. Instead she was replaying the conversation with Inaya about the trainers, and trying to work out why it felt so important.

At last, Fiona stopped shouting. Zoe hung up, relieved but knowing she hadn't heard the end of it. She still wasn't sure why the trainers were relevant.

But she'd crack it eventually.

CHAPTER EIGHTY-ONE

ZOE KEPT FISHING FOR IT, like a tooth that needed a trip to the dentist.

She sat behind her desk, closed her eyes, and tried to think back. It had been in Nina's report, whatever it was. Phrases she hadn't got, local dialect she'd thought at first. But it had just been the language of youth, something Nina understood, something Nicholas would have understood. But that Zoe didn't stand a chance with.

It wasn't coming. She'd distract herself.

She started by calling Olivia Bagsby: number unobtainable, still. Then she dialled Jake Frimpton.

"Zoe," he said. "Good to hear from you. Did you read my piece about last night's trouble?"

"Sorry, Jake. I haven't had a chance. I hope we came out of it well."

"Very well. Your DC Kapoor is building a bit of a name for herself."

"Good. Thanks. Look," she said. "Can I pick your brain? This planning application."

"What planning application?"

"The Mosque development. It was at the centre of the trouble, the site. What do you think are the chances of the application going through?"

"Until this week," he replied, "hardly anyone knew about it. Not a great deal of local interest, for or against. I know it's close to the town centre, but it's not *close* close, is it?"

"So you think there's a chance it'll be passed?"

"I dunno. The only people with any real interest in it, apart from those putting it forward, will be Conway Homes."

"Conway Homes?" Zoe asked.

"Sinead Conway. She's got a development going up in the area. If the Mosque doesn't get built, she'll want the land. She doesn't need it, but you know what those property people are like."

Zoe remembered the signs up near the community centre – Conway Homes – on a scrap of wasteland between the railway and the sea.

"What's she like, this Sinead Conway?" she asked. "Local, is she?"

"No," Jake told her. "I met her once, briefly. Seemed pleasant enough. Irish, I think, although I might just be guessing from the name. You free for a drink later this week?"

She laughed. "Wish I was. It's work, and when it isn't work, it's this bloody charity auction on Thursday."

"Whitehaven Golf Club?"

"Yes, why?"

"I'll see you there."

At least there would be one friendly face.

"Thanks, Jake. That's good news, at least."

Zoe went back to thinking about Nina's report. Where had she been reading it?

She closed her eyes and went through it. She'd been at home, in the...

She had it.

She stood up and grabbed her jacket.

Hurrying to the car, she checked her phone. Two missed calls. One from Aaron, one from Fiona.

Aaron first.

"Are you in your office, boss?" he asked.

"Just off checking something. I won't be long. Listen, do you know anything about Sinead Conway?"

"Name isn't familiar."

"Conway Homes."

"Oh, that I know. Well, I've seen the signs. And they've done a few small developments around the area. But that's all I know about them. Is everything OK?"

"Yes, I think so."

"Only you left without telling anyone where you were going, and the super's been up asking where you are..."

Zoe pushed down irritation. "I'm fine, Aaron. Between the three of you, I want someone updating the case notes, someone chasing the lab for an update on the DNA, someone trying to find out where this orange bloody jumper came from, and if we can't identify who it was that got Mulcaster, I want to know how they found out. Where did the leak come from? We need something, Aaron."

"Got it, boss."

Zoe turned into the estate her new house sat in. There was yet another missed call from Fiona. This time, the super had left a voicemail.

"Where are you, Zoe? I was expecting to see you when you got back, but I understand you've disappeared again. It would be good practice to inform your team of your whereabouts..."

Zoe glanced at the phone in its holder, half-wishing she hadn't listened. But Fiona had more to say.

"I understand from a little birdie that you were in Workington yesterday morning. Near the port. Now, where you go in your investigations is, of course, entirely up to you, but don't forget that Ralph doesn't want us stepping on his toes. Do come and see me when you're back."

Zoe turned into her road, running over Fiona's words, and the leads they had – or didn't have. She looked ahead, realising she was on autopilot.

She frowned.

What was Carl's car doing in their drive?

CHAPTER EIGHTY-TWO

"I've got your number, Detective Sergeant," Stella told Aaron.

"Sorry?" he asked.

"I mean, if I have news, I'll tell you. You don't need to chase me. The DNA's still being tested. If there are any matches on the system, I'll phone you and text you and if you want, I'll hire an aeroplane to fly over the police station announcing the news. But until then—"

"Understood, Stella. Speak later."

Stella Berry spoke like that to everyone. Didn't she?

Aaron brought up the case folder and added the latest: nothing from Stella, nothing on Mulcaster's attackers or the petrol bombers or the murderer. A lot of nothing. He shook his head and went back to the beginning, reading everything, looking for things that had been missed, leads that hadn't been followed.

There were none that he could see.

Tom was working on the orange and white jumper,

muttering in frustration. His phone rang. He listened for a moment then stood up.

Aaron looked up. "Everything alright?"

"That was Harriett. There's been a fight. Reports of a fight. Warehouse in Arrowthwaite."

Aaron knew the industrial park there, towering high above the town centre.

"What's that got to do with us?" he asked. "Surely Uniform can deal with that sort of thing?"

"It's looking like a racist incident. Bunch of people turned up, not employees or anything, just to cause trouble."

"OK. Thanks, Tom." Aaron grabbed his jacket from the back of his chair. "Which one of you is coming with me?"

Nina stood up and Tom stayed put: no surprise there.

"Come on then, Nina," Aaron said, "you can drive." Then he remembered that driving with Nina meant he'd have to listen to Elvis.

At least it would be a short drive.

CHAPTER EIGHTY-THREE

"CARL?" Zoe called as she opened the door. "Are you here?"

"In the living room."

She walked in to find him lying on the sofa, the TV quietly stuck on that same news channel. He wasn't watching. She wasn't even sure he'd been awake.

"Carl?" She sat down next to him. She'd seen Carl looking tired before. But now he looked more than tired.

He looked defeated.

"What are you doing here?" she asked.

He shrugged.

"What?" She put a hand on his arm.

He stared ahead, up at the ceiling. "Taken off the case."

"What case?"

He sat up. "You know I can't tell you that." He pulled in a long breath. "They called me at half seven and told me not to come in today."

"Not to come in today?"

"Oh, don't worry. They'll have something new for me tomorrow. Plenty of dodgy coppers to go round, aren't there?"

"How should I know?" She pulled back her hand.

Carl looked at her at last. "I'm sorry." He sat up and put his arms around her. "It's not your fault."

"Of course it's not my fault. Why would it be my fault?"

He shrugged.

Zoe pulled away. "What aren't you telling me, Carl?"

"I'm sure it's nothing."

"If it's nothing then you might as well say it out loud."

Her phone vibrated in her pocket. She ignored it.

"Aren't you going to answer that?" Carl asked.

"No," she replied.

That look returned. Defeat.

"They just said the wrong people had been asking questions," he said. "Said someone had been sticking her nose where it—"

"'Her'? They definitely said 'her'?"

Carl nodded. "You're not the only woman in Cumbria, Zoe."

"This is ridiculous." She took a few steps away, then turned and looked him in the eye.

"I know," he said. "Believe me, I know. It's nothing. Forget about it, OK."

"How can I forget about it, Carl? Someone... What, your DCI? Your Super? Someone's suggesting that I'm getting in the way of your investigations, and I'm supposed to just forget about it? Is this Ralph Streeting? Is it something to do with him?"

Carl shook his head. "Streeting doesn't have any authority over PSD. Look, it's inevitable, isn't it? When you've got relationships between coppers, and one of them does the job I do, then every now and then the paths are going to cross."

"This case you've been taken off. Was it someone on my team?"

"You know I can't tell you—"

"Was it someone on my team?" she repeated.

"No," he said. "No."

Her phone buzzed again and this time, she checked it. Aaron. He could wait.

"Look, Zoe. This isn't about you, OK? Or your team. It really isn't."

"When you say things about someone sticking her nose in—"

He walked to her and put his arms on her shoulders. He stared into her eyes. "It's not about you."

Zoe watched him disappear into the kitchen.

"D'you want a coffee?" he called.

Coffee? She couldn't think about coffee.

But she had to. This kind of thing would keep happening. Carl could never tell her what he was working on. And there would be times when...

She shook her head. She'd come here for a reason. Might as well get on with it.

She found the chest of drawers, dug through it, and pulled out Nina's report.

"Here you are." Carl was back with the coffee.

"Put it on the table." Zoe gestured with her head.

"Of course." He sounded wounded.

But she had it.

She looked up.

"Trainers," she said. "Shoes."

"Huh?"

She looked back down at the report, at a passage she'd circled, meaning to ask Nina what it meant.

They discussed their failure to loot a shoe shop, and refer-enced expensive trainers worn by Goldie and Plumber.

Goldie and Plumber. Rappers, she'd thought. Or YouTu-bers. But then she'd forgotten about it, because whatever it was, it wasn't important. Not then.

It might be important now.

Zeps, Inaya had said. Zoe pulled out her phone and looked them up. Expensive. Limited stock, and only available from the more high-end shops. Huge white sole, an upper that was mostly solid black with thin white lines down the sides and a lime green band in the middle.

She found the CCTV image she'd shown Inaya and zoomed. The shape was unusual.

And yes, it was a match.

Two of the figures in the video were wearing Zeps.

CHAPTER EIGHTY-FOUR

THE WAREHOUSE WAS IN ARROWTHWAITE, near the site of the old mine and just off Solway Road, which rang a bell. Aaron had told Nina to slow down half a dozen times on the short drive and made her turn the Elvis down, if not off.

She parked behind two police vans and an unmarked car.

Men were climbing into one of the vans, five of them. As Aaron and Nina got out of the car, the men turned and started shouting racist insults. The kind that Aaron thought had gone out before he'd been born.

He sensed Nina slowing as they passed the van. He shot her a warning look but she walked on anyway. *Well done, Nina.*

A woman was coming out of the main entrance, walking towards them: Tracy Giller-Jones. Aaron felt his heart sink.

"DS Keyes. DC Kapoor." Giller-Jones stopped and looked down at them.

"DS Giller-Jones," he replied.

"Out for a jaunt?"

"We were called in," he told her.

"This is my crime scene, Aaron." She smiled. Aaron didn't like it when Tracy Giller-Jones smiled.

"We'll see, Tracy." He continued walking.

The manager was a white man in his fifties, who looked confused. "I already spoke to another detective."

"Sorry," said Aaron. "We'll try not to keep you. Could you run through what happened again?"

The man gave him a peevish look. "No idea who they are, not from round here. They turned up during a shift break."

"How many of them?" Nina asked.

"A dozen, maybe? They stood outside, didn't try to get in. Shouting abuse, they were."

"And you called the police," Aaron said.

"We waited a bit. Then Dave – the shift supervisor – stuck his head out and asked them to leave. Politely, like. One of the buggers threw a rock at his head." He looked between Aaron and Nina. "*That* was when I called the police."

"Anything else we should know?"

"A couple of my lads went out there, just to try and break it up." He looked Aaron in the eye. "Not their fault. There were a couple of scuffles. Nothing serious."

"Thanks," Aaron said.

"Did you recognise any of the men in that van?" he asked Nina.

She shook her head.

Aaron turned back to the manager. "Have you got an employee called Ibrahim Bashir?"

"Yeah, I do. Not in today, though. He worked last night. Why? Is he in trouble too?"

"Not that I know of."

"Coz," continued the manager, "you can't tell with that lot, right?"

The manager looked at Aaron, then Nina, grinning. His grin turned to a look of horror.

"I mean, teenagers, you know. I didn't mean... You know I meant teenagers, right? You know what they're like, Officers?"

"They're usually perfectly pleasant, to be honest," said Nina. "The main problem tends to be middle-aged white men who think they're better than everyone else."

Aaron suppressed a smile. He should stop her.

He didn't.

"So if you come across anyone like that," she continued, "do please keep an eye on them."

She turned and walked out. Aaron followed.

Back in the car, he remembered where he'd heard about Solway Road. It was where Mick Halfpenny lived.

"You need to calm down," he said to Nina. "You handled that well, but getting yourself wound up won't help anyone."

She stopped the car on double yellows. She turned to him, her face hard.

"With respect, Sarge, that's easy for you to say. You don't understand what it's like, though."

"Really?"

"If you'd faced the sort of prejudice I've faced..."

She stopped, realising what she was saying to a black gay police officer.

"I'm sorry," she said.

Aaron laughed. Nina joined in. Horns sounded behind them.

He shook his head. "Sorry, Nina, but that was priceless."

CHAPTER EIGHTY-FIVE

ZOE ENTERED the team room at the same time as Aaron and Nina, noticing that Nina was chuckling. She flashed Aaron a look but he said nothing.

Tom was inside already. As they entered, he straightened with the guilty look she'd noticed when someone caught him behind a computer screen.

"Have you found anything, Tom?" she asked.

"Nothing on the jumper, boss. But the trouble last night, yes. More videos. And I've traced the way the accounts interact with each other. There's one that's running the show. They post something, and the others take it up."

He pointed to the big screen, and the account. The Knights of Whitehaven.

"That's one of the ones I saw," said Nina.

Tom nodded. "Yep, I read your notes. Anyway, look at this."

He scrolled down and highlighted a tweet.

Don't allow them to take over. Meet in town to #MarchOn-TheMosque – details to follow.

He clicked on the hashtag, and a dozen tweets appeared.

"These are all from the night before last. They use similar words, but not identical. They all use that hashtag. And that's the first time it's been used."

He showed two more examples, then clicked through to the website linked in the account bio.

"It's a single page. Not much more than a blog, but they haven't used any of the usual blogging platforms. They probably knew they'd be kicked off. It's more of the same stuff, but here's the thing, it predates the murder."

"What?" said Zoe.

"It predates the murder. Here's a post from eight days ago, telling people to protest against the expansion of the community centre. Here's one a few weeks before that with a link to the planning application, suggesting people send in their objections."

"So," she said, "this wasn't a response to the murder at all. It's being made to *look* like a response to the murder, but it started before." She folded her arms. "Let's see these videos."

The same man, the same balaclava, the same sort of message. The specific lines – the one that had included the word *kafir* and the one about the knife – they'd already seen. The rest were all general, and the sort of thing you could find on a million social media posts: *they're* taking over; *they're* not like us; *they* want to kill our women.

"Watch those videos," Zoe told Tom. "Try to isolate details. The clothes, the voices, the room, background noises. Anything that might tell us who this is."

Tom nodded and returned his focus to his screen.

"Nina," Zoe said, "I want to ask you about your report."

She'd put it on the table near the board. She picked it up now, and a look of recognition passed over Nina's face.

"Tell me about these trainers," Zoe said.

Nina frowned. "I'm sorry?"

Zoe opened the report. "The trainers. I need to know what they said. If you can remember, *exactly* what they said."

Nina was trying to read the words upside down. Aaron watched, puzzled.

"Here." Zoe put the report on Nina's desk. Nina bent to read the page she'd turned to. She read out a line.

"They discussed their failure to loot a shoe shop, and referenced expensive trainers worn by Goldie and Plumber."

Nina turned to Zoe. "I remember this. It was... I can't remember who said what, but I think it was Davey and Mal."

"Yes?"

Nina shut her eyes. "Yes." She opened them. "I knew roughly what they were talking about because my little cousin's been going on about these things."

"Things?"

"The trainers. Zeps. Mal was messing around, trying to wind me up, complaining he hadn't got the chance to smash up a shop that night. The night it all happened."

Zoe nodded.

"He was just taking the piss, really. Sorry, boss."

"What's this about?" Aaron asked.

Zoe raised a finger, her gaze on Nina. "It's OK, Nina. Carry on."

"So Davey laughed at him. He said, *You might wanna prance about like Goldie and Plumber, but you wouldn't get a pair of Zeps if you robbed every box in Shoe Zone.*"

"Shoe Zone?" Zoe asked.

"It's a shop. In town."

"And they sell these Zeps there?"

"No, boss. I think that was the joke. They're trendy.

Expensive. People round here don't tend to wear gear like that."

Zoe frowned. "OK. But Goldie and Plumber? Who are they? Rappers or something?"

"No idea, boss."

Zoe considered. "But this conversation, they're saying that Goldie and Plumber, whoever they are, they have these trainers, right? These Zeps?"

"Yes, boss. But I'm not sure—"

"OK, Nina. I want you to go and have a word with them. Davey, was it? Mal, Jay, whoever you have to speak to, find out who Goldie and Plumber are."

Nina stared at Zoe. She looked like she was about to object. Then she spotted Aaron giving her a nod.

"Got it, boss," she said, stood up, and walked out.

CHAPTER EIGHTY-SIX

"Everything alright?" Aaron asked. "The trainers?"

Zoe sniffed, thinking. "It might be nothing. Let's see what Nina comes up with."

He nodded. "The warehouse we just went to. It's near Solway Road, where Mick Halfpenny lives."

"The history buff?"

"That's him. It's just... It might be connected. Probably not."

Zoe put a hand on the desk next to him. "Tell me."

"Mick said there was a warehouse keeping him awake at night. It's the only one on the site. And Ibrahim works there." He looked at her. "Why would it be so loud at night?"

"The council would put a lid on that, I imagine."

Aaron nodded. "I don't think Ibrahim's involved, but..."

She pursed her lips. "Run a check on him. It's probably nothing."

"Yeah." He fired up his computer and ran Ibrahim's name through the system.

Nothing of interest; nothing at all, in fact.

"What about Mick Halfpenny?" he muttered.

"What's your thinking?" Zoe asked.

"I'm not sure."

Zoe leaned over and watched him change the name to Mick Halfpenny. A host of hits appeared: local newspaper articles, tours of the town, comment pieces. Posing with a couple of councillors. At a business forum. Talking about the heritage of the Cumbrian coastline, alongside a striking dark-haired woman. Sinead Conway, of Conway Homes.

"That's the company that wants to develop the land near the community centre," said Zoe.

Aaron nodded and looked up. Tom was staring at his screen, intent on the videos and the social media posts. Nina was still out.

He returned to the searches, finding seven separate occasions on which Mick Halfpenny and Sinead Conway had been photographed together or mentioned in the same article.

"OK." Zoe placed her phone on Aaron's desk, hit speaker, and dialled.

"Jake Frimpton, Whitehaven Chronicle."

"Jake, it's Zoe. I've got my DS with me, Aaron Keyes. I was wondering if you could tell me anything more about this Sinead Conway."

"Not really," replied Jake. "Like I said, she's not local. But she lives locally, been around a few years, done some small estates. Bracklington's one of hers, not far from your place."

"She linked to anyone in particular?" asked Zoe.

Jake laughed. "She's a property developer, she's linked to everyone. Politicians, business, you know what they're like."

"Myron Carter?"

Aaron tensed beside her.

"They've probably met," said Jake. "I think they're part of

the same business advisory group for the council. Pretty sure I've seen them together at some event or other."

"Thanks, Jake." Zoe drummed a fingertip on the desk. "Do me a favour, will you? If you hear anything about her, anything of interest, let me know, will you?"

"Sure. Tell you what, I'll have a dig through the archives," replied Jake.

"Thanks." She hung up.

"I don't—" began Aaron.

Zoe eyed him. "It's OK, Aaron. It's just Jake Frimpton. Don't worry."

CHAPTER EIGHTY-SEVEN

Nina watched Mal McDonald's mum give him a slap as he slunk past her out of the house. "What the fuck you been up to this time?"

"Nothing, Mum." Mal looked at Nina, who hadn't even stepped away from her car. He ambled along the path and she opened the back door for him to get in.

As she walked to the driver's door she heard his mum mutter, "That fucking dickhead."

"What is it this time?" he asked as they drove.

"Just a little chat," she replied. "Me, you, and maybe one or two of your friends."

In the rear-view mirror, she saw his jaw clench.

"I mean your actual friends, Mal. Not people you owe money to."

He relaxed. She stifled a laugh.

On Foxhouses Road, Davey answered the buzzer after a minute, smiling like he was expecting someone else. Dealer or girlfriend?

"What is it this time?" he asked.

Nina pointed to the car, to Mal, waving from the back seat. Davey sighed and joined them.

"I've got some questions," she said, still parked up.

"Why should we tell you anything?" replied Davey.

"Because you might be a piece of shit, Davey Grant, but you're not a murderer, and you're not the sort that wouldn't help the police when they're trying to catch one."

"Eh?" asked Davey.

"I think," Mal said, "she's trying to say she likes us."

"I like you more than I like whoever butchered that girl at the marina," Nina said. "And if the feeling's mutual, you'll want to help me."

"You lot got our mate beaten half to death," said Davey, his expression sullen. He kept glancing out of the window, towards the road. Dealer or girlfriend, he'd have some explaining to do if they saw him in the back of a CID vehicle.

"Your mate?" she asked.

"Rich Madsen. Remember?"

Nina raised an eyebrow. "No such person."

"What?" asked Mal.

"He lied to you. Sorry, lads. Even his girlfriend didn't know his real name."

She watched the surprise on their faces. So they hadn't known about the girlfriend either.

"I'm betting none of you knew he was out on probation, or what he'd been in for, so I'm not sure he's earned your loyalty. And anyway, it's not him I want to talk to you about. It's Goldie and Plumber."

"What?" they said together.

"You mentioned them in the station. Something about robbing shoes, and Zeps. Davey, you mentioned those two names. Goldie and Plumber. Who are they?"

The two of them exchanged looks. Nina waited.

"Just a couple of dickheads," said Davey. "Posh kids. Wankers."

"Local?"

"Yeah. Goldie's actually called Charles Bexley. Wears chunky gold bracelets like that fella from The A-Team, remember?"

"I'm not fifty, Davey."

"He's a prat, anyway. The other one's Adrian Hargreaves."

"That's Plumber?"

Davey nodded.

"Why's he called Plumber?"

"His dad's a plumber."

"That's it?"

"Well, yeah. I mean, he's got a big business, loads of people working for him. But he's a plumber. Why do you want to know about these two? They killed her?"

Nina shook her head. "It's not that. These trainers. Zeps. Do these two, Goldie and Plumber, do they wear them?"

"Yeah," said Davey.

She turned to Mal in the back.

He nodded. "Never stop going on about them. Wankers."

"Wankers," agreed Davey.

CHAPTER EIGHTY-EIGHT

Aaron looked up as the boss walked into the team room. "Tom, Nina's on her way back. I want the two of you to carry on working on this jumper, and keep an eye on the social media feeds. Aaron, I'd like you to come with me."

"Again?"

She eyed him. He looked downwards. She said nothing, but turned away.

What now? It was bound to involve the Port of Workington. Myron bloody Carter.

"Yes, boss," Tom said.

"Good. I want to see some results. We'll be in touch."

The DI led Aaron to her car and gave him a smile as he buckled in.

"We're not going to see Carter, don't worry. I just want to take a look at that spot again. Where we saw Olivia Bagsby. And see if there's anywhere else that offers a decent view."

Aaron knew there wouldn't be, but he also knew she wouldn't be deterred.

"There's something else, though," she said. "I've been told

not to investigate the port, or anyone linked to it. Told to steer clear of organised crime, basically. Someone else's turf. Which would be fine, except when it crosses into my turf."

"So you're making a point?"

They left the police station. The roads were quiet.

"I want them to see me," the DI said. "Ralph Streeting and his people. I want it to get back to the super, so I can explain to her that I'm trying to solve this crime."

"You're engineering a showdown?" Aaron wasn't sure that was a good idea.

She shrugged. "I'm just telling you to give you the choice. You can stay in the car, sit it out. I can drop you somewhere else, come back and pick you up, I can—"

"No."

"No?" She glanced at him. He stared ahead at the road, wishing she'd do the same.

"No," he repeated. "I'm with you on this, boss."

"Thanks. As long as you know what you're getting into."

He swallowed. "I want to find out who killed Daria Petrescu."

She smiled. "So do I."

CHAPTER EIGHTY-NINE

Tom was fed up.

They were getting nowhere on the Knights of Whitehaven, and the jumper was a dead end. He knew exactly how many of them had been manufactured, but it wasn't like that was any help.

There was good news though: he'd called the hospital and discovered that Mulcaster was out of danger, and conscious. The PC with him hadn't been able to get him to say who'd beaten him up, though.

"I don't really care who did it," said Nina.

He stared at her. "What?"

"It'll just be a bunch of thugs, won't it? We won't get any evidence, and even if we do, it'll be a few months inside for one or two of them and the rest'll get away with it."

Tom felt his shoulders slump. "True."

"What I want to know is, who leaked?" Nina said. "How did they know who he was and where he lived?"

"Ilkley might have some idea."

Nina sat up. "Why?"

He sighed. "There was talk about the dungeon. The sarge said something about it. He looked worried."

"Worried, how?"

"I don't know. It's nothing. Don't worry about it."

"Right." Nina stood up and marched out of the room.

Shit. He shouldn't have said anything.

Tom returned to his screen. He'd messaged Romania about Daria Petrescu. Anything was better than looking for a jumper no sane person would dream of wearing.

While he waited to hear back, an idea occurred to him.

The website: Knights of Whitehaven. It would be registered with ICANN. Or at least, it should be.

He brought up the WHOIS website and typed in the address. While he waited for it to search, he looked at the door.

Nina was down there, having a go at Ilkley.

Nina could handle herself. She'd stood up to those thugs the other night.

But those thugs weren't Ilkley.

He sighed, glanced at his screen – still processing – and stood up. Nina needed his help.

CHAPTER NINETY

THE CAR PARK near the not-quite-lighthouse was almost full. Bike racks on all the cars; some kind of cycling meet.

Zoe slung her bag over her shoulder and strode towards the point and the tiny lighthouse, Aaron a few steps behind her.

She climbed the single flight of metal steps and walked around the upper level. A low haze lay across the sea to their west, while to the east it was clear, a good view of the rooftops and the hills beyond them. If you had a telephoto lens, you could see inside the port.

But what had Olivia Bagsby seen? Women, a minibus, maybe even Daria Petrescu among them. If Zoe could get hold of those photos...

She fished in her bag for binoculars. Carl had bought them when she'd landed the job and agreed to move up here. Something to do with birdwatching or taking in the views.

She raised them to her eyes and adjusted the focus. She could see men, cranes, boats, forklifts, and warehouses. More boxes than she could count. None of it meant a thing to her.

"Sod this," she said.

Aaron stiffened beside her. She turned to him.

"You're not from here, are you? Elterwater, was it?"

"Yes, boss."

"Is it nicer there?"

He screwed up his face. "I suppose so."

"I've been here a week," she said, "and I'm feeling hemmed in already. There's the sea on one side and the hills on the other, and in the middle there's us, and a bunch of crooks, sex offenders, and racists. Please tell me there's more to it than that."

"There is." His eyes crinkled.

"Good. Hopefully, I'll get a chance to see it." She sighed and looked back at the port. It was tempting to ask him if they could take a detour, but there was too much to do. Too much pressure from all sides.

"Come on," she said. "Let's go back."

CHAPTER NINETY-ONE

TOO LATE, thought Tom.

Nina was at the desk, talking to Clive Moor, her expression a snarl, her voice low. Tom approached, hoping the half dozen or so officers in the custody suite weren't listening.

Clive stood up. "How fucking dare you?"

His voice was level, but it carried. Everyone in the room fell silent and turned towards them.

"How fucking dare you?" He shook his head, gaze on Nina. "I know I take the piss a bit, but how dare you accuse me of leaking to the press."

"Not the pre—"

"I take my job very seriously, NIna. And if anyone else doesn't, and I find out about it, I come down on them like the angel of fucking death. Now, if you're planning on making a formal accusation, you'd better get on with it. And if you're not, you'd better explain what the hell you're playing at coming down here making this sort of allegation."

Nina retreated, mumbling apologies.

Tom stepped past her to the desk. "She didn't mean it."

"I should think fucking not." Ilkley gave him a look that would melt steel and sat down. Behind them Tom could hear the Uniforms talking.

He turned.

"Served the fucker right," said a voice Tom didn't recognise. "Nonces get knives."

Laughter.

"Who sa—" Nina began.

Tom shook his head. "No."

She sighed, but turned and stalked away.

As Tom followed her up the stairs, he heard Ilkley's voice.

"That woman might have got me wrong, but she's got bigger balls than the lot of you."

The sniggering and chatter stopped.

Tom looked up. Nina had rounded the corner to the first floor and wouldn't have heard. *Shame.*

Back in the team room, she was in her chair, shoulders shaking. As he entered, she stopped shaking.

"I'll tell you what," she said. "That wasn't a complete waste of time."

"No?"

She shook her head. "While I was talking shit to Clive Moor, I spotted a couple of names on the custody sheet. Charles Bexley and Adrian Hargreaves. Better known as Goldie and Plumber."

CHAPTER NINETY-TWO

"Do you want to see some of it?" Aaron asked as they got back into Zoe's car.

She looked at him. "See some of it?"

He nodded. "Cumbria is beautiful. It's sad that you've only seen" – he gestured outside the car – "well, this."

She smiled. "We don't exactly have a lot of spare time."

"I'll just take you on a detour. Won't take long."

She eyed him. "OK."

"Right," he said. "I'll take you up via Branthwaite Edge. The roads are narrow though. You'll need to take care."

She stifled a laugh. "You think I'm a boy racer, don't you?"

He said nothing.

"I'll take it easy, Aaron. You direct me."

He directed her away from the port and out of Workington. As they reached the A595 he told her to turn left.

"That's the wrong way."

"Trust me."

Zoe shrugged and turned left. Moments later he pointed out a right-hand turn signposted to Branthwaite.

The road was bordered by hedges, but up ahead she could see mountains, and the sky had widened out. Zoe felt herself breathing again.

The sun was low in her rear-view mirror, and the sky was darkening.

As they approached a right-hand turn, her phone pinged.

She glanced down: three missed calls, two from Fiona, and one from Jake Frimpton.

Damn.

Jake had left a voicemail.

"I'll play it," said Aaron. "You keep your eyes on the road."

The road they were on was only wide enough for one car. Zoe gripped the wheel tighter. He had a point.

"Hi, Zoe," Jake said. "I've been digging through the archives, looking into Sinead Conway, and I've found something that might interest you. You mentioned Mick Halfpenny. I've got a photo of the two of them together. Like I say, she's the sort of person that knows everyone, but I've sent you the photo anyway, just in case."

Aaron ended the message and Zoe glanced at the info screen. There was a text.

"I want to see this," she said.

"There are no passing places that I can see."

She checked her mirrors. "There's nothing around. I'll stop."

She pulled over, the Mini still taking up most of the road. It was a straight section: any cars approaching would see them in time. She grabbed her phone and opened Jake's attachment.

It was a photo. Sinead Conway, a mass of dark hair coiled around her shoulders like a snake. Standing beside her was a man with curly hair, wearing thick red-framed glasses. He looked like a kids' TV show host.

"That's Mick?" she asked Aaron.

He nodded, his eyes wide.

She felt her pulse pick up.

It wasn't the fact that Mick Halfpenny was in the photo that had made Aaron's eyes widen.

It was the jumper Mick Halfpenny was wearing.

The orange and white argyle jumper.

CHAPTER NINETY-THREE

"The jumper," Aaron said.

Zoe nodded. "We need to get back." She looked at him as she started the car. "How do we turn round? We don't have time for the scenic route."

Aaron looked ahead, then turned in his seat. "There's nowhere to turn. We'll have to keep going."

"No." She squinted in her rear-view mirror. "We need to take the main road."

She could hear his breathing, slow and steady. Was he humouring her?

"We need to go straight on, boss. Have you got satnav?"

"Yes. But I was hoping your local knowledge might be of more use."

"I'm pretty sure there's a turnoff about a mile ahead that'll get us back to the main road." He looked at her. "To be honest, it's probably quicker going the way I was planning."

"Fine," Zoe said. She still hadn't started moving. She was trying to decide if she could turn in this narrow lane. The road was tight, but her car was small. And she knew from the times she'd manoeuvred it around Birmingham that it had a tight turning circle.

"I'm turning around," she said.

"If you're sure..."

"Yes." She turned to look behind them, throwing her arm over Aaron's seat to get a better angle.

"Shit," she said.

"What?"

"Is that a car behind us?"

He turned to follow her gaze. It was almost dark; there wasn't much to see. "What the...?"

Zoe placed her hand on the centre of the steering wheel and hit the horn.

Something was advancing on them, a dark shape. No headlights.

"Have they seen us?" Aaron asked.

Zoe said nothing. Instead she continued leaning on the horn.

Right. Move.

She hit the accelerator with her foot. It slid off.

Focus, Zoe. Concentrate.

All she had to do was drive.

She hit the accelerator again. The car jolted forward, just as light filled the Mini.

The vehicle behind had turned on its lights, full beam, and was almost on them.

She yanked the wheel to the left, sending the Mini into a ditch. She yelled.

"Down, Aaron! Get down!"

CHAPTER NINETY-FOUR

Nina watched Tom's face crack into a smile.

"Better see what they've been arrested for," she said.

"Sure," Tom replied. "Want to go and ask your new best friend Ilkley?"

She laughed.

"I'll go," he said.

As he left the room she turned to her screen, already bored of the dead ends she knew she'd find. There was a beep from Tom's desk.

She looked over. His screen was dead, but she knew his password, and when she'd woken it, she saw what the notification was about. WHOIS. One of his endless internet hunts.

She opened it anyway. A response to a WHOIS request on the Knights of Whitehaven website. As if the sort of person who'd run a site like that would give their real name.

She scrolled down. The site was, supposedly, run by 'Whitey Whitehaven', operating from an address on Winder Grove. Windup Grove, more like. She emailed the information to herself, shaking her head.

She was back on social media digging through the rumours about Mulcaster when Tom returned.

"You've met them, I think," he said.

"Met who?"

"Our Baxter and Hargreaves. Goldie and Plumber."

"Have I?"

"Your trip to the warehouse, earlier. With the sarge. Weren't there some lads who gave you grief while they were being nicked?"

"Nothing out of the ordinary."

"Baxter and Hargreaves were among them. That's why they're here. Chucked some rocks, threw a few punches, them and a bunch of their mates."

CHAPTER NINETY-FIVE

"Aaron?" Zoe said.

"I'm OK."

She could hear him moving, checking himself for injury. She took a moment to do the same.

"Me too," she said.

Her eyes were beginning to adjust to the gloom, but not enough to see where they were.

"What happened?" he asked. He sounded strained, tense.

"You sure you're OK?"

"Yes." His voice cleared. "Yes, boss. Just a bit of a shock. That's all."

Zoe reached forward, found the key, turned it. Nothing. She reached up for the internal light switch, found it, and pushed. Nothing again. The car was at an angle, front wheels in the ditch.

"Someone came straight for us," she said. "No lights, then suddenly full beam right at us. I managed to steer to the right, and they went by. Didn't hit us. But the car's not happy."

She released her belt, then reached over and did the same for Aaron.

"Thanks, boss." His voice shook. "That... That can't have been an accident."

"I know." Zoe felt something pressing into her leg. She reached down and was relieved to find her phone. She tapped the bottom of the screen.

Nothing.

She pushed the button on the side. Held it in. Still nothing.

She ran her fingers over the screen and felt bumps and ridges where there should have been smooth glass.

"OK, Aaron. The car's dead, we've got no light, and my phone's smashed. Is yours OK?"

A moment's fumbling, and then, blessedly, she saw a square of light to her left.

"Yes, boss. But no signal."

Zoe looked out of her window. There was no sign of another vehicle. But the person who'd driven them off the road might still be around.

And might come back to finish the job.

She reached for the door handle, pulled at it, and pushed the door. It opened an inch or two, then stopped.

"Can you open your door?" she asked. She heard a bang.

"Sorry, boss. I'm in the hedge."

Shit.

"Wait here." Zoe clambered into the back seat. The door behind hers opened fully.

Two minutes later, they were both out on the road and she was waving Aaron's phone at her car, checking it for damage.

The side panels had scratches and dents and the bonnet was dented. There seemed to be bits of car sticking out where they weren't supposed to be.

My poor car. It was a link with Birmingham, with her dad...

Get a grip. It was a car.

"Let's walk," she said. The road was quiet, no sign of the other car. Whoever it was, they thought they'd done the job.

She hoped.

They walked in silence, Aaron's phone switched off to conserve battery. It felt like she could hear every owl, every gust of wind, every unaccountable noise in Cumbria.

After fifteen minutes they stopped. Aaron checked his phone: a signal. He dialled the office.

"Tom," he said. "The boss and I have been in a car accident. Branthwaite Edge." He gave him a WhatThreeWords reference. "Can you send Uniform out to pick us up?"

He hung up. "We'll have to stay put."

Zoe nodded and settled in for the wait.

They chatted, avoiding talk of the case for once. He asked her about Birmingham, what it was like to work in a city. He talked about his experience as a copper coming out in an area like this, how he'd decided to take up mixed martial arts, just in case. She smiled and told him about her black belt in karate. He asked about her family and she gave him just the lightest of details: Nicholas at university, parents no longer around. She didn't talk about her mum's alcoholism and neglect, or her dad's long illness. Her dad's job at the Leyland factory in Longbridge, then the Austin factory, the inspiration for her beloved Mini...

It was nearly half an hour before they heard the first car. They moved to the edge of the road and crouched down, watching.

As it drew level, Zoe spotted the markings and the logo. She leapt out into the road, Aaron right behind her.

"Hope you're both OK, Ma'am," said the PC, once they

were in. Zoe didn't recognise her. "Your car'll be recovered later tonight. I've got a phone for you."

"Thanks."

"Do you need medical treatment?"

"No. Back to the station, please." Zoe called Carl, just to tell him she'd be late, and then she dialled Nina.

"We're on our way back," she said. "Stay where you are. We've got work to do."

CHAPTER NINETY-SIX

Zoe sipped the coffee Nina had made her, trying not to grimace. It was kind of Nina to do that, but in future she'd offer to make drinks herself.

They were in the team room. Zoe had spoken to Fiona, who'd managed to show concern. She'd heard from Inspector Keane, who'd said his team was at her disposal if she needed them for an arrest. And now it was nearly ten pm, and she was briefing her team.

"Item one," she began. "Bexley and Hargreaves. I want to talk to them."

"They're not your arrests," said Aaron.

"So?" She looked around the room. No one met her gaze. "What? Do I have to make nice with DI Markin if I want to talk to someone he's nicked?"

Aaron shrugged. "Markin doesn't like to share."

"I'll just have to have a chat with the super."

"Markin's the super's blue-eyed boy."

"They're probably out by now," Tom added. "They were in for, what, affray? Not serious enough to keep them in for long."

"OK. We'll park that. Item two. I want to know who forced me off the road."

"You're sure it was deliberate?" asked Nina.

"One hundred per cent," Aaron replied.

"How long will the road be sealed off?" asked Zoe. "What are the investigation protocols?"

More grimaces and shaken heads.

"What is it?"

"The road won't have been shut," Nina told her. "It's the only route in and out of that valley, and the farmers need it even more than the tourists do."

"So, what, life has to go on?"

"Afraid so, boss."

This is ridiculous. Zoe turned away from their stares to gather her thoughts.

If those bastards had killed her Mini....

"Right. Tom, find out what you can, which I presume will be absolutely nothing. Can someone at least go out there in daylight and see if there's anything at all?"

Tom nodded.

"Item three, then. I want someone to bring in Mick Halfpenny."

Nina and Tom both frowned. Zoe pulled out her newly issued phone and showed them the photo. She'd managed to get hold of Jake from the response car and asked him to resend it.

"I should have known," Tom said.

"Was there reason to suspect him?" asked Zoe.

"Not really. But I couldn't think of anyone who could pull off wearing that jumper. He wouldn't pull it off either, but he wouldn't care."

"Remind me," Zoe asked, "what he was doing in town the

night of the murder?"

"It's the warehouse, boss," Aaron said. "The one me and Nina were at this morning, the one Bexley and Hargreaves were arrested at. It's just round the corner from Halfpenny's house. The noise keeps him up at night, so he goes for late-night walks until he's exhausted."

"Right. You can bring him in."

Aaron nodded. "Are we arresting him?"

"Not yet. Just bring him in for a chat. From what you've told me, he sounds like he'll come willingly. Now, item four. Knights of Whitehaven. Keep looking, Tom, Nina. That should be your focus for now. But first, Nina, come with me."

"Where are we going, boss?"

"Well, you might be right, they might be out by now. But they might not. Let's see if we can have a word with Goldie and Plumber, shall we?"

CHAPTER NINETY-SEVEN

ZOE WATCHED the two young men at the custody desk, Tracy Giller-Jones standing behind them. One of them had his arm in the air as he fastened a chunky gold bracelet around it.

"That must be Bexley," whispered Nina.

Zoe approached and tapped Giller-Jones on the shoulder. As she did, she caught a smell. It reminded her of...

The DS spun around like she'd been punched.

"Oh," she said. "It's you, Ma'am."

"Yes, Tracy. Are you releasing these two?"

"Yes, Ma'am."

"Can I have a quick word with them?"

Giller-Jones pursed her lips. "I'll just have to call the DI."

Zoe slumped. She'd thought she would get away with it.

"I'm sorry, Ma'am," Giller-Jones said. She passed Zoe her phone.

"Zoe?"

"Alan."

"I gather you want to talk to Bexley and Hargreaves. Is that right?"

"If you don't mind."

"Oh, I don't mind at all." He chuckled. "But it's not really up to me. You see, we've released them both without charge. We can hardly go harassing innocent members of the public can we, Zoe?"

"No, we can't."

Zoe passed the phone back to Tracy Giller-Jones. The two men stepped away from the desk and towards the exit, where a woman stood waiting for them. A tall woman, with blonde hair and glasses.

Clarissa Bexley. Charles Bexley. The family resemblance was obvious.

Nina looked at Zoe. "Can you smell that, boss?"

Zoe nodded. "It's—"

"Nina?"

Nina turned to see the custody sergeant, Clive Moor, waving at her. She shrugged at Zoe then approached the desk, glancing behind her and to each side as if suspecting a trap.

She bent and spoke quietly with Moor. When she straightened up, she was smiling and her eyes were wide.

Zoe could hear Tracy Giller-Jones, still on the phone. "Yes, boss. They're on their way home now."

Zoe felt someone grab her arm and looked around. Nina.

"Follow me, boss."

Nina turned and ran out of the custody exit, into the car park. Zoe had no choice but to follow.

Nina had caught up with Clarissa Bexley and the two young men. The four of them stood by a new-looking BMW. Clarissa Bexley was sneering, muttering something about harassment.

Nina ignored her, addressing the men.

"I'm arresting you for aggravated arson," she said.

"What?" demanded Clarissa Bexley.

"What?" muttered Zoe.

"With intent," added Nina.

"What do you think you're playing at, Constable?" said Clarissa.

"You do not have to say anything. But it may harm your defence if you do not mention when questioned something that you later rely on in Court. Anything you do say may be given in evidence." Nina paused. "Come with me."

The two men followed her back to the custody suite with Clarissa Bexley shouting behind them, and Zoe trailing a few paces back.

Inside, there was a flurry of voices.

Clarissa Bexley announcing that she would be filing a complaint.

Charles Bexley wearing a sneer a lot like his mother's, telling Nina she had nothing on him. Adrian Hargreaves, looking confused, asking what was going on. Tracy Giller-Jones muttering into her phone.

Nina turned to them, a smile on her face. She leaned towards the younger Bexley, then sniffed loudly.

"Next time you set fire to a place of worship, lads, you might want to think about washing your hands afterwards."

She turned back to Clive Moor and shook the custody sergeant's hand.

CHAPTER NINETY-EIGHT

Aaron parked a moment's walk form Mick Halfpenny's house, within sight of the warehouse. Above the sound of the wind and the waves crashing against the seawall, he could hear the clank and rattle of things being moved, and the shouts of the people moving them. It might be irritating enough to keep someone awake, to drive them out for long night-time walks.

Or they could just shut their window.

Uniform were at the house ahead of him: Roddy Chen standing by the front door, Harriett Barnes approaching, shaking her head.

"There's no one—" she began.

"It's a waste of time, mate. No one here."

Aaron turned to see Tel Cummings approaching from the side of the house.

"I told these two," continued Cummings, jerking his thumb towards Roddy Chen, "to keep an eye while I went round the back. No lights, nothing."

Cummings wasn't anyone's senior officer. Roddy, despite his size, was easy-going enough to do what he was told, and

Harriett was still learning the ropes. Hopefully, given time, she'd realise she didn't have to take orders from the likes of Tel Cummings.

Aaron pulled out his phone and called the DI. "No one here, boss."

"Shit," she muttered. "Any way you can get in, have a look around?"

"Not really, boss. I mean, it's not like we've got a warrant. And we won't get one, just on the fibres. Even if it puts him at the hardware store, it's not the primary crime scene."

"What about the paint?"

"Don't get me wrong, boss, I can see the connection. Mick probably broke into the hardware store, and whoever broke into the hardware store probably stole the paint, and whoever stole the paint probably wrote on the body. But it's too many *probablies*."

She sighed. "You're right. I've crossed enough lines already. Head back and you can help me with Baxter and Hargreaves."

He approached Tel Cummings.

"Tel, want to show me what you saw round the back?"

"Not much, really. Follow me."

Cummings unlocked the side gate by reaching over and lifting the latch. Beyond it, lit by a dim moon, Aaron could see a small patch of well-tended garden.

"Got your bodycam on, Tel?" he asked. "We might need to get in and search, and we'll need to record everything if we do."

Cummings leaned against the house, sneering. "Fuck that thing. Doesn't work half the time, and when it does work, you don't want it to. Got to get physical sometimes, right?"

"Right."

Aaron took a step towards Cummings, spun him and lifted

a knee into his back to bring him down a little. He snaked his left arm across the PC's throat, grabbed his own right bicep, and gently tightened.

He leaned forward, his mouth millimetres from Cummings's ear, and whispered.

"Was it you that leaked?"

He could feel movement in the man's throat but heard nothing. He loosened his grip, just a little.

"Was it you?"

"I don't know what—"

Aaron tightened again.

He hoped his hunch was right. Cummings was a homophobe, a racist, a sexist, and he wasn't even a competent copper.

But it wasn't like Aaron made a habit of assaulting people, coppers or civilians.

"Was it you that leaked the story about Mulcaster?" he said.

Cummings nodded. Aaron loosened a little.

"Yes," gasped Cummings. "I know I shouldn't, but the guy was scum and—"

"Enough." Aaron released Cummings and pushed him away. "Yes, the guy was scum, and we don't like scum. But you know what else we don't like?"

Cummings stared at him, eyes narrowed. Aaron took a step towards him and watched him shrink, his back against the wall.

"We don't like dodgy coppers. Proper coppers, we catch people like Mulcaster and we deal with them properly. Dodgy coppers ruin it for the rest of us."

Especially for coppers like me.

"You've stepped over the line," he said, echoing the DI's

words from earlier. "Do it again, and it's over for you. You don't want everyone knowing you're dodgy do you, Tel?"

Cummings shook his head.

"Good. And you'd better hope Mulcaster's lawyer isn't hungry, because she'd have you for breakfast."

He walked away, leaving Cummings catching his breath in the alley. He rubbed his hands against his trousers, trying to wipe away any traces of the man.

He'd done the right thing, but that didn't stop him feeling sick about it.

CHAPTER NINETY-NINE

THE BOSS WAS WRONG, thought Nina.

Back in the team room, the DI had taken one look at her, reminded her she'd spent the last two nights facing down racist mobs, and sent her home.

"You need to sleep," the boss had said.

Sitting around at home, when all this was going on? She wouldn't be able to sleep even if she wanted to. But the boss hadn't been prepared to discuss it.

It wasn't fair.

She opened the door, poured herself into her car, and plugged in her phone. She let the opening chords of *Jailhouse Rock* wash over her.

She was tired, she couldn't deny that. But she was on a high, too. What she'd done there, with Bexley and Hargreaves, the way Ilkley had helped her out, the look on Giller-Jones's face.

The perfect end to the perfect day for a normal person. But Nina Kapoor wasn't a normal person.

Nina Kapoor was better than that. And there was one last

triumph she could add to the day's list. A long shot, but worth it.

She grabbed her phone and tapped in the address.

Winder Grove was real after all. A tiny street between the back roads and the station at Corkickle. She'd never been there before. But it wasn't too far out of her way.

Whitey Whitehaven wouldn't be real. And the address would probably turn out to be a dead end, plucked at random from the web. But still.

One full round of the *Jailhouse Rock* EP later, she arrived. The street itself was a tiny alley with no vehicle access. She found a spot to park on Esk Avenue and walked down.

It was dark, the streetlights broken. Quiet, too. Nina could hear her footsteps echoing as she approached the house.

There were four buzzers, labelled not by name but by floor: two, one, ground, basement.

23D, the register had said. She took a stab and pushed the button for the basement.

Nothing.

Damn.

CHAPTER ONE HUNDRED

HARGREAVES AND BEXLEY were sitting together in room three. There was a green metal table in the middle, bolted to the floor, and plastic chairs at the side of the room. They'd taken a chair each, with an empty one between them. They weren't saying a word.

Aaron arrived as Zoe was watching them on the video feed. "What's the plan, boss?"

"You and Tom can do the interviews."

"Really? It was Nina who made the arrest."

"I've sent her home. And I think they'll respond better to men, anyway."

"OK." He scratched his nose.

"Remember, the focus isn't the community centre bombing. It's not even the Knights of Whitehaven. It's the murder. I want to know about the group of men dragging a holdall through the streets of Whitehaven shortly before a dead body was found there." She indicated the screen. "Those trainers. Hargreaves is wearing his right now."

Aaron nodded.

"Good luck," she said. "Keep me informed."

Back in her office, Zoe sat back and thought about calling Carl. But what would she tell him? She had no idea when she'd be home, and it wasn't like they weren't used to unpredictable hours.

She closed her eyes and sat back, thinking through the day. The community centre. Inaya. The trainers. Carl, at home, and whatever had happened to him. Workington, again. The port. The drive. Her car, her wonderful car, alone up there in the fells....

"Boss?"

Tom was at the door, looking concerned.

"You OK, boss?"

"Yes." She'd fallen asleep.

She sat up and brought her thoughts into focus. "What's happening down there?"

He shook his head. "Bexley's mum's telling him to say nothing, and he's sticking to it."

"Have you mentioned the trainers? The holdall?"

"Yes. He might have been thrown by it but I can't be sure. Didn't make him open up, though. I'd like to show him the video. The man in the balaclava."

"Why?"

"The voice. I think it might be him."

"OK. What does the sarge say?"

"He said to ask you."

She screwed her eyes shut and wondered what it would take for Aaron to make some decisions on his own.

"Yes," she said. "Do it."

Zoe sat back again. She was worried about Carl.

What had happened to him? What was he working on?

He'd denied that it involved her team, but...

Tom was back. It had been less than five minutes, and he was grinning.

"He cracked, boss. I played him the video. He admitted everything."

She sat forward wide awake. "Everything?"

"Not everything. But he admitted the petrol bombing. Admitted being the bloke in the video, the Knights of White-haven stuff. His mum's going mental. She keeps swearing at him and calling him a disgrace, and then she remembers where she is and hisses at him to shut up. So that's as far as we've got."

Everything, he'd said. Nothing about the murder.

"It's a start, Tom. Good work. Has the lawyer for Harg-reaves arrived?"

Tom nodded.

"Let's let the Bexleys stew. I want to watch the two of you take on Hargreaves."

Zoe watched from an unlit side room in the custody suite as Aaron went in for the kill. Hargreaves sat next to Stan Basham, the duty solicitor called in to represent him. The lawyer looked bored and disinterested. No Clarissa Bexley, then.

"Your mate, Bexley," Aaron began.

"What about him?" drawled Hargreaves.

"He's already talking."

"Sure," said Hargreaves.

"He's told us about the bombing. I wouldn't be able to say this if we didn't have video of him admitting it, Adrian. Ask your lawyer."

Stan Basham nodded.

"And he's told us about the Knights of Whitehaven stuff, too. It's not looking good, Adrian."

Adrian Hargreaves slumped in his chair, the swagger gone.

"Tell me about the holdall, Adrian," said Tom. He leaned forward, eyes wide.

"What holdall?" said Hargreaves. Zoe waited for Basham to ask the same question, but he sat in silence.

"The one you and your mates were dragging around town the other night," Tom said. "In your fancy dress."

"Dunno what you're talking about, pig," said Hargreaves. He smiled, his eyes wary.

In the darkness, Zoe's phone buzzed. She ignored it.

"Your trainers." Aaron shook his head. "Look at your trainers, Adrian. And look at this video."

Hargreaves looked up from the video, fear all over his face.

"It was just a joke," he said. "A laugh, like. No one was supposed to get hurt."

"Really, Adrian?" said Aaron. "That's all you've got? A woman's been murdered, and you're telling us it was a joke?"

"We didn't know."

"Didn't know what, Adrian?" Tom leaned forward.

Good work, thought Zoe.

"We didn't know what was in it," said Hargreaves, looking from Tom to Aaron and back to Tom.

"Bingo," Zoe whispered to herself.

CHAPTER ONE HUNDRED ONE

BESIDE NINA's feet was a grille, a metal grid the size of a paving stone. Using her phone as a torch, she crouched down and peered into it. A small window was below it.

The basement flat, she assumed. 23D.

She swept the light from side to side. She couldn't see the walls or get a sense of scale. There was something there, or some things. She squinted and dropped her head even lower.

Boxes. Cardboard boxes. Four of them, in two piles of two. A box on top was open, and she could see paper in there.

Black paper, white text.

She stood and called the DI. No answer. Of course not. She'd be busy pulling the truth out of Bexley and Hargreaves.

She tried the sarge, then Tom. Voicemail. She crouched down again and looked at the box and the two sheets of paper spilling from it.

Could this be where those posters had come from?

She closed her eyes and saw them, all of them, *FREE THE NORTH, WE WILL NOT BE ENSLAVED, THE NORTH IS WHITE, THEIR WAYS ARE NOT OUR WAYS, WHITE-*

HAVEN FOR THE WHITES, FIGHT THE ISLAMISA-
TION OF YOUR HOMELAND.

She opened her eyes and looked again.

From here, there was no way of knowing for sure.

Nina took a step back and looked up and down the short street. There was no one around. She pressed the buzzer for the basement again and waited. Silence.

She crossed the road and looked at the house. The first-floor curtains were drawn, a narrow strip of light leaking from under them.

Back at the front door, she pressed all four buzzers at the same time. She waited.

After thirty seconds, the door buzzed. She pushed at the door, and it gave.

She was inside.

She took a step forward, and the door fell shut behind her.

Darkness.

"Hello?" she called.

Someone had let her in.

As she reached for her phone, she heard a footstep from behind, then a cough. She spun around, but too late.

She felt something slam into the side of her head.

And then she felt nothing.

CHAPTER ONE HUNDRED TWO

Stan Basham spoke, at last.

"Shut the fuck up," he muttered to his client.

Hargreaves did so.

Clarissa Bexley had given similar instructions to her son, and he'd listened.

Five minutes later they were in separate cells. Zoe was left with *we didn't know what was in it.*

She texted Fiona to update her, then followed up with a call. She wasn't surprised when the super picked up.

"That's all very well, Zoe," the super said, "but I hope you're not forgetting what started all this. You're investigating a murder."

"Yes," Zoe told her. "I know. We're making progress."

"I hope I don't have to bring Alan Markin in on this, Zoe. Not on your first case."

"We're getting closer, Fiona. We think there's a link between the murder and the kids who did the bomb."

Putting down the phone, she thought back to Hargreaves and his *we didn't know what was in it.*

Zoe had watched him, and she thought he was telling the truth.

She'd watched when Aaron and Tom had gone back to Bexley, and Tom had opened things by asking, "Your pal Adrian says he didn't know there was a dead body in that holdall you two were dragging around town. Did you?"

Bexley had said nothing, but if he hadn't been sitting down, he'd have fallen.

He knew now. They both did. But they hadn't known at the time.

There was still no sign of Mick Halfpenny. Roddy Chen and Harriett Barnes were outside his house, waiting. Zoe was convinced that Mick Halfpenny was the key to all this. But she couldn't prove it.

She could hold Hargreaves and Bexley until morning. She'd send the team home, hope they got some proper rest. Hopefully, something would turn up.

CHAPTER ONE HUNDRED THREE

Zoe blinked away tiredness as Mick Halfpenny's answerphone picked up her call. She was driving home in the pool car, trying not to think about her poor Mini.

"Mr Halfpenny," she said, "it's DI Finch, from Whitehaven Police station. We've got something we'd like your help with. If you could drop by in the morning, we'd be grateful."

She hung up. Hopefully that would appeal to the man's ego. She'd told Uniform to stand down from his house and was relying on his eagerness to help.

The car was a shiny new Range Rover. Certainly a car fit for a DI, but not her thing.

She drove slowly, tiredness and an unfamiliar vehicle conspiring against her. But she couldn't deny how smooth the thing was compared to her Mini.

Stop it.

The Mini would be fixed. It would all be fine.

She pulled up outside the house. *Carl.* She hoped he would be fine.

The front door opened and he rushed outside, pulling open her door handle. He was puzzled for a moment by the unfamiliar vehicle, but when he saw her looking back at him, his face collapsed in relief.

He pulled her out of the car and held her, standing on the drive.

"I was so worried." He pulled back, holding her at arm's length and looking her over. "They called me and told me what had happened."

She sighed. "I'm sorry. My phone broke. And then we were... We made some arrests."

"The killer?"

"No. But we're getting closer. I think."

He pulled her to him again, and she shivered. "Can we go inside?"

"Of course."

The cat was in the hall miaowing like she'd been away for years. She ruffled its ears. "Silly Yoda." She looked at Carl. "Have you fed her?"

"Of course I have."

She nodded and went through to the living room, where she let herself slump onto the sofa.

"Just tell me next time. If something happens to you. I was worried."

Zoe held his hands. "I'm sorry. I didn't... We're used to each other getting in late."

"You were in a car accident. You're driving a bloody Range Rover, for God's sake."

She smiled. "I'm sorry, Carl." She leaned against him. "About everything. I know it's not easy."

"Shush." He kissed the top of her head. "We'll work it out."

She shifted her weight. "Could you get me a coffee? Please?"

He laughed, softly. "Still my Zoe Finch." Another kiss. "Of course. And food. You need to eat."

He walked through to the kitchen. Zoe lay on the sofa. Moments later, she was asleep.

CHAPTER ONE HUNDRED FOUR

Nina woke shivering.

She reached to pull the duvet over her, but there was no duvet.

There was no reaching.

It was dark and she was cold and uncomfortable, but that wasn't what was bothering her.

It was the fact that she couldn't really move.

She opened her mouth to call out and felt something slip into it. She pushed it back out with her tongue and tried again, with similar results.

Her left side was pressed against something hard. She twisted so that the hardness was on her right, easing the discomfort.

Nina couldn't see a thing. She was tied up and gagged, and she was starting to panic, breathing hard and far too fast.

She forced herself to slow down, to inhale for a count of three and exhale for a count of three. Slowly.

Are You Lonesome Tonight floated through her head. A good, slow beat. She ran through the whole song once, then twice. By the time she'd finished the encore she felt a little calmer.

She tested the extent of her movement. Her wrists were tied together. Her ankles too. She couldn't see what was binding them or what sort of knot had been used. It felt like rope, and it was tight.

But she could twist and wriggle. After a minute, she'd pushed herself onto her back and used her core strength to force herself up towards a sitting position.

Something stopped her halfway. Her head and face met something soft, with a little give in it, but not enough for her to push through.

She tried again. This time she got a little further, but found the same substance pushing back at her, around her legs.

She lay back down and moved her upper body from side to side.

It was there, too. It was all around her.

It was fabric.

Nina fought back panic as she realised she wasn't just tied up and gagged in the dark.

She was tied up and gagged. In a holdall.

CHAPTER ONE HUNDRED FIVE

Tom had been at his desk for twenty minutes when the sarge showed up and nearly half an hour when the boss walked in, and it was still only half past seven.

No sign of Nina yet.

"Should I call her?" he asked. It would make a change.

"No," said the boss. "Leave her a bit. She was shattered yesterday."

We were all shattered yesterday. He was sure he'd caught the boss napping in her office. Alright for some.

"Anything from the accident investigation?" she asked.

He shook his head. "Not yet. But there's some good news. The motor crew have been at it since dawn and they think they'll have your car back for you later today."

The boss nodded and turned to Aaron. "What about Mick Halfpenny? Has he shown up yet, or called?"

"No sign of him."

She clenched a fist. "Right. Aaron, you and me are going down to have a chat with Bexley and Hargreaves. Tom, see if you can find out any more about Mick. Why he'd be involved in something like this, who his connections are. This Sinead Conway woman keeps coming up. There's some shared interest in local heritage. See what else you can find, OK?"

"Yes, boss."

Tom tried to read about Mick Halfpenny and Sinead Conway, but found the words and sentences blurring together into one long, senseless rant about preserving historic beauty while moving forward.

He couldn't focus. He kept thinking about Nina.

This wasn't like her. Tired, hungover, she'd always be at her desk or her post or wherever she was supposed to be. But now they were in the middle of a murder investigation, and she was nowhere to be found.

The boss had said to leave it. But the boss didn't know Nina.

He picked up his phone.

No answer.

That wasn't like her either. Nina didn't turn her phone off or leave it on silent. He'd teased her about her FOMO.

He was trying again, listening to it ring out, when he heard his name.

Mick Halfpenny was standing at the entrance to the team room, smiling at him.

Tom smiled back. "Hello, Mick."

Shit. Don't look at the board. Mick's face was all over it. That jumper.

He tapped at his keyboard, his fingers moving fast, his eyes on Mick. He found the escape key and breathed a silent sigh of relief as the screen went blank.

"What... How come you're here, Mick?" he asked.

Mick walked in and looked around, nodding approvingly as if he understood what he was looking at. A bunch of locked screens, thank God.

"Well, you know," said Mick. "People just know me, I suppose."

Tom didn't know.

How did someone like that have the confidence to walk into the restricted area of a police station? How did they get past the front desk, past the other officers?

He could see Mick doing it: *It's only me; they're expecting me; I've been helping Zoe, Aaron, and Tom.*

Mick walked around the desks and sat at Nina's. Tom opened his mouth to speak.

"I gather your boss wants a word," said Mick.

"I'll call her. Bear with me."

Please answer, he thought, *please answer the bloody phone.*

She picked up. Tom breathed out, his gaze on Mick, trying not to give himself away.

"Boss, it's Tom."

"What is it? I'm in the middle of talking with our suspects."

"I've got Mick Halfpenny here. In the team room, boss."

Mick was looking around the room like he owned the place, tapping his fingers on Nina's desk.

"What?" said the DI.

"Yes, boss. Mick. Here in the team room."

Mick looked over and smiled at him again, and he smiled back.

"On my way," replied the boss. "Keep him there. Offer him tea or coffee, but don't leave the room without him, just stall. And make sure the screens are all locked."

"That's all taken care of," said Tom. "Still no sign of Nina," he added, his voice light.

"I'm sure she's fine. Up in a minute. Don't let Mick out of your sight."

CHAPTER ONE HUNDRED SIX

CALM DOWN, Nina told herself. *Stop panicking.*

She took three deep breaths, counting as she exhaled. Hyperventilating wouldn't help her get out of there. And it wouldn't help her stay conscious inside the bag.

She blinked up into the darkness, pushing away the fear that nagged at her every time she allowed herself to think.

Don't think about Daria.

She was going to get out. She just needed to focus.

She twisted, feeling the fabric push back against her. She recoiled.

Focus. Don't panic.

She closed her eyes, tongue between her teeth, and ran her hands around the inside of the bag. She couldn't get at it all, so she shifted her weight and used her face too, trying to feel what she could through her cheeks.

How much time did she have?

She stopped.

Silence. There was no one in the building.

Either that, or there was someone right next to her, watching her in silence.

Nina felt bile rise in her throat.

Stop it.

Elvis would help.

She started running through *Love Me Tender* in her head, working her way around the bag methodically and repeating the song over and again.

She was halfway through her eighth silent rendition when it happened.

Something cold, against her right hand.

She froze.

Moving carefully, she shifted so that the thing, the strip of cold, was between her hands.

Whatever it was, it might be sharp enough, or rough enough, to break the rope around her wrists.

She switched to *Hound Dog*, hoping its upbeat rhythm would help her physically and emotionally. It wasn't until she'd been through the song three times that she realised it wasn't working.

Yes, the holdall had a zip opening. And yes, Nina had found it, and a little lump in it that seemed to protrude inward.

But it wasn't sharp enough to damage the rope binding her wrists.

She slumped back. It was still dark, the building was still silent. Her bladder ached and her muscles were taut from all the wriggling.

Sleep, maybe? Recover her energy?

No. She didn't know when they'd be back.

She'd kept hold of the zip. She lay there, running over her options in her mind.

Of course.

Instead of using the zip to cut herself free, she could use it to open the bag.

Bloody idiot. Why hadn't she thought of that before?

Her hands were already in the right place. She started working at the zip, pulling it towards her. She switched to *Heartbreak Hotel.*

But she couldn't get enough strength into her fingers to pull at the zip.

Her mouth was still gagged. She couldn't shake the gag, couldn't bite her way through it or push it clear with her tongue.

But she could bite *around* it.

She started shifting position, ignoring her muscles screaming at her. *Heartbreak Hotel* repeated in her mind.

Three *Heartbreak Hotels* brought her face into contact with the metal protrusion. Once she'd manoeuvred into the right position, she clamped her jaws around it. She could hold the tiny bit of metal in place through the gag, the same way she used a towel for grip with a screw-top beer.

Nina had refused to let go, however much her mouth ached.

And it ached.

She could sense daylight, the darkness inside the bag receding. Not enough for her to see anything useful, but enough to tell her she might not have much more time.

After what felt like hours but was probably minutes, she let go, the force with which she was dragging her head backwards overwhelming the strength of her jaws.

She gasped for breath, her mouth sore.

Ignore it. Keep going.

It took two more *Heartbreak Hotels* to get herself back in position.

But she could feel something, a slight difference in the quality of the air. She'd started to make an opening.

And the daylight kept getting brighter.

Nina lost her grip two more times, regaining it more quickly now she had a little light and a better sense of her position, as well as some extra manoeuvring room. Another time she slipped with such force, she felt the zip cut into her face as it flew past.

She gasped, unsure if the pain was from the zip or the cold air.

That cold air told her she was alive. It told her she had to hurry.

And then, at last, the holdall fell open.

She pushed herself out, squeezing through the gap, and tumbled onto the floor.

She lay panting. Something crept across her face. Blood?

No matter. If she hadn't been so tired, she'd have laughed for joy.

After a few breaths, she sat up and opened her eyes.

She shut them. Even the dim light of the basement was too much after that darkness.

She opened them again, giving herself time to adjust.

The first things she saw were the flags. They were draped against the walls, but invisible from the street. She could see why.

A Confederate Flag. A huge Nazi Swastika.

She kept scanning the room, her eyes growing accustomed to the light. There was a small wooden desk with a can on it, three old wooden chairs, and the boxes she'd seen last night. One was open, its contents visible.

WHITEHAVEN FOR THE WHITES, said the poster on top.

There was a door.

Half stumbling, half crawling, she made her way to it. A round wooden handle. Hard work, with her wrists still bound, but at last she turned it.

Shit.

Nothing happened.

She turned again and pushed against the door.

It gave, just for a moment, then stopped.

Nina turned a third time. She pulled.

No movement at all.

The door was locked. It was a wooden thing, old, probably flimsy, but Nina was tired, her ankles and wrists were still bound, and she was hungry and thirsty and she really needed the toilet.

She was trapped.

CHAPTER ONE HUNDRED SEVEN

"You believe them?" Zoe asked.

Halfway up the stairs, Aaron turned to face her. "Yes, boss. Don't you?"

She nodded. "They're dumb enough. They've admitted they're in this group, they've admitted they dragged that bag around town, and yes, they probably are dumb enough to have done it without asking what was in it."

"And they don't know who gives them their instructions either," added Aaron. "They probably like that. Makes them feel like a terrorist cell or something."

"They *are* a terrorist cell, Aaron. They might not have killed Daria Petrescu, but someone in their gang did, and they did it to spread terror. Just because they're stupid, just because they didn't know what they're doing, doesn't stop them being terrorists. We can work out the charges later. In the meantime, let's have a little chat with Mick Halfpenny."

The historian was sitting in Nina's chair, smiling to himself, when they entered. He spun around and stood up as Zoe approached him.

"Mick Halfpenny," he said, offering his hand.

"Detective Inspector Zoe Finch." She shook it. He was still smiling. "Have you offered our guest a drink, DC Willis?" she asked, and Tom nodded. "Better go and get it."

She gestured for Mick to sit. She chatted with him, mainly about her impressions of Cumbria. *Keep him here. Avoid alerting his suspicions.*

At last, Tom returned with a cup of tea. Zoe nodded at Aaron and he took over the conversation, steering onto the safe ground of local history.

She beckoned to Tom and spoke quietly into his ear.

"Have a word with Ilkley, will you? Get our two trouble-makers out of their cells."

Tom looked at her, recognition dawning on his face. He slipped away. Zoe turned back to Aaron and Mick, who seemed not to have noticed.

She looked at Mick. "Right, Mr Halfpenny."

"Mick, please."

"I was hoping we could pick your brains about all this." She smiled. "Do you mind coming downstairs with us?"

"Not at all."

Zoe led the way, with Mick in the middle and Aaron bringing up the rear. They used the internal corridors instead of going outside and back in through the custody reception area.

Mick had no idea where he was going.

CHAPTER ONE HUNDRED EIGHT

Tom finished talking to Ilkley and raced back up the stairs. There was no sign of either the boss or the sarge.

Or of Nina.

He called down to the main reception, and the custody suite. The boss and the sarge were in with Mick Halfpenny. Nina hadn't checked in yet.

He tried her phone again. It rang eight times then went to voicemail.

"I don't know where you are, but you'd better get in here," he said.

He woke up his screen and returned to the search results. Mick Halfpenny. The same thing, over and over again.

He has to be involved.

The fact that he'd been on the scene, or close by. The fibres from the hardware store. But there was nothing in his documented history that suggested he'd ever get mixed up in something like this.

Tom couldn't focus. He'd messed up. Forgotten calls.

Made mistakes. And now Nina had disappeared. Was it his fault?

He picked up his phone again and scrolled through numbers, considering them, dismissing them.

There.

Should he?

He pressed the button before he could talk himself out of it. The phone was answered on the third ring.

"Hello?" said a familiar voice.

"Mrs Kapoor? It's Tom. Tom Willis. Nina's—"

"Tom? I recognised your voice. How lovely to hear from you. What can I do for you? Is everything OK?"

"Yes," he said. "I was just wondering..."

"Yes?" prompted Mrs Kapoor.

"Just wondering if you'd heard from Nina."

"Yesterday, I think? Maybe the weekend? Why? Is there a problem?"

"No problem at all." He forced a laugh. "We're just... It's fine. She's not actually supposed to be here. I was just thinking she, er, she might want to be around."

"You know Nina. She's probably sleeping through a hangover, silly girl."

His phone buzzed. A text, from the boss. He read it twice, then thanked Mrs Kapoor as he ran downstairs and jumped into his car.

Whatever her mother might say, Tom knew Nina. She didn't sleep through hangovers. And he couldn't shake the nagging feeling that whatever had happened to her, it was all his fault.

CHAPTER ONE HUNDRED NINE

LYING ON THE GROUND, her head propped against the door, Nina was startled by a familiar noise.

A ringtone. A very specific ringtone.

Always On My Mind.

Elvis, not the bloody Pet Shop Boys.

She pushed herself up as best she could against the ropes and shuffled towards it.

It was coming from the desk. She was close. It was still ringing. Closer, now. If she could just—

It stopped.

She dropped to the floor just as it started up again. She lifted her head and scanned the room. Why couldn't she see it?

It was in a drawer.

There were three drawers in the desk.

Sitting up, she got one hand around the top one and pulled. It opened and flew right out of the desk, landing on her foot with a crash.

Empty.

The second contained nothing but an assortment of pens.

The third was locked. As she pulled at it, the paint can on top of the desk tipped and began to roll towards her.

Nina recognised that can. She'd taken an identical one from Jackson Liddell's hardware store. This one was open, and rolling towards her, and she didn't have time to get out of its way.

She lay on the floor, panting, her face flowing with blood and red paint. More noises.

Footsteps.

She froze.

Was there someone in the building?

Were they coming to finish her off?

Nina pushed herself up onto her knees. She was tired and weak, bound hand and foot. But she wasn't about to make it easy for them.

She waited.

The sound stopped, started up again. It was at its clearest not overhead, but by the window.

People. There were people on the street, walking by, walking almost over her head. If she could get the gag off and call out...

She shuffled over to one of the wooden chairs. If she could break it, get an edge, something sharp, she could use it to loosen her gag, possibly even to cut the rope around her wrists and ankles.

She started working at it.

By the time she'd lost count of her renditions of *Are You Lonesome Tonight?* there were three chairs on the floor. Two tangled together, the other alone by the door.

She lay beside it, sobbing silently into the gag. Her phone hadn't rung and she hadn't heard a sound from outside since she'd started trying to break the chairs. The ropes, the gag, the chairs, all were intact.

The only damage she'd done was to herself, adding an extra cut or two to her face, grazes to her legs and arms, and what was bound to be a black eye later.

If she lived till later.

"Oh."

Mick Halfpenny cleared his throat as they arrived in interview room two. He took in the bare walls, the metal chairs, the plastic table. "I do hope I'm not under arrest."

Zoe reassured him. "No, not at all."

Not yet, at least.

She gestured for him to sit. He lowered himself into a chair on one side of the table, by himself, with Zoe and Aaron opposite him. He was still smiling.

Zoe wondered what it would take to knock that smile off his face.

"I'd like to thank you for your help, Mr Halfpenny," she said.

"Mick," he reminded her.

"And I also want to reiterate, in case it hasn't been made clear already, that you're here entirely of your own free will, you're not being interviewed under caution, this is nothing more than a casual conversation. But you're still entitled to legal representation, if you want it. And of course, this conversation will be recorded, so we don't say or do anything we shouldn't. Is all that OK?"

"Of course," said Mick. The smile tightened. "Please, do carry on."

"Now, Mr Halfpenny, can you tell me: do you still own this jumper?"

Aaron pulled out a plastic wallet containing an A4 copy of the photograph Jake had sent them, while Zoe described it for the benefit of the recording. Aaron placed it on the table and slid it over to Mick.

"Please, take your time," said Zoe. "And remember, any time you want a break, or to take legal advice, you just let us know."

He wouldn't. Not yet. Mick Halfpenny's bluff still had some way to run.

But she'd be calling it today.

"Well," he said. "That does bring back memories."

"This photograph is only four years old," Zoe pointed out. "It was taken at the launch of a heritage trail around the town."

"Yes, yes. I remember, of course." Mick looked into the middle distance, as if thinking back.

Zoe didn't buy it. The man was playing for time.

"The jumper, Mr Halfpenny," she said, gently.

"It was hardly one of my prized possessions." He chuckled. "And I've never been one to care about clothes. As you can probably tell." Another chuckle.

He was playing it well, thought Zoe, but that was fine. The moment he caved, she'd have to caution him. And at that point, things would move out of her hands. The more she knew before then, the better.

"I was wondering," Aaron said, "about that night. The night the body was discovered."

"Yes?" said Mick.

"You were in town quite late, weren't you? Can you remind me why?"

"I live on Solway Road. Just opposite the Enterprise Park. They do late nights in the warehouse, and sometimes the noise means I can't sleep, so I go wandering."

He inclined his head to one side, eyebrows slightly raised, still smiling.

Time to take stock.

Zoe stood up. "I think we should take a little break. Do you mind waiting here for a minute, Mr Halfpenny?"

"Well." He looked from her to Aaron, and back again, and scratched his head, his eyes narrowed.

"It would be helpful," she said.

"I really am rather busy," he replied.

She raised her eyebrows, feigning surprise. "We'd really appreciate it, Mick. You've been immensely helpful so far."

He nodded.

Good. Zoe headed out, Aaron behind her.

CHAPTER ONE HUNDRED ELEVEN

AARON WAITED while the boss spoke briefly with Clive Moor. So far, things were going to plan, but there was no sign of Mick Halfpenny caving, and until he did, all they had was coincidence. Not enough to search the man's house, or to arrest him.

The boss and Aaron took the stairs up to the team room. Tom was in the doorway, holding a plastic bag and shifting his weight from one foot to the other. The bag looked heavy.

"Still no sign of Nina," he said, handing the bag to the boss. She peered into it and nodded.

Arron frowned: surely she didn't have Tom doing her shopping?

"What's—"

"I've called her," interrupted Tom. "Called her mum. It's not like her not to be here, boss. Right, Sarge? It's not even like her not to answer her phone."

Aaron nodded. Nina was almost Pavlovian, always ready to respond to the right noise.

Noise. What was it about noise?

What had he heard?

Of course.

It was what he hadn't heard. Or what he wouldn't *have* heard.

"Tom," he said. "We'll find Nina. But I need you to do something for me, right now."

Zoe turned to look at him. "What is it?"

"It's Mick Halfpenny's excuse, boss. I think it's bullshit. Tom, get the number for the warehouse, the one me and Nina were at yesterday. Find out if they were open the night of the murder, or if they were shut for maintenance."

Tom pulled out his phone. Aaron turned to Zoe. "The warehouse. Mick says it's too noisy at night, that's why he was out walking. Right?"

"Yes," agreed the DI.

"But that's the same warehouse Ibrahim Bashir works at. I checked yesterday, when I was there with Nina. And remember what Ibrahim said, the first time we were at the community centre?"

She smiled. "Inaya said Ibrahim had been at work the night before. She was fishing for an alibi. He told us he hadn't, because the place was shut for maintenance."

Aaron nodded. "Second Friday of the month, he said."

Tom put the phone down and turned to them. "It was shut."

Zoe exchanged looks with Aaron. A lie on top of a coincidence. Of course, Mick would deny it, say it was an honest mistake.

"Good work, Aaron," she said. "Now, Tom, let's set your mind at rest. Want to speak to Uniform and get them to send someone round to Nina's house?"

"I'll go myself, boss. If that's OK?"

She sighed. "OK. You find her, get her out of bed or wherever she is, and the two of you get back here as soon as you can. I want Mick Halfpenny so deep in this, he can't even hear the way out."

CHAPTER ONE HUNDRED TWELVE

MICK HALFPENNY LOOKED up as they entered the room. Zoe nodded at him and sat down. Aaron pulled the door half-closed behind him.

Round two.

"Mick, thanks for waiting," she said. "Would you like another drink?"

He shook his head and smiled at her. Confident again.

"I have to remind you, you're being recorded, you're not under caution, and you can end this whole thing or ask for legal representation whenever you want. You can stand up and walk out right now, if you want to."

He stayed put. He saw this as a challenge, she reckoned: was he good enough to withstand being questioned by a DI and a DS, without a lawyer on his side?

"Now, Mr Halfpenny."

She hesitated. No *call me Mick* this time.

Good.

"Can I refer you to our conversation a little earlier?" she asked.

"Certainly." Halfpenny leaned forward.

"My colleague DS Keyes asked what you were doing in town so late last Friday, and you said, and I quote, *I live on Solway Road. Just opposite the Enterprise Park. They do late nights in the warehouse, and sometimes the noise means I can't sleep, so I go wandering.* Does that statement ring a bell?"

"I think that sounds like what I said."

"I can play the tape if you'd like?"

He waved dismissively.

"Is the noise really so loud?" she asked. "I understand that their overnight operations are extensive. Do you *go wandering*, as you put it, every time this happens?"

He sat back and pretended to think about the answer.

"Well," he said at last, "not *every* time. Sometimes, if I've been kept up late the previous night, for instance, I'm so tired I'll sleep through anything. Sometimes I put gentle music on, sometimes I even watch TV. And yes, sometimes I go wandering. Quite often, as it happens." He leaned forward and smiled at her. "Surely that's not a crime, Detective Inspector?"

She returned the smile. "Of course not. But I'm a little confused, Mr Halfpenny, because we've just had it confirmed that the warehouse was closed last Friday night."

Mick Halfpenny blinked at her.

She waited.

"Closed, you say?"

"Yes, Mr Halfpenny."

"Well, I *am* surprised," he said. "I suppose I'm so used to hearing the noise, I just assumed it was happening and set off before I realised it wasn't. How extraordinary!"

The smile was taut now.

Zoe coughed and took a sip from the bottle of water she'd brought in with her.

"Well, yes, I suppose that's possible," she said. "We do get used to doing things, seeing things, don't we?"

Mick Halfpenny nodded enthusiastically. He paused as the silence was broken by Clive Moor's voice outside the room.

"This way, you two."

Zoe turned her head towards the door, and then back again, watching Mick Halfpenny. This was what she'd asked Tom to speak to Ilkley about. She hoped it would work.

Halfpenny turned towards the noise. Aaron had left the door half open, a gap just big enough for Halfpenny to see Clive walk past.

And the people Clive was with.

Bexley and Hargreaves.

Halfpenny exhaled. He gave a small, involuntary murmur.

"Are you OK, Mr Halfpenny?" Zoe asked.

Mick turned back to her, nodding, a fraction too earnestly.

"Are you sure you wouldn't like a break? Or would you like us to call a lawyer for you, perhaps?"

"A lawyer? Do I need one?"

"I'm afraid I can't say." Zoe sat back while he pretended to laugh.

"I don't think I do," he said. "I'm Mick Halfpenny. I'm just here to help."

CHAPTER ONE HUNDRED THIRTEEN

Tom pressed the bell for the fourth time, allowing his finger to linger on it.

He banged on the door and shouted her name through the letterbox.

No one answered.

He looked up and down the street. No one was standing outside, watching him. No curtains twitching. This was Nina's house, and the neighbours were probably used to a bit of noise.

He'd checked the cars parked on both sides of the road, been up and down a hundred yards to either side of the house.

No sign of her Fiesta.

Tom gave one last look each way, pulled out his key, and let himself in.

It was dark inside: it always was in Nina's house. She kept the curtains drawn, *just in case*, as she put it. Just in case she had a hangover, he reckoned.

He could feel something under his feet. He reached for the switch and the hallway light came on, dim and murky.

"Nina?" he called.

Silence.

What he'd felt underfoot was paper. Post; fliers for take-aways, club nights, handymen; the *Whitehaven Chronicle*.

He picked up the newspaper, walked into the kitchen, looked around. Nothing out of place, in that everything was a mess anyway. He felt the kettle: cold, but if she'd been up and out that would have been hours ago.

But the newspaper. It was yesterday's.

For all her faults, Nina liked to keep the hallway tidy. Empty, usually. "Clean line of escape," she joked. The truth was, she'd let things pile up before, and she'd paid the price. Missed bills. Her old Fiat had been repossessed. She wasn't letting that happen again.

Tom stood up, went to the stairs, called her name every third step.

Nothing.

Upstairs he checked her bedroom, the bathroom, the tiny guest room he'd crashed in more times than he could remember.

Nothing.

Downstairs he took a final look in the kitchen and then examined the living room and toilet. There was nothing to say she'd been in, but there was nothing to say she hadn't.

But the hallway told its own story. Nina might have left the paper and post out overnight, but she wouldn't have left it there this morning.

Which meant Nina hadn't been home last night.

He dialled her number again. No answer. He tried the boss, the sarge.

No answer.

He felt himself breathing fast, too fast, the breaths coming with the words in his head.

My fault, my fault, my fault.

In the hallway he leaned against the wall and dropped to a crouch, his head between his legs.

Fix it, he thought. *Stop panicking. Just fix it.*

Nina couldn't be dead. He wouldn't allow it.

My turn, thought Aaron. They'd planned out the order of things. They'd considered contingencies and plotted alternatives, in case things went better than expected, but that hadn't happened.

"Mr Halfpenny," he said, his expression neutral. "Can you tell us anything about this?"

The DI reached under the table and produced a white plastic bag. She put it on the table and pulled out a paint can.

Halfpenny's jaw clenched. His body jerked back and forward again before he could get it under control.

"Where..." he began. He shook his head, sat forward again. "Where did you get that?"

They waited.

"Have you been in my property?"

"No," said Aaron. "We just bought it."

"Oh." Mick sat back.

"We got it from a hardware store on Queen Street. Do you know the place?"

Mick's face creased.

"Only," Aaron continued, "someone broke into this hardware store. On the night Daria Petrescu was killed. And there are some curious things about that person, the one who broke into that hardware store. Do you know what those things are, Mr Halfpenny?"

Mick shook his head and tried a smile.

"Well, the first thing is, that person was wearing an orange and white argyle jumper. Just like the one you're wearing in this photo." Aaron picked up the photograph, waved it in front of Mick, and put it down.

"I'm sure there are thousands of people who own that jumper, Detective Sergeant," Mick replied.

"Two hundred and forty-seven," Aaron told him.

Mick's eyes widened.

Good work, Tom, Aaron thought.

"Only two hundred and forty-seven of these jumpers were ever sold, across the whole of the UK, over nineteen years. They stopped making them over a decade ago, Mr Halfpenny."

"Well, I mean, that's just a coincidence, isn't it?"

Aaron ignored him. "The second thing is that the person who broke into the hardware store on Queen Street, on the same night Daria Petrescu was killed, that person stole a can of paint. Paint just like this, Mr Halfpenny." He indicated the can on the table. "Same colour. Same brand. Do you know what they did with that paint?"

Mick shook his head.

"They used that paint to write a slur on Daria Petrescu's body."

Mick was still shaking his head. "That's appalling. Utterly appalling. How people could do something like that..."

He trailed off and looked Aaron in the eye.

"I can see what you're doing, Detective Sergeant. You're

trying to lead me somewhere. But it's just coincidences. I had nothing to do with any of this. I'm just trying to help."

The DI cleared her throat. "Thank you, Mr Halfpenny. We're really very grateful. But we haven't quite finished. You see, whoever this person was, they thought they were being clever. Writing a word on the body, a foreign word, and I'm sure they looked it up and practised writing it. But the thing is, Mr Halfpenny, this person made a mistake."

"A mistake?" Mick looked affronted.

"Yes," continued the DI. "It seems he wasn't as bright as he thought he was. He got the word wrong." She shrugged.

"Who told you that?" asked Mick. "How do you know it was a man?"

"The local Imam. Maybe you've come across him. Lovely people, him and his wife. They run the—"

"Oh, I know who they are," said Mick Halfpenny.

Only it wasn't Mick Halfpenny.

The words had come from his mouth. It was the same man sitting there, in the same clothes, the same glasses, the same curly, greying hair.

But the voice was different. The whole manner.

There was a size to him now, a scale, a sense of menace, like he'd ripped off a mask and revealed the true man beneath it.

"Oh, I know them, Detective Inspector," he snarled. "Filthy scum, they are. They're here now, of course. It was inevitable. They've taken over all the cities and now they're here, breeding like rats."

Aaron glanced at the DI. Was the shock on his face as obvious as it was on hers?

"They won't get away with it, you know." Mick looked at each of them in turn, waiting.

"Why's that, Mr Halfpenny?" the DI asked.

"Hah!" He almost spat it. "Hah! There's so many of us, Detective Inspector. So many more of us than those scum could imagine, even in their darkest nightmares, and that's what we'll be, for the likes of them, for those who enable them. We will be their nightmares."

He rose from the chair. Was he taller than he had been, too?

"Mr Halfpenny," said the DI, her face composed despite the man leaning over the table towards her. "Are you willing to provide fingerprints and DNA samples on a voluntary basis, and consent for your property to be searched by our officers and forensic teams?"

Halfpenny shook his head. His smile had more teeth now.

Aaron could feel his pulse rising.

Don't react. Stay calm.

"Fine." The DI tilted her head. "Mick Halfpenny, I'm arresting you on suspicion of perverting the course of justice."

Mick Halfpenny said nothing while the arrangements were made, other than to name his lawyer. Trevor Singleton.

"Know him?" Zoe asked Aaron as they took the stairs back to the team room.

"Name's familiar. I think he works a bit further north."

"You mean Workington?"

Aaron nodded.

Ilkley would take prints and DNA samples from Mick within the hour. Right now, the man's personal possessions were being catalogued, and CSI and Uniform were en-route to search his house.

She hadn't added murder to the list of charges, not yet, but it was only a matter of time. A sense of wary euphoria bounced between Zoe and Aaron as they entered the team room and pulled up the case notes, ready to be updated.

Halfpenny was the killer. She was sure of it.

Tom walked in thirty seconds later. Zoe felt her mood plummet as she saw his face.

"She's not there." He looked from her to Aaron and back again. "And she wasn't there last night."

"How do you know, Tom?" she asked, keeping her tone gentle. "Are you absolutely sure?"

He nodded. "The mail. And the paper, the *Chronicle*, it was all there, in her hallway. She wouldn't leave it like that."

"You've seen her car, Tom," said Aaron. "A bit of paper in the hallway isn't exactly out of character."

"No." He shook his head. "Her car's not there. And I've spoken to her mum, her old schoolmates. No one's heard a thing."

"Is she seeing anyone?" asked Zoe.

"No," replied Tom. "Have you checked your phones?"

He pulled out his own phone and thrust it towards them.

Zoe exchanged looks with Aaron. "Tom, why don't you sit down? I—"

"With respect, boss. Your phones. I've got missed calls from her last night. Have either of you got anything like that?"

Zoe sighed. She pulled out her phone. Two missed calls, about half past ten last night. She held out her phone.

"Me too," said Aaron.

"That's what I had," Tom told them. "Twenty-seven minutes past. So she called all three of us twice, in, what, the space of a few minutes?"

Zoe felt her jaw clench. She nodded. Aaron did too.

Tom hurried to Nina's desk. He scanned through her notes. Zoe watched as he woke up her screen and typed in a code.

"You know her password?" she asked.

"Yeah." He didn't look up. "She knows mine, too. We're mates."

"That's not—"

She stopped herself. This wasn't the time for a lesson in password security.

"I'm calling Inspector Keane," she said.

"Leave it with me," Keane said. "My boys and girls'll be out there looking for Nina and her car before you've put your phone down. I'll sort CCTV checks, anything that might have picked up her car's reg. And we'll check mobile towers."

"Thanks." Zoe was impressed.

"I'll put it in as a Grade 1 priority request," he said, "and the towers should tell us if she's in Whitehaven. Not much more than that. It's a long shot."

Tom sat at Nina's desk, shaking his head as he alternated between interrogating the screen and rifling through her papers.

It would be fine. Zoe was sure of it. Nina would turn up, drunk, hungover, tired, maybe. Or...

Don't show them how worried you are.

Zoe picked up her phone, strolled out of the room, and called Keane again. "Do you have someone at the hospital you can check with?"

"Already happening, Zoe. I'll let you know. And don't worry."

"No?"

"No. Nina Kapoor's one of ours. We'll find her."

CHAPTER ONE HUNDRED SIXTEEN

Halfpenny's lawyer was a quiet man whose almost white hair belied his youthful face. He seemed friendly and knew his stuff.

One thing Trevor Singleton didn't know, however, was his client. *Interesting*, thought Zoe, given Mick had asked for him by name.

There was a murder case to build. But right now, that wasn't her priority.

"Where's Nina Kapoor?" she asked.

Mick said nothing.

"Who is this Nina Kapoor?" asked Trevor Singleton.

Zoe turned to him. "She's a colleague. She's disappeared whilst investigating your client."

Singleton shuffled through the few sheets of paper he'd been given. "There's nothing about this here, Detective Inspector. I'm sorry your colleague's missing, but do you have any reason to believe Mr Halfpenny is involved?"

"It's new," she replied. "That's why it's not in your—"

She was interrupted by a knock at the door: Morris Keane, beckoning her out.

"Interview paused," she snapped, and hurried out.

"I've spoken to the CSI lot," Keane said. "Halfpenny's DNA won't be processed for a bit, but there's a match for the prints. Your Mick Halfpenny had that knife in his hands."

Zoe smiled. "Thanks. I realise this isn't your job.." She thought of Alan Markin. *Thank God I've got Morris Keane here.*

"Don't be silly. Nina's one of ours. If he's got her..." He cleared his throat. "My team's been in his house less than twenty minutes and they've already found the jumper, plus a bag of an unidentified substance that I guarantee will turn out to be heroin. It's on the way to Stella's lab and she's already liaising with Chris Robertson to get it matched against the substance found in Daria Petrescu's system."

"This is great," Zoe told him, as her phone rang.

She reached for it so quickly she almost dropped it. It wasn't Nina.

It was Jake Frimpton. She signalled for Keane to wait a moment.

"Zoe," Jake said. "I assume you're busy."

"Like you wouldn't believe."

"I'll be quick. There's a lot of police in town and there's rumours an officer has been murdered."

Zoe let the phone fall from her grasp, rescuing it before it hit the ground.

"Where did you hear that?"

"Just the rumour mill."

"You're not going to print that, are you?"

"Of course not. But if I've heard it, then it's all over social media."

"OK. Understood. And thanks."

She ended the call and turned back to Morris Keane.

"Nina's car," he said, without preamble. "We've found it."

"Where?"

"Car park by the offices off North Shore Road."

"Near the community centre?"

Keane nodded.

"It's bullshit," she told him. "Whoever left it there, it's the same thing as the men in white and the knife being found nearby. It's a diversion."

He nodded. "But I've pulled some of the team out of the town centre to focus on that area, just in case. We found the keys, too. Your Mick Halfpenny had them in his pocket."

Zoe felt her mouth fall open. "Thank you."

She turned back to the room.

"Mr Halfpenny," she began. "We've now confirmed your prints match those on the knife that was used to cut Daria Petrescu's throat."

Mick smiled at her.

"We've also found a bag of heroin at your property, and we're having that tested against the substance found inside the victim."

Still smiling.

"There are a few other items, like the jumper, but I think we're past the jumper now. I'm more interested in what you were doing with Nina Kapoor's car keys in your pocket."

Mick put his fingers to his lips and leaned forward.

Zoe waited.

"Nina Kapoor is a slug," he said. "Part of an infestation. And the only way to control an infestation is to eliminate every trace of it."

He sat back again. Still smiling.

Zoe noticed a movement to her side. Aaron's fists were clenched and he'd drawn his right arm back.

She turned to him and shook her head.

"Interview paused." She all but dragged the DS out of the room with her.

In the corridor, she turned to face him. "I know it's personal, Aaron. I know you want to beat the answers out of that man. But it won't work."

"Boss," he replied.

"Come on, Aaron. You're not just a good copper, you're an excellent copper. Stay calm, keep your head, and we'll find her. OK?"

CHAPTER ONE HUNDRED SEVENTEEN

Nina had rolled over to the window. She couldn't communicate, but the sound of people walking by was keeping her sane. That, and the way the light dimmed every time someone went past the grille.

What she could hear now gave her more than sanity, though. It gave her hope.

It was a conversation.

"It's no use, Rob," said a female voice. Was it familiar? "How are we supposed to know if she's been round here?"

"I don't bloody know. She could be anywhere. I don't even know the woman."

"Well, I do. She's alright, is Nina."

Through her gag, Nina smiled. Harriett Barnes.

Harriett would find her. She wouldn't give up on her.

Slowly, painfully, Nina raised herself against the wall and kicked against the floor. Whoever had tied her up had taken her shoes, and her socks didn't make much noise. She cast around for something that might.

The can.

"I know," Harriett was saying. "But this is where Minor wanted us looking, so this is where we'll look."

Stay there, Nina thought.

She slid to the floor and wriggled her way over to the now-empty can of paint. With some twisting and turning, she could just about get it between her hands.

She heard a crackle. Radio. Had someone figured out where she was? She couldn't hear.

"Understood," she heard. Harriett's colleague. Rob something. "ASNT."

Area Searched, No Trace.

Shit.

Nina lifted the can above her head and dropped it onto the floor.

A small bang. Nothing more.

"OK. We'll head over."

Head over where?

"Reckon they've found something?" asked Rob. "This new search area, it's over by the Mosque, isn't it?"

"Community centre," replied Harriett.

Nina paused, then raised the can again.

New search area, she thought. *Shit.*

"Whatever," she heard from outside. "Anyway, if her car's there, chances are she is too. Let's go."

Nina dropped the can, lifted it, dropped it again. It was pointless. Even Harriett and Rob's receding footsteps were louder than any noise she was capable of making.

She fell to the floor, silently sobbing.

CHAPTER ONE HUNDRED EIGHTEEN

Nina's computer held nothing useful.

Well, not *nothing*. Tom had found case notes, web pages for the Knights of Whitehaven and social media accounts for their friends and associates. A page was open with Stella Berry's contact details, another with the orange and white jumper, a list of club nights in town, a photo of the knife, videos of the press conferences, Elvis lyrics...

Nina's browser habits suffered from the same problem as her car and most of her house. A lack of discipline.

Tom resisted bookmarking everything and shutting it down. Everybody had their own way of working. And he wasn't here to tidy up Nina's computer.

He was here to find her.

He moved on to Nina's messages: emails and internal communications. He browsed through them. Nothing surprising.

Except there was a message from him.

Sent the previous evening. Before she'd gone home. Before the boss and the sarge had their accident.

Tom didn't remember sending it.

He clicked it open.

A WHOIS link. An address. 23D Winder Grove. He thought he recognised that. Corkickle, wasn't it? And a name, *Whitey Whitehaven.*

He called the boss. No answer. Same for the sarge. They'd be questioning Mick Halfpenny.

He didn't have time.

He grabbed his coat, checked for his car keys, and ran out of the team room.

CHAPTER ONE HUNDRED NINETEEN

"Mr Halfpenny," Zoe began. "Are you the leader of the Knights of Whitehaven?"

Silence.

She looked across the table at the lawyer. She wanted to take hold of him, show him Daria Petrescu's body. Not the cleaned-up images. The real ones. Show him what he was part of, the man he was helping.

"Mr Halfpenny," she repeated. "Where is Nina Kapoor?"

Nothing. Not even the smile now.

"Are you the leader of the Knights of Whitehaven?" she asked.

Nothing.

"How did you kill Daria Petrescu?"

He gazed back at her.

"Where is Nina Kapoor?"

"Did you even know Daria Petrescu?"

"Are you the leader of the Knights of Whitehaven?"

She took a breath.

"Where is Nina Kapoor?"

Her voice was strangled. *Keep going.*

"Why did you cut her throat?"

"Are you the leader of the Knights of Whitehaven?"

"YES!" he shouted, finally. "Yes. I am. You'll find out eventually."

He turned to his lawyer. Singleton rested his head on the tips of his fingers, trying not to look disappointed.

"I'm sorry, old chap," Halfpenny said, "but all this, it's bigger than you and me. They've got my fingerprints, all their clever scientists and DNA analysts will be able to put me there, so there's not a lot of point prolonging it."

"So you give them their instructions?" asked Zoe.

"Yes, yes. I did it. I told them to carry it around town."

"It?" said Aaron.

Mick Halfpenny flicked his hand dismissively.

"It, her, whatever. I told them to carry her around. I cut her throat. It was a shame, really."

"What was?" asked Zoe.

"Her. What did you say her name was? Daria, wasn't it? She wasn't supposed to be dead already. I must have given her too much of the heroin, I suppose. But she should have bled more. If she'd bled more, I wouldn't have needed the paint."

He looked up at them, smiling.

"Did you know her, then?"

He shook his head. "I simply had her delivered. And before you ask, I won't be telling you who delivered her. She was in the bag already, lightly sedated, it was so convenient. A little like your friend."

Zoe's skin ran cold. "What do you mean?"

"What I mean, Detective Inspector, is that I strongly suggest you find your Nina Kapoor soon. Because I've seen just two of my Knights in this police station, which leads me to believe there are plenty more outside it."

He paused and licked his lips.

"And if I can't finish off the job, you can be sure there are others who will."

CHAPTER ONE HUNDRED TWENTY

MORE FOOTSTEPS, above.

The first sound since Harriett and Rob had left.

How long had it been? Nina had no idea. She'd spent too long sobbing, too long contemplating her own death. Picturing Daria Petrescu's body.

She wriggled back towards the window. Was it her imagination, or had the rope around her hands loosened a little?

The footsteps had come closer, closer even than Harriett and Rob's. They stopped.

There was a loud noise from close by that had her turning sharply around.

The buzzer. Someone had pressed the buzzer for 23D.

Someone was trying to get in.

The can, Nina thought. *Drop the can.*

She picked it up, then dropped it in surprise as she heard the voice.

"Come on," he was saying. "Open the bloody door."

It was Tom.

"Come on," he repeated.

Press the other buzzers, she thought. *Just press them all. Someone'll let you in. Press the buzzers.*

A moment's silence, then his voice again. He was talking to someone else this time.

"Boss, it's Tom."

He was on the phone.

"I think it's a dead end," he said. "There's no one there."

Footsteps, again. Moving away.

No.

Nina lunged for the chair by the door. She threw herself at it, threw her face at it, slamming her own mouth down on the square end of one of the legs.

"Shit," she shouted in pain, then realised she'd heard herself. Not loud, but there.

She'd loosened the gag.

"Tom!" she shouted.

Her throat was so dry, the word came out as a rasp, interrupted by what little cloth was still around her mouth.

"I'll let you know more when I get back," she heard him say. "I hope this is all nothing. That he's told you where she is."

"I'm bloody here," she tried to shout.

But the words were muffled. Tom's voice moved away, his footsteps receding.

CHAPTER ONE HUNDRED
TWENTY-ONE

Zoe terminated the interview and walked straight out, her gestures and stance making it clear Aaron was to follow her.

Her first call was to Morris Keane, who received the update calmly.

Next was Tom. He didn't pick up, but she'd expected that. He was out. Following up a lead, he said. The address for the *Knights of Whitehaven* website.

Fiona answered on the first ring. "I hear you have a missing detective, Zoe."

"Yes. I was hoping maybe a press conf—"

"I can't quite believe I'm having to tell you this, but you really have to learn to look after your team. First, your DC gets herself in a fight, and now she's decided to disappear."

"Yes, Ma'am, and we're doing all we can to—"

"Do better, Zoe. We're the police. We're supposed to solve problems. Not create them." She hung up.

Zoe stared at the phone, incredulous. She looked at Aaron.

She took a breath. Whatever issues she had with Fiona, they weren't Aaron's concern.

Go back in.

She strode back into the interview room, turned on the tape.

"Who delivered her, Mick?"

He pursed his lips and shook his head, glancing at his lawyer.

"That foreign girl, so pretty, so dead," he said. "So disappointing she didn't survive the drugs."

"What did you do with her?"

Zoe could sense Aaron next to her, struggling to maintain control. *Keep it together, Aaron.*

Mick shrugged. "I left the bag in the agreed place, gave my instructions, took photographs." He smirked. "Then once I knew my Knights would be all over CCTV, I recovered it."

Was that *it* the bag, or Daria herself?

"Who brought her to you?" she repeated.

A shrug. Silence.

"Your Knights, as you call them. We already have two of them. Who are the others?"

He sat back in his chair. "There are others besides me who would like to preserve this nation's great heritage."

"Give me names."

Halfpenny shook his head. Trevor Singleton sat beside him, mute.

"Where's Nina?" asked Aaron.

Another shake of the head. "If you'll just let me go, I can put an end to all this. Put her out of her misery. As it is, she'll have to wait until one of my Knights finds her. And they might not be as considerate as I am."

Aaron gasped. He leaned forward.

Zoe put a hand on his arm. She'd had enough.

"Mick Halfpenny," she said. "I'm arresting you on suspicion of kidnapping and murder."

CHAPTER ONE HUNDRED TWENTY-TWO

"Tom!" Nina shouted, one more time.

Too quiet.

She reached for the chair. Her hands were looser now. Perhaps she could...

Another noise.

Always On My Mind. From the desk.

She stopped, holding her breath. It was loud. She always had it set to loud. She could sleep through quiet things.

"Hang on," she heard. "I can hear—"

Tom's voice, louder. And the footsteps, approaching, fast, running.

The ringtone stopped.

A moment later it started again, rang for a minute. Above it, she could hear Tom shouting.

"Are you there? Nina? Are you in there?"

Finally.

CHAPTER ONE HUNDRED TWENTY-THREE

Zoe leaned back against the wall outside the interview room and read the text again.

She'd read it six times in the last minute. Aaron had received the same text, and he'd read it aloud twice. Just to be sure they hadn't somehow misunderstood, she'd called Tom to check.

It was true.

She dialled the super's number.

"Zoe. I hope you've got some positive news for me. I've got Alan Markin on standby. I can't let this whole thing spiral out of control."

"You can have him stand down, Ma'am. My team's tracked Nina down. She's safe and well. And we've arrested Mick Halfpenny for murder."

She only half-listened as Fiona poured out her congratulations.

"Thank you, Ma'am." Zoe ended the call.

She turned to Aaron and let out a long, slow breath.

"So, how did we do for our first case?"

He laughed. "Not bad, boss. Not bad at all."

It was fitting, Zoe thought, that she'd be eating a cheese sandwich when Nina walked into the team room. No gulls in here, at least.

She, Aaron, and Tom stood and applauded. Nina gave a little bow and almost fell into her seat. The paramedics had tidied her up, but she'd refused to go to hospital.

She shouldn't be here, not in this state. There were cuts and bruises all over her face, two black eyes, and flecks of red paint in her hair.

But Zoe had learned enough about Nina Kapoor to know she couldn't keep her away. And now there was cheap wine in plastic cups, and Tom was pressing one into her hands.

"No, it's OK," she said.

"Come on, boss. One drink won't hurt you."

"Leave it, Tom," said Aaron. He swept up the cup and knocked it back.

A scrunched-up piece of paper hit Tom square in the face, distracting him.

"What?" He turned to Nina.

"Two talents, mate."

"What d'you mean?"

"I said you had two talents. Good hearing, and one other. Remember?"

"Yeah." He took a swig from his own cup. "Then you said it was only one, after all."

"Yeah, well. I was lying. You're solid."

"Solid?"

"Yes. Solid."

"That's all you can say about the bloke who dragged you out of a psycho's basement? Solid?"

"Yeah. You know. Reliable."

"Reliable? Christ, Nina, that's even worse. Solid and reliable with good hearing. I should probably apply to the dog division."

Zoe stifled a laugh.

"You're a good copper," said Nina. "I wouldn't have tracked me down with the information you had. But you did. I owe you one, mate."

"That's better."

"Think you might be up to giving you-know-who a call?"

"I don't..." began Tom. He grinned. "Yeah. Maybe I am."

They were interrupted by a knock on the door. Zoe turned to see Fiona Kendrick standing there, her hand raised in greeting.

"May I?" she asked.

"Of course, Ma'am," replied Zoe.

"I just wanted to offer my congratulations in person, Zoe," she said. "I hear there's a match for the DNA now, too."

Zoe nodded. Mick Halfpenny had been a match for the samples taken from the sweater fibres, and also from the body.

And, of course, they had his clear and unambiguous confession.

And she'd had more good news: her Mini was fixed and ready for her to take home.

"Thanks, Ma'am," she said. "Even if he tries to retract his confession, we've got too much forensic evidence for him to wriggle out of it. He's not implicating anyone else yet, but we're hopeful."

"Well, that's something for another day. Anyway, it's not just congratulations I'm here for. The fact is, Zoe, I haven't made your first week here particularly easy."

Zoe opened her mouth to protest.

"Don't argue. It's not my job to make your job easy, it's just my job to make sure you can do it, and if I've been hard on you, it's because I was concerned that you couldn't."

Zoe stared, open-mouthed, as the super continued.

"I misjudged you, Zoe. I should have had more confidence in you. I won't underestimate you again."

The entire room seemed to let out a collective sigh of relief, before falling into low, muttered conversation.

"Thank you, Ma'am," Zoe said.

Tom approached with another cup for Fiona.

"Thank you, Tom." The super turned to Zoe. "I've just heard from Mr Mulcaster's lawyer, by the way."

Zoe waited. She could see Aaron watching them.

"He wants everything forgotten about," Fiona continued. "As much as it can be. He's not coming after us, anyway."

Zoe saw Aaron breathe out, slowly. She frowned at him and he looked away.

The super drained her cup and thanked the team. At the door, she stopped and addressed them all.

"There's a memorial being held for Daria Petrescu next

week," she said. "Her parents are being flown over. I hope you can—"

"Of course," said Zoe. She smiled as the rest of the team answered in unison.

If you want a good team, you've got to have good people in it. That's what Carl had told her.

These were good people.

CHAPTER ONE HUNDRED TWENTY-FIVE

ZOE HAD FORGOTTEN about the charity auction.

Fiona wasn't going to let her get away with that though, and sent her a text ten minutes after leaving the team room. Zoe slumped. She'd just solved a murder, for Christ's sake. Couldn't she just rest?

She called Carl as she headed for the stairs, to remind him, but he already knew.

"It's OK," he told her. "I'll probably have to go straight from work. I'll see you there."

So he'd gone to work that morning. *Good.*

Zoe felt her step lighten as she left the building. Her phone rang as the main door swung shut behind her and she answered it without looking at the screen.

"If you want me to dig out a bow tie from somewhere in those boxes, I'm telling you now you're better off trying to buy one instead," she said.

"Zoe Finch?" replied a female voice.

"That's me." She glanced at the screen: number withheld.

"Who is this?" she asked.

"We met. On Sunday."

There was something familiar about that voice. A southern accent. The days had blended together lately. Sunday…

She had it.

"Olivia," she said. "I've been trying to get hold of you."

"I know. Please stop."

"Where are you?"

A short, sad laugh. "Nowhere close. Listen, Zoe, I know you mean well, but I really don't want to speak to you."

"What do you mean?"

"Please. Stop trying to contact me. Don't try to find me."

"This is ridiculous. Talk to me, Olivia. Tell me what you know."

Silence.

"I'm a police officer. I've got a good team here. We can keep you safe."

Another laugh, longer. "What, like you kept Ahmed Hosseini safe?"

"Who?" Zoe asked, but the line was dead.

CHAPTER ONE HUNDRED TWENTY-SIX

Zoe couldn't help worrying about the chandeliers.

The size of them, and the fact that one of them was right over Carl's head, left her feeling jittery.

The fact that everyone else was either drunk or on the way to drunk didn't help, and nor did the way people kept pushing glasses into her hand.

Carl had been waiting for her at the entrance, thank God, and he'd had his own bow tie after all. He looked good, she thought, the white tie setting off his light brown skin and dark eyelashes. The way his eyes roamed from her head down to her feet and back up again made her feel better about the blue dress she'd tracked down in a box right at the back of Nicholas's room.

She'd been late, but only because Nicholas had called just as she was about to leave. She'd asked how he was, and he'd been coy. She wanted to know more about this Fox person he'd mentioned, but she wasn't about to pry.

She sat next to Carl, polishing off a chicken salad. She'd not realised how hungry she was until it arrived. Now she eyed

Carl's plate and grabbed a piece of meat while he was distracted by someone collecting a winning bid.

They hadn't bid for anything themselves. The lots were out of their league: not just boat trips but actual boats, dinners that came with three-night stays in luxury hotels, holidays in the Caribbean. But it was entertaining to see the tension as each lot was unveiled, and amusing to watch the bidders' excitement.

There were plenty of people she knew, more than she'd expected. Fiona, of course, who'd flirted with Carl, and who'd introduced her to the Assistant Chief Constable Joseph Carghillie. He was an enormous man, friendly, too, pumping Zoe's hand and congratulating her on her success.

"Why do people call him Little Joe?" Zoe whispered to Carl after he'd been guided away by Fiona.

"To distinguish him from Joanne."

"Joanne?"

Carl turned to her, an eyebrow raised. "I know you don't like to play politics, Zoe, but not knowing who your own Chief Constable is... Joanne Ainsworth. They call her Big Jo because she's the boss."

Zoe laughed. She'd never liked politics, and up here she thought she'd like them even less. But she could leave all that to the likes of Fiona.

Streeting was there, too. He approached her and Carl, booming out both their names. He congratulated her loudly and with little sincerity, then left them.

"I don't like that man," she told Carl, who nodded but said nothing.

Jake Frimpton was at their table, drinking orange juice and lemonade. He and Carl hit it off from the moment she introduced them. Jake pointed out Sinead Conway, talking to two men, one silver-haired, the other bald, both spending big on auction lots.

Zoe was sitting by herself while Carl queued at the bar and Jake spoke to the local MP's campaign manager. The bald man who'd been talking to Sinead Conway approached her, his hand outstretched.

Zoe pasted on her friendliest smile.

"Myron Carter," said the man. "I've been looking forward to meeting you."

Zoe forced the smile to stay put. "Mr Carter. Nice to finally put a face to the name."

He took Carl's seat and leaned in. Zoe smelled wine on his breath, but he didn't look drunk.

There was something about him, so obvious she could sense it before he'd even spoken. Power. Confidence, bordering on arrogance.

Danger.

"Call me Myron," he told her. "I hear congratulations are in order, Detective Inspector."

"Thank you. It's been an interesting first week."

He chuckled, then looked up and exchanged a nod with someone across the room. Zoe followed his gaze.

Ralph Streeting.

Carter leaned in further, so close she could see the pores in his skin and the flecks of green in his grey eyes.

"I heard about your little accident," he said. "I hope your car's all better now." He stood up.

Zoe nodded dumbly, as he bent down, smiling, and whispered into her ear.

"Those roads can be dangerous, you know. Best stick to the safer parts of town."

CHAPTER ONE HUNDRED TWENTY-SEVEN

ZOE CHECKED THE CLOCK: 3am. She'd been trying to sleep for more than two hours, Carl snoring beside her.

She squeezed her eyes shut and tried to wipe her mind clean, yet again.

It didn't work.

There was too much to process.

A new house in a new town. A new job with a new boss and a new team.

A fresh murder, a new set of crime scenes, a hospital, a pathologist, a lab and forensic team, a port and everything that came with it. All the politics. Her car.

Myron Carter's warning. It *had* been a warning. Or a threat.

And a name. A name she didn't recognise.

Ahmed Hosseini. The name Olivia Bagsby had thrown at her as if she'd know it.

She eased her way out from under the duvet, grabbed her phone, and tiptoed downstairs.

Google threw up a few thousand Ahmed Hosseinis. She narrowed her search to the UK, then clicked on the News tab.

There were a handful of stories from a couple of months back.

She remembered it vaguely. A man being stabbed to death was, sadly, nothing unusual. A man being stabbed to death and having his eyes removed was something that would stick in the mind. Ahmed Hosseini, butchered, in Kent. The case unsolved. Not a local, Hosseini had moved south from Nottingham a year or so earlier.

There was a photograph of him, taken two weeks before the murder.

Zoe knew that face.

To her, his name wasn't Ahmed Hosseini, but Ahmed Iqbal. Zoe had watched him giving his evidence, from behind a screen, during the latter stages of the Canary trial. She'd watched as he'd condemned his former employers, and she'd known the screen wouldn't stop them figuring out who he was.

He'd known that too. He'd entered Witness Protection and disappeared as soon as the trial was over.

And that should have been it. New name, new identity, new city.

But someone had found Ahmed Iqbal. Or Hosseini. His name didn't matter. Someone had tracked him down and killed him.

The same person Olivia Bagsby was running from.

Zoe could see why the woman was so scared. Why she'd laughed at the idea that Zoe could protect her.

Olivia had known the name, and she'd known that Zoe would know it, or at least that she'd know the man.

How?

Zoe leaned on the table, hunched over her laptop. Her breathing was shallow and thin.

Had Olivia been warning her?

Was there a link between what was happening here in Cumbria, and the people she'd put behind bars in Birmingham?

———————

Thank you for reading *The Harbour*. We hope you enjoyed it. Zoe Finch returns for her second Cumbria murder case in *The Mine*.

Rachel and Joel.

READ A FREE PREQUEL NOVELLA, THE CASTLE

DI Zoe Finch has a big decision to make.

Will she stay in Birmingham, clinging to the wreckage of her beloved team as it breaks up and leaves her behind? Or will she follow her partner Carl to Cumbria, a new job and a new life?

Carl's already decided. He's heading up north, revelling in the lakes and fells and excited about his new job chasing down dodgy coppers.

And Zoe's future colleague DS Aaron Keyes is perplexed. A man has been found dead at Egremont Castle – a man who left a voicemail for him just before he died.

Can Aaron track down the killer? Will Carl be able to work out exactly why members of Cumbria police are acting strangely? And will Zoe decide to make the move up north?

Find out by reading *The Castle* for FREE at rachelmclean. com/castle.

READ THE CUMBRIA CRIME SERIES

The Harbour, Cumbria Crime Book 1
The Mine, Cumbria Crime Book 2

Buy now in ebook or paperback.

ALSO BY RACHEL MCLEAN

The DI Zoe Finch Series – Buy now in ebook, paperback and audiobook

Deadly Wishes, DI Zoe Finch Book 1

Deadly Choices, DI Zoe Finch Book 2

Deadly Desires, DI Zoe Finch Book 3

Deadly Terror, DI Zoe Finch Book 4

Deadly Reprisal, DI Zoe Finch Book 5

Deadly Fallout, DI Zoe Finch Book 6

Deadly Christmas, DI Zoe Finch Book 7

Deadly Origins, the FREE Zoe Finch prequel

The Dorset Crime Series – Buy now in ebook, paperback or audiobook

The Corfe Castle Murders, Dorset Crime Book 1

The Clifftop Murders, Dorset Crime Book 2

The Island Murders, Dorset Crime Book 3

The Monument Murders, Dorset Crime Book 4

The Millionaire Murders, Dorset Crime Book 5

The Fossil Beach Murders, Dorset Crime Book 6

The Blue Pool Murders, Dorset Crime Book 7

The Lighthouse Murders, Dorset Crime Book 8

The Ghost Village Murders, Dorset Crime Book 9

ALSO BY JOEL HAMES

The Sam Williams Series – Buy now in ebook, paperback and
audiobook

Dead North

No One Will Hear

The Cold Years

The Art of Staying Dead

Victims, a Sam Williams novella

Caged, a Sam Williams short